THE RANCHER'S DREAM

A Crimson Rose Novel Book 2

CATHRYN CHANDLER

BOOKS BY CATHRYN CHANDLER

The Circle of Friends Series:

Believing in Dreams (Maggie & Ian)

Believing in Love (Beth & John)

Believing in Promises (Abby & Cade)

Only One Dream (Lillian & Charles)

Only One Love (Rayne & Tremain)

Only One Promise (Shannon & Luke)

Only One Beginning (Dina & Cook)

Box Sets:

The Believing In Series

The Only One Series

The Crimson Rose Novels:

The Marshal's Promise (Dorrie & Jules)

The Rancher's Dream (Brenna & Robbie)

Loving Amelia Coming in August, 2018

Be the first to receive notification of new releases. Subscribe to the mailing list here:

http://eepurl.com/bLBOtX

CHAPTER ONE

"I'm tellin' you, we have a problem. And it's one the boss needs to be fixin'." The gangly cowboy glared at the man squatting on the ground in front of his horse. The target of his complaint had his head down and wasn't paying attention to anything but the cougar tracks they'd been following for the last hour. "Are you listenin' to me?"

"Nope." Robbie Smith stood to his full six feet and a bit more. He rolled his wide shoulders back and forth before flashing a broad grin that had his blue eyes crinkling at the corners. "I don't have to listen to you, Toby. You've been saying the same thing for the last hour, and I heard you the first time."

Toby, who was built like a string bean, with muscular arms attached to a whip-thin body, shifted in his saddle. "I had to talk over the grumblin' of your stomach, so don't tell me it don't concern you. It's a wonder you have any strength to hunt that cattle-killin' cougar, and I'm goin' to be skin and bones if we have to eat Hopper's cookin' all the time. And that's what's goin' to happen if Shue ups and leaves the way she keeps talkin' about."

Robbie laughed. Toby was already as skinny as any full-grown man he'd ever seen, but his ranch foreman was right about a couple of things. Hopper's cooking was barely edible, and the cougar they were hunting had developed a real taste for cow meat. So far, the animal had managed to stay ahead of them and out of their sights, but from what Robbie could tell, the big cat was slowly circling back toward the herd. He sighed and pushed his broad-brimmed hat back further on his head.

"Well? What are you goin' to do about it?" Toby demanded. "Yer're the boss, ain't you?"

Robbie gathered up the reins of his horse before looking back over his shoulder. "I'm the boss. And right now, what I'm going to do is mount up and follow those tracks before we lose any more cattle." He rolled his eyes at the long dramatic sigh that came from behind him. Toby's stomach had always been a major concern for the foreman. Probably a leftover from the days he'd been abandoned at a young age and had been lucky to scrounge up any kind of meal.

But that was a long time ago, and right now the two of them had bigger problems.

Thirty minutes later they left the gently rolling hills covered in green from the winter rains, to enter a long and narrow wooded area strewn with large rocks and heavy undergrowth. Toby hung back, covering their rear with his shotgun, while Robbie followed the tracks which had skirted around a collection of stacked-up boulders.

He felt his horse quiver beneath him and stroked a soothing hand along its sandy-colored neck. "It's all right, Hayseed." A second tremor beneath his hand had Robbie reaching for the rifle attached to the back of his saddle.

He'd barely managed to pull it free when he heard the low guttural growl coming from over his head. He and Hayseed both froze. Robbie twisted slowly in his saddle while his gaze lifted rapidly upward along the boulders forming a wall on his left. The cougar was crouched on top, his muscles bunched as he fixed his yellow, unblinking stare on the rider below.

Robbie carefully brought his rifle around, but it was too little, too late. The cougar let out a bone-chilling cry as it launched itself into the air. Hayseed bolted at the first sound, his movement so sudden and violent that Robbie's desperate grasp for a handhold swished through thin air as he was tossed backward. The body of the cat flew right over him, his claws missing Robbie's chest by a fraction of an inch. Man and animal hit the ground to the sound of Hayseed's hooves pounding through brush. The lithe cat did a quick roll before coming up on its feet. Robbie wasn't so lucky. He landed on his back as the rifle flew out of his hand. His leg slammed against the sharp point of a rock, sending a shearing pain up his thigh and hip. With the wind knocked out of him, Robbie fought to drag air into his lungs, his eyes fixed on the cougar who'd dropped into a crouch.

Fully expecting to be ripped apart, the rancher automatically lifted his arms as the only defense he had to protect his head and throat, when a shot rang out. The ground spit up a small fountain of dirt barely a foot in front of the predator, who instantly shied away from the unknown threat. A second shot barely grazed the animal's shoulder, but it was enough to have it pivoting on its haunches and disappearing into the trees.

Robbie's head dropped back to the ground and he closed his eyes. It seemed he wasn't going to be that cat's dinner after all.

"You should'na gotten so far ahead of me like that." Toby dismounted but kept his rifle raised and his eye on the spot where the cougar had melted out of sight. He made a quick glance to where his boss lay in the dirt. "Are you gonna get up? He didn't get a claw into you, did he?"

"No claws."

Blowing out a breath to control the pain in his leg that was throbbing with an unrelenting beat, Robbie reached a hand down and gingerly felt along his thigh. He didn't need to look to know what that warm stickiness meant. He gritted his teeth and flexed a foot. At least his leg wasn't broken. Aware that it was dangerous to stay there, especially when the scent of his blood would be carried in the air, he pushed himself to his elbows and then slowly to a sitting position. That's as far as he could manage on his own.

"I'm going to need some help, Toby."

The foreman's head snapped around, his gaze immediately going to the bloody pant leg.

"Well, hell." Toby inched his way backwards to where his horse was standing, watching the two men with large brown eyes. "I'm gonna put Rosie in between us and where that cougar slunk off, and then have a look at you."

Robbie nodded while his gaze lifted to the rock wall towering over him. He wouldn't put it past the four-legged hunter to make its way back to the top of those boulders.

Once the foreman had maneuvered his horse into a position to offer them some protection, he knelt beside Robbie and stretched a supporting arm across his back. "Let's take a look."

While the lanky foreman leaned over until his nose was barely an inch away from the wound, Robbie untied the bandanna he wore around his neck. His pant leg was shredded, so he pushed aside the tattered pieces and wrapped the kerchief around his thigh, frowning when it was soaked through in less than a minute. Toby silently handed over his own bandanna, which Robbie used as a second bandage, hoping the two scraps of cloth would hold back the bleeding until he could return to their camp.

Toby got to his feet and held out a hand. "Yer too big for me to carry, boss. Yer goin' to have to stand up. Good thing that's your right leg. It'll make it easier to get you on top of Rosie."

Not wasting his energy with an answer, Robbie grabbed the offered hand and pulled himself to a standing position. He swayed in place for a full minute, all his weight on his left leg and his eyes closed, as he waited for the lightheaded rush in his head to fade away.

"Yer sure you can stand on your own?" Toby looked worried as he kept a firm hold on Robbie's hand.

The rancher nodded. "Go get Rosie." A few seconds later Robbie had to grit his teeth as he shifted his weight to his right foot so he could step up into the stirrup. Even with Toby's arm curling under his shoulders and across his back, the pain was burning a wide path up his leg and spine. He landed in the saddle with a grunt, but managed to stay upright, sliding forward as Toby hauled himself up to sit behind him.

"Where do you figure Hayseed got off to?"

Robbie shrugged. "He's most likely halfway home by now. After we get to camp, you go on ahead to the ranch. I don't want Shue worrying when my horse shows up there without me."

"With that leg the way it is, yer goin' to have to ride in the chuck wagon with Hopper. At least we only got another four hours to get to the ranch, so that's a good thing."

His leg was on fire, his horse was missing, and the cougar was still on the loose. Robbie couldn't see one good thing about any of this.

Silently cursing his own carelessness, he settled for a grunt as Toby set his horse into motion. The foreman kept Rosie to a gentle walk, but even so, every step sent a shot of misery up Robbie's leg. By the time the camp came into sight, his face was sheet-white and covered in sweat. Since the rest of the hands were still out driving the herd to a feeding ground closer to the ranch, only Hopper was in camp. The man rarely said a word, and didn't utter eve one as he rushed forward to help his boss off the horse and into the wagon.

Once his leg was raised up on a couple of full sacks of flour and he could rest his back against the wagon's wide wheel, Robbie managed a grin for his foreman.

"You go on ahead and let Shue know I'm all right."

Toby's mouth twisted into a scowl. "I'll let her know what happened, but you ain't all right. I figure you'll have to go into town and get Doctor Abby to look at that leg."

"I'm not taking a two-day wagon ride into town, Toby." Robbie rubbed his leg just above his wound. "I don't have the time or the inclination."

Toby's chin stuck out and he wagged a meaty finger at his boss.

"You don't want infection settin' in and you endin' up losin' that leg and bein' a cripple, now do you?"

Robbie rolled his eyes. His foreman always did have a good imagination. And whenever he used it, it usually took him right to the gloomy side of life.

"I'll have the doc look at it when I go into town at the end of the month to see to my usual business."

"Why didn't you tell me that before?" Toby groused. "I wouldn'a been yappin' in yer ear for the last few hours if I'da known that. So while you're there, *boss*, you can take care of that other problem."

Rubbing his neck at the base of the skull to try and fend off the headache he could feel forming there, Robbie was only half-listening to his foreman. "What other problem?"

Toby looked around to be sure that the silent Hopper wasn't within hearing distance. "When yer in town, you'd better find us a cook so Miss Shue can be on her way if that's what she wants. We won't have no hands left if they have to eat Hopper's food."

CHAPTER TWO

Robbie strode up the boardwalk lining either side of the steep hill. It rose above the city, like a sentry guarding the frenzied activity on the banks of the sparkling blue bay below. He was glad he didn't have to haul himself all the way to the top, where several of the newly wealthy railroad barons were building their enormous mansions. Robbie much preferred the smaller, more friendly homes where many of his extended family members lived. Their houses had porches running across the front, and small patches of grass leading into rows of flowers lining their short walkways.

Climbing the three steps to reach the porch, Robbie turned to look at the spectacular view out across the crowded buildings and busy docks, to the water stretching out below him in a deep blue carpet that separated the city from the green and gold of the hills on the other side of the bay. Covered with trees and long stretches of open country, he couldn't imagine how anyone could look at those distant hills and then choose to live in the city.

Out of habit, the tall, lean rancher looked north. Out there beyond his vision was a piece of land he was working to make his own. It was nestled in a wide valley, beyond the played-out gold fields and the busy silver mines, along the route to the border of

Oregon. Every ache and pain from a horse he broke, or spending the day chasing down stray cows, earned him the pay he'd taken faithfully to the bank every month to put toward the price of the land.

Starting his own place was now a dream within his reach, thanks to the generosity of the two people who had done more for him than anyone else in his life. He'd never be able to repay them. But he'd never stop trying. And when his honorary Aunt Lillian needed someone to manage her new cattle ranch while she remained in town to help her husband run their gaming hall, Robbie had never even considered saying "no". He owed Lillian and Charles more than he could ever put into words.

The door behind him opened and Jules, his close friend going all the way back to childhood, stood in the doorway. He had one eyebrow raised as he looked around Robbie toward the street.

"Were you planning on coming in, or are you waiting for someone?"

Robbie grinned at his boyhood friend who'd followed in his older brother's footsteps and become a US Marshal. "Just making sure none of your customers were sneaking up behind me."

Jules snorted. "They aren't 'customers', they're criminals, for the most part."

"For the most part?"

The tall, dark-haired marshal shrugged. "Decent citizens also stop by to see me on occasion."

"More likely they stop by to see your wife." Robbie smiled at the pretty woman, with the soft brown eyes and hair the color of melted caramel, who'd stepped up beside Jules. She smiled as she slipped one hand around her husband's arm.

"Hello, Dorrie." Robbie patted a hand against his chest. "My heart's still broken that you chose Jules over me." He let out a loud dramatic sigh. "I'd never have believed such a thing in a million years."

"I'm sure you've recovered from your disappointment by now." Dorrie's tone was laced with amusement. "Probably before you'd reached the edge of town on your way back to the ranch after the wedding party."

The marshal laughed and put an arm around his wife's shoulders. "It seems your reputation hasn't changed much, Robbie. I think every lady in town has figured out that you aren't the marrying kind."

"Only the ladies I grew up with." Robbie winked at Dorrie. She and Jules, along with Dorrie's best friend Ammie and another good friend of his, Ethan, had spent their childhoods together. They were all part of the large extended family Robbie was very grateful to be a part of, although none of the five of them were related by blood.

Theirs was a family by choice, since many of them had been either abandoned by their blood families, or were orphaned at a young age, which only made the bonds of love and friendship that much stronger. And not being blood relatives had been a good thing, since Dorrie and Jules' childhood friendship had grown into love, and the two of them had married just over a month ago.

"Why in heavens are all of you out here?"

Dina, who was one of the few who could claim a blood relation to Jules even though she was more than twenty years his senior, peeked over Dorrie's shoulder. The short, stocky older woman had managed the McKenzie household for Jules' father when the family had lived in Chicago. Now she looked after the next generation of McKenzies, including Cade and his wife and their two children, as well as Jules and his brand-new wife, Dorrie.

"You'd better not think you're going to simply give a wave and a 'hello', and then go off somewhere else, Robbie Smith." Dina lifted a hand and wagged a finger at him over Dorrie's head.

Laughing, the new bride nudged her marshal husband in the side. "Why don't we move out of the doorway, so Robbie can greet Dina properly?"

Jules gave his wife a quick kiss on the cheek before he stepped inside, pulling her with him. Robbie quickly crossed the porch and caught the plump Dina up in a huge bear-hug, ignoring her squeal of protest.

"I've missed you. And your cooking. Why don't you come out to the ranch where your talent in the kitchen would be really appreciated?"

"Why don't you come into the parlor and have a drink before I have to punch you in the nose?" Jules asked.

"Jules, you behave yourself." Dina frowned at her much-younger cousin before she turned a motherly smile on Robbie. "You come right in and tell us everything that's going on at the ranch." She paused and narrowed her eyes, dropping her gaze to his leg. "Including why you're limping."

"It's hardly noticeable," Robbie protested. He'd tangled with that cougar almost three weeks ago, and except for a twinge now and then, he'd healed up nicely. Or for the most part. He intended to ask the family doctor to have a look at it, since he was in town anyway.

"I noticed it," Dina declared.

"And I'm sure Abby will too, and she'll be home soon," Dorrie said, referring to Cade's wife who was also known as "Doctor Abby". Dorrie let go of her husband's arm and stepped forward to latch onto Robbie's. "Come on. Our family doctor can look at it later. Right now, I want to hear why you're still looking for a cook? Has Shue left?"

Robbie walked easily beside her, letting her lead him over to one of the divans in front of the fireplace. He wouldn't mind sitting on a soft cushion for a bit. It had been a long ride from the ranch, and the truth was that his leg was aching. Which was why he'd been limping enough for Dina to notice.

He nodded his thanks for the whiskey glass Jules held out to him before turning his lazy smile back to Dorrie. "Shue hasn't left. At least not yet, but she'd like to go home." He looked down at the amber liquid in his glass. "She says she wants to do more hunting and panning for gold, but she's getting on in years. I can't expect her to keep cooking for seven men along with taking care of the ranch house, although I try to do most of that myself." He sighed.

Toby was right in nagging him to find another cook. Shue had made it clear from the beginning that she was only there to help out on a temporary basis. He'd hoped she'd stay until the fall when they left for his new spread, but every day he could see the work was getting to be too much for her. Shue needed to carry a lighter load, so he needed to find another solution. He perked up and glanced over at Jules.

"Do you think Cook might know someone, Shue came with me to check on the supplies, and to talk to him about it?"

Cook was Dina's husband, and was known for putting out the best meals in the city. Robbie and every other hand on the ranch would give their right arms to have him put up all their meals, but the former sailor only worked at Charles Jamison's gaming hall.

"I can certainly ask him," Dina said. "But let's discuss that later. We should get you settled in."

Robbie shook his head. "Thanks for the offer, Dina" He included Dorrie in his smile. "But I'm not staying here with a couple of newlyweds. That's Cade and Abby's burden to bear and I have no desire to share it." He grinned when Dina simply shook her head as she leaped up from her seat and scurried out of the parlor, declaring she could smell her biscuits burning, while Dorrie blushed at his comment and Jules rolled his eyes.

As the sound of Dina's footsteps faded away, Robbie took a quick glance around the parlor. "Speaking of places to stay, how is that new house you're building coming along?"

Dorrie immediately brightened. "Da is doing a wonderful job."

That wouldn't have surprised anyone. Dorrie's father was a master carpenter, and very much in demand all over the city. He was helping build his daughter and her new husband a home on a piece of land Jules had bought. It was just a little further up the hill from Cade and Abby's place.

"Since you don't want to stay here, where are you staying?"

Jules' blunt question was a sure sign he wasn't going to let the topic go until he had an answer. "With Uncle Charles and Aunt Lillian?"

"Nope."

"There's no reason to go to a hotel, Robbie. There's plenty of family in town who'd be happy to have you stay with them," Dorrie said.

"Which is what I'll be doing." Robbie took a slow sip of his drink while Dorrie bit her lip and Jules gave him a questioning look. Deciding he'd made them wait long enough, he broke out into a wide grin. "I'm staying with Ammie and her Aunt Charlotte."

"Ammie?" Dorrie blinked.

"Aunt Charlotte and Miss Helen are there, so it's perfectly proper. Besides, like you said, we're all family." Robbie kept his expression bland but was careful not to look over at Jules. If he did, Jules would know in an instant that his old friend was up to something.

"That's fine. Much better than a hotel." Dorrie's smile returned. "But can you at least stay for supper? Ethan is coming into town and promised to be here before sundown."

Jules crossed his arms over his broad chest and fixed a stare on Robbie. "Which I suspect Robbie already knows."

"You do?" Dorrie's eyes widened as she also stared at their old friend.

"He does," Jules confirmed when Robbie decided it would be more prudent to stay quiet. "Don't you?"

Robbie tried a casual shrug. "He might have mentioned it when he stopped by a few weeks ago."

Dorrie put her hands on her hips and turned an exasperated look on her husband. "How did *you* know that Robbie already knew about Ethan?" When Jules only grinned at her, she pursed her lips. "You know what I mean." When Jules and Robbie started laughing, she glanced between the two men. "What are you both up to?"

Jules held his hands up, palms out. "Not me. Ask the lonely rancher over there."

"Lonely?" Dorrie was silent for a long moment, and the look she sent Robbie was full of worry. "You don't have an attachment to Ammie, do you?"

Robbie frowned in confusion. "A what?"

"She wants to know if you're in love with Ammie." Jules shrugged at the horrified expression on Robbie's face.

"Of course not," Robbie instantly denied. "She's like a sister to me. You know that."

The marshal stepped behind his wife and pulled her back against his chest, wrapping his arms around her waist. "Robbie's just trying to annoy Ethan, honey." He shook his head at his friend. "You always did like to poke at bears."

The easy-going rancher shrugged. "Some bears need poking."

"And you two are acting like meddling old gossips," Dorrie declared. "I forbid you to bait Ethan that way while he's a guest in our house." She smiled to soften her words. "And I won't let Ethan insult you at supper either."

"You're taking away all my fun," Robbie complained. When Dorrie started to tap one foot against the floor, he gave in. "All right. No mention of Ammie at dinner."

"Good. Because I'm happy to have Ethan back for a while and I don't want you to give him any excuse to go storming off again." Dorrie sighed and leaned back against her husband. "He's been gone so much the last five years, it's been hard to keep track of him."

The sadness in her eyes had Robbie's gaze snapping over to Jules. He gave his friend a questioning look. Something was clearly wrong in Dorrie's life, and Robbie expected her husband to fix it.

"One of Dorrie's good friends has gone missing. At least my wife thinks she has, so she's glad she doesn't have to worry about Ethan's whereabouts too," Jules offered by way of an explanation.

Dorrie turned in her husband's arms so she could look up at

him. "She *is* missing. She always comes to market and hasn't been for over a month."

"Market?" Dorrie's words rang a faraway bell in Robbie's mind. He searched his memory and a name popped up. "Brenna? You're talking about Brenna?"

One of Jules' eyebrows shot up. "You've met her?"

Robbie shook his head. "No. But I remember Dorrie talking about her over the years. She used to come to market with her grandparents, wasn't it?" He looked over at Dorrie for confirmation.

The young woman nodded, but her eyes were still troubled. "Her grandparents can't make the trip into town anymore, so she comes by herself. But I haven't seen her since we've been married."

"Honey, you've only been down to the market once since then," Jules said patiently. "She might have just missed that one week."

Dorrie stepped away from him and faced the two men. "I asked some other farmers there who are acquainted with her. They said they hadn't seen her in weeks." She rubbed her hands together. "Something's happened to her, I know it."

"If she doesn't come this week, I promise I'll make the trip out to her farm to check on her." Jules reached a long arm over and gave his wife a gentle pat on the shoulder.

"There you go." Robbie considered that the perfect solution to the problem of the missing Brenna.

"*We*, Jules," Dorrie insisted. "We will go out and check on her."

"Even better," Robbie declared, winking at Dorrie when she smiled at him.

"Since you've both settled that," Jules said dryly, "tell me what happened to your leg?"

Robbie was back to his easy-going grin. "It seems a cougar took issue with me following it around."

CHAPTER THREE

"IT'S A SAD DAY."

Brenna kept her head bowed and hands clasped in her lap. She'd been sitting in the same chair for over three hours. That's how long it had been since the midday meal had been finished, but still Daniel Tolan went on throwing out his views on how the family should view death. At least that's what he was telling the other three people in the room. He kept his back to Brenna, completely ignoring her presence in the kitchen. It didn't surprise her since Daniel had made it very clear from the moment he'd politely introduced himself that she wasn't a member of his family. Which is why she had a chair near the stove while all the Tolans sat together at the rough-hewn wooden table.

There was a persistent ache in the small of Brenna's back, and a headache lurked behind her eyes, but she didn't make a single sound of complaint. How could she? Even her quiet weeping whenever she was swamped by the memory of digging the graves for Meemaw and Gramps, and then gently placing them into their final resting places, had drawn head shakes and frowns from the others. But then they'd made it quite clear from the moment they'd arrived at the small farm owned by Daniel's parents for

almost fifty years, that they'd expected her to prepare their meals
and do all the housework and chores. Daniel, his haughty daughter,
and her husband seemed to consider her as nothing more than a
servant in their parents' home. At least Daniel's wife had given her
a sympathetic look or two.

Brenna had lived on the farm for eighteen years, ever since her
own parents had perished in a fire when she was seven years old.
Despite their advancing years, the elder Tolans had taken her in
when no other relatives had presented themselves. To Brenna, they
were Meemaw and Gramps, and she'd been happy to gradually take
on most of the work on the farm as she'd gained in years and experience. But in all the years that she'd lived on the farm, this was the
first time she'd ever met Meemaw's and Gramp's only child,
Daniel, or any of his family.

It hadn't been a pleasant experience. They'd arrived two days
ago, and she hoped they'd be leaving soon. It hadn't been easy
waiting on four demanding adults, as well as feeding the animals,
and seeing to the very large vegetable garden that had kept the
small farm going for the last decade.

"Yes, a very sad day," Daniel repeated as he slowly looked
around the cozy kitchen. Most of the floor space was taken up by
the table in its center and the four straight-backed chairs
around it.

Brenna kept her head bent and mentally rolled her eyes. This
sudden devotion on Daniel's part was hard for her to swallow,
considering he hadn't made the effort to see his parents in at least
last eighteen years. In fact, Brenna wasn't at all sure his grown and
married daughter had ever met her grandparents. Which would be
a real shame. Meemaw and Gramps Tolan had been wonderful
people, and no matter how little their nearest kin felt about their
passing, Brenna was going to miss them. Just as much as she still
missed her own parents.

"That was a fine meal you prepared today, Brenna." Daniel
stroked a beefy hand down his thick brown beard that was liberally
shot through with streaks of gray.

While her shoulders tensed at the rare compliment, Brenna did what was expected and lifted her head to nod at the new head of the Tolan family.

"Thank you." She kept her voice low and polite, not that it did any good. Daniel's daughter, Roberta, still pursed her lips while she shot the only non-family member a glare. It was the only expression Brenna had seen on the sour woman's sharp, angular features. At least whenever Roberta deigned to look her way. Her flat brown-eyed gaze was usually focused somewhere over Brenna's head.

"It's time to put our sadness away and tend to the pressing matters at hand." Daniel pushed his shoulders back and took a thorough, visual inventory of the kitchen.

Brenna stayed silent, watching all four of the Tolans relax in their chairs and smile at Daniel.

Shortest mourning period I've ever heard of. Brenna sighed. Meemaw and Gramps deserved better, but there wasn't anything she could do about that. At least she hoped that it signaled Daniel's intention to put his hat on and take his family home.

"We've come to a decision about the farm."

Decision? Brenna's head snapped up. She caught the smug-looking smile on Roberta's thin lips. Worried at what the whiny woman and her father were up to, Brenna fixed a stare on Daniel and waited.

"Well then. We'd best get on with it." The heavy-set man stood and tucked his thumbs into the waistband of his pants. When he cleared his throat, he didn't even glance in Brenna's direction, but kept his back to her. "As the only son, I inherit all of my parents' worldly possessions, which is this farm and everything on it." He ignored the sharp sound of protest that came from behind him. "Since I already have a farm to run, I'm giving this one to Roberta." He glanced at his daughter and stretched his thick lips into a smile. "You and your husband should do well here."

Having heard more than enough, Brenna shot to her feet. "Meemaw and Gramps promised the farm to me."

Daniel slowly turned around. "You will use a proper address when you speak of my parents, girl."

"That *is* the proper address, since it's the one they asked me to use." Brenna straightened her back to her full height so she was eye-to-eye with the short and hefty Daniel Tolan. "They promised the farm to me."

"Do you have a piece of paper that states you're entitled to the farm?"

"Neither of your parents could read or write, Daniel Tolan. You know that." Brenna sent him a cold stare.

"Then you have no claim." Daniel waved a hand to emphasize his point. "My parents never told me you were to receive the farm, and they would have if that had truly been their wishes."

Brenna's eyes narrowed. "They would have if you'd ever come to visit them. But they couldn't send you a note, could they?"

"A neighbor would have written it down for them if that's what they really wanted," Roberta sniffed.

"Or *you* could have written it down and had them put their mark on it," Daniel pointed out to the dark-haired woman who was staring at him with ice in her blue eyes. "I know their mark."

If only I could. The elderly Tolan parents weren't the only ones who couldn't read or write, but Brenna wasn't about to mention that particular flaw of hers to Daniel, and most certainly not in front of Roberta.

"Pa has every right to give the farm to us. And we don't need you here." Roberta pointed to the stick-thin man scrunching down in the seat beside her. "Harlan can work the land just fine."

Brenna doubted if the always silent Harlan knew which end of a horse to put the harness on, much less how to work a farm. She was sure the animals would die from neglect within a month. But that was the least of her worries at the moment.

"You're telling me to leave?"

"My wife will help you pack while I ready the horse and wagon." Daniel placed a hand on his wife's shoulder. The plump woman immediately shifted her weight as she pushed herself to her feet.

"Now?" Brenna's mouth dropped open and she gave them both an incredulous look. "You're expecting me to leave now?"

Lizzy Tolan waddled her way over to Brenna and slipped a hand around the younger woman's upper arm. Brenna could feel the callouses on them, attesting to Lizzy's life of hard work. "No one's expecting you to walk all the way into town. That's why Daniel is getting the wagon ready."

She gave a firm tug on Brenna's arm. With little choice left to her, Brenna allowed herself to be led away to her small room in the very back of the house.

"It will be good riddance to her." Roberta's voice filled the small kitchen and followed Brenna down the hallway. "With all that black hair and those eyes, she has the look of a witch about her. It wouldn't surprise me if she put some kind of spell on Meemaw and Gramps, so they'd let her stay here for nothing."

"Your grandparents were always too charitable," Daniel said.

Brenna's chin snapped up, and she held her head high as she marched away. Nothing? She'd worked day and night to keep the farm going and his parents sheltered and fed. Not that Daniel or his daughter believed that. And she was not a charity case. Or a witch.

"Come on, Brenna. There's nothing to do but make the best of it."

Lizzie's voice held a warmth that surprised Brenna. The woman had hardly spoken at all since she'd arrived with her family three days ago, and Brenna had assumed she held the same low opinion of her as her husband did.

The older woman stepped into the small space that Brenna had called her own for the last eighteen years, then moved to one side to allow Brenna to squeeze in next to her. A narrow bed, made of wooden bars and slats, with a thick blanket over a layer of straw, jutted out into the center of the room. Hooks lined up on the wall at the foot of the bed held all of Brenna's clothes, and the rest of her meager possessions were neatly stacked on the floor in the far corner, next to a basin and a water pitcher. Brenna's gaze immediately went to the burlap sack lying on top of her bed.

Lizzie sighed. "I brought that in earlier, so you'd have something to put your belongings in." She looked around before turning a sympathetic eye on Brenna. "Doesn't seem like you have much. Do you keep some things stored in another room? Or maybe the barn?"

"No." Brenna walked over to the hooks and started gathering her clothes. Since she was wearing the only skirt and blouse she owned, it didn't take long to fold the shirt and britches she wore to work on the farm, or the one dress she had that Meemaw had made for her on her eighteenth birthday. "Just in case a young man comes around," the old woman had told her with a smile.

But that had never happened.

Still, Brenna cherished the dress simply because Meemaw had made it. Aside from a locket her mother had given her and that she always wore, it would be the only reminder she had of the life she was being forced to leave behind, for the second time in her twenty-five years. Brenna had to rapidly blink back the tears forming at the thought.

Lizzie put a gentle hand on her shoulder. "Don't you go out into the world with nothing but worry, Brenna." She gave Brenna's shoulder a motherly pat. "I know how hard you worked here, and how you took care of Daniel's parents when he wasn't here to do it." She nodded when Brenna stared at her with wide watery eyes. "My Daniel can be a stubborn man. He wants our daughter and her useless husband out of our house so there'll be room for our son and the new wife he'll be marrying soon." She looked around the tiny space and sighed. "He took this farm as a sign from heaven answering his prayers, and it blinds him to how unfair this is to you."

Grateful for even a little understanding, Brenna managed a smile. "Thank you. I loved Meemaw and Gramps. They took me in when I had nowhere else to go and were always good to me."

"It's not the Christian thing to say, but I wish my daughter appreciated everything we've done for her as much as you did my in-laws." She raised an eyebrow when Brenna picked up a stack of letters tied together with two pieces of twine. "What's that?"

"Letters that belonged to my pa. I don't have much of my parents besides these letters and the locket Ma gave me just before she and Pa died in the fire." Brenna lifted the locket as Lizzie leaned forward for a better look.

"Looks like two women carved on the front of it." The rotund woman glanced up at Brenna and smiled. "It's sure pretty." She turned her head and leaned over to peek down the hallway outside the door before lowering her voice to a whisper. "You should have something from Meemaw and Gramps, too."

"I don't think your husband or daughter would let me take anything." Brenna was certain about that.

"They don't need to know." Lizzie reached into the pocket of the apron she always wore and held out a round gold coin. "Daniel knew where his father kept his money, and he told me the hiding place long ago. This is a five-dollar gold piece from the box Gramps kept under his bed. I took it before Daniel got to the box, so he doesn't even know it was in there. It will help you get a new start."

Brenna gasped and stared at the coin as Lizzie held it out to her. Taking it gingerly between two fingers, she stared at the gift in wonder. "I don't know what to say."

Lizzie reached out and engulfed the much taller Brenna in a hard hug. "Maybe you'll save some of that appreciating you have in your heart, for me," she whispered before stepping back and cupping her hand beneath Brenna's chin. "I'll think of that from time to time. It will be something to make me smile as the years go by."

"You've been very kind, Mrs. Tolan."

"Nonsense." Lizzie stepped back and rubbed her hands together. "Have you got everything? Daniel doesn't like to be kept waiting, and I imagine Roberta is champing at the bit to have your beautiful face away from her husband."

Harlan? Brenna was quick to raise her hand and disguise her laugh behind a cough. She couldn't imagine anyone less appealing than Harlan. At least it gave her the reason for Roberta's obvious dislike, and why the Tolans' daughter wanted her gone in such a hurry.

"You mentioned town. Will your husband be taking me to San Francisco?" Brenna asked.

The older woman nodded, setting the gray frizz around her face bouncing up and down. "I told him if he and Roberta want you gone today, he'd have to drive you into town. It wouldn't be right to set a young woman out of her home and then have her get caught on the public road after dark."

Brenna appreciated the thought, but it was late afternoon now she was facing a three-hour wagon ride into town. It would be getting dark by the time they reached the city. And she had nowhere to go. The only place she ever went in San Francisco was to the open market by the docks. And she was sure that wasn't a somewhere she wanted to be at night. Realizing there wasn't a thing she could do about it, she bit her lip and concentrated on arranging her belongings in the sack so the weight was evenly distributed and would be easier to carry.

"Ma!"

Roberta's voice echoed loudly down the hallway. "Pa's outside with the wagon. He said the girl can either get out there right now or she can walk to town."

Lizzie shook her head but yelled back at her daughter. "Tell him she's coming right now." She waited as Brenna picked up her sack and took a last long look around the tiny room. It wasn't much, but she'd spent many nights lying in her lumpy bed, dreaming of far-off places and handsome men who came calling with flowers in their hands. It was likely she'd never have been more than the girl who went to market once a week during the spring and summer, but she'd enjoyed the hours she'd spent in this room with nothing but her imagination.

Brenna didn't bother to wipe away the tears trailing down her cheeks as she quietly walked through the farmhouse for the last time.

CHAPTER FOUR

Brenna stood on the dark road, her burlap bag clutched to her chest, and watched the wagon disappear into the night. She could still hear the rattle of the wheels against the rough-packed dirt long after she'd lost sight of it. But even those sounds finally faded away, leaving her standing alone with nothing but the surrounding darkness. The night was made softer by the gentle kiss of the fog rolling in from the bay in the distance. Brenna rubbed her arms against the rapidly cooling air and eyed the dimly visible road stretched out in front of her.

Daniel Tolan had considered his duty done at the very edge of the city where there were only a few scattered shacks, most of which were abandoned. The ones that showed signs of life most likely had occupants Brenna would just as soon avoid. A tremble of fear raced through her, and she had to fight the urge to turn around and walk back to the farm. But knowing she'd find no welcome there had Brenna's feet staying rooted to the ground.

Forcing herself to breathe slowly, her nerves gradually settled down. Thinking this was as calm as she could get for the time being, Brenna moved off toward a fallen log that was lying by the side of the road. She carefully lowered her weight until she was sure it wasn't rotted through, then set her bag on the ground beside her.

It was a trick she'd learned long ago, to sit quietly and breathe deeply whenever she was confronted with something that worried her. Like being stranded in the city where the only place she knew to go was the marketplace, and the only person she knew was Dorrie. And she had no idea where Dorrie lived.

She drew in one deep breath after another, closing her eyes and picturing her mother's face. She'd had light hair and blue eyes that were always sparkling with amusement. Brenna had inherited her father's dark hair and her mother's eyes, and her imagination. But right now, all she saw was her mother's smiling face, and all she heard was the one thing her mother had always said to her.

Don't waste time being scared, Brenna Roberts. There could be an adventure around the corner. Be sure you grab it whenever you can.

"Yes, Mama," Brenna automatically whispered, just as she always had those many years ago.

Brenna opened her eyes and stared down the road. An adventure? She wasn't so sure. While she might have inherited her mama's vivid imagination, the years of scraping out an existence on the farm had also ingrained a practical streak in her. And right now it was telling her to get moving, or she'd be spending the night in the woods.

Just then a low mournful howl came from the trees behind her. Brenna jumped up and grabbed her bag, backing away from the log until she was again standing in the middle of the road. With the decision of whether to move or stay made for her, she started to walk toward town.

———

FORTY MINUTES LATER, Brenna stepped off the road as a lone horse came plodding toward her. The heavily sway-backed animal, as well as the rickety wagon it was pulling, had definitely seen better days. As the contraption passed, the driver leaned over the side to peer at Brenna. She could see the streaks of dirt across his face and the sudden leap of heat in his eyes.

Drawing her bag up against her chest as a makeshift shield, Brenna ducked her head and kept walking, holding her breath since she half-expected the filthy driver to stop his wagon and leap out after her. But when the sound of the horse's hooves kept up a slow but steady beat against the packed earth, she let out a huge sigh of relief. She took a quick peek behind her to be sure they'd kept on their way out of town.

"I'll be lucky to stay in one piece tonight," Brenna muttered under her breath. She needed to come up with a plan on how to walk safely around the city. She glanced down at the skirt swaying gently back and forth as she walked. What she needed was to look less female. And it just so happened that she'd had years of practice doing exactly that.

When she came up on an empty shed five minutes later, Brenna looked up and down the road to be sure she was alone before walking behind the sagging structure and stepping into its deep shadow. Within a few minutes she'd discarded her skirt and pulled on her britches. Shrugging into a bulky coat that reached to her knees, Brenna tied back her long dark hair with a short piece of twine and stuffed the thick mass into a large wool cap. Her spirits rose a notch now that she was dressed in her much more familiar attire, but she frowned at the burlap bag at her feet. *It's only inviting trouble to carry it around.*

Resigned to leaving at least some of her precious belongings behind, Brenna sat on the ground and dug into the bag. She put the packet of letters into the one pocket of the oversized coat, then shoved a small comb, her only hair ribbon, and another short piece of twine into the pocket of her britches. Carefully rolling up the dress Meemaw had made for her, Brenna flattened it as much as she could, then stuffed it down the back of her pants, with half of it sticking out the top. Her coat would cover it up, and no one would be the wiser.

Satisfied that was the best she could manage, Brenna carefully tucked the bag with her skirt, hand mirror, and a handkerchief up next to the shed, covering it with leaves and the small bit of dirt she managed to pry loose with her hands. Maybe if she had a chance to come back for it, it would still be here. At least she hoped it would be.

Without the skirt to impede her, Brenna made better time. When she finally reached the docks a good hour later, she picked up her pace. The creaking of the ships straining against their mooring ropes, and the occasional sound of rats scurrying over the wooden walkways, set her nerves on edge. She was very glad when she passed the last berth and moved deeper into the city.

The marketplace was only a ten-minute walk from the wharf. During the daylight hours it was a beehive of activity with farm wagons coming in to sell their produce, and the maids and cooks from the big houses that dotted the hills around the bay, crowding around to haggle for the best prices. But at night the market was as quiet as a graveyard, and Brenna quickly crossed over the deserted place to stand on the far side.

She was sure she at least knew the general direction of Portsmouth Square, located in the center of the town. Dorrie had told her it was always busy. Maybe someone there could help her find her friend. She already knew what questions to ask, all Brenna had to do was find someone to answer them.

On the long walk into town, she'd had time to try to remember everything her only friend had told her about her life. Brenna knew Dorrie worked at her ma's dress shop, but Brenna didn't think her friend had ever told her where the shop was located. And besides, it wouldn't be open at this time of night anyway.

Dorrie had also talked quite a bit about her large family, which had fascinated Brenna since in one way, at least, they were much like she and Meemaw and Gramps. Not related by blood, but still a family. There had been Ammie, who Dorrie had grown up with, and Ammie's aunt and uncle, Charles and Lillian. Or was her aunt named Charlotte? She couldn't be sure. But Brenna was certain that Dorrie had mentioned the uncle owned a gaming hall. And she'd never forget the hall's name. Dorrie's uncle had called it "The Crimson Rose". Brenna had loved the name. It conjured up images of dashing young men falling madly in love with beautiful women, offering them a single rose as a sign of their devotion.

Shaking off her silly fantasy, Brenna only remembered two more names Dorrie had mentioned. There was the handsome marshal, Jules, who Brenna had actually met, and the marshal's sister-in-law, who was a doctor.

It stuck in her mind because Brenna had never heard of a female doctor before. Dorrie had called her Doctor Abby. How hard could it be to find a US Marshal, a gambling hall, or a female doctor? Surely lots of people would be able to help her.

An hour later, Brenna wasn't so certain about her grand plan. The square was bustling just as Dorrie had claimed, and no one paid any attention to the tall boy in the bulky coat. There were certainly a large number of people there, but so far Brenna hadn't been able to get up the courage to stop and ask anyone if they knew where the marshal's house was, or a gaming hall called The Crimson Rose.

She walked along with the crowds, going around the entire square twice before she saw the old man, sitting on an upended barrel. His clothes were baggy and patched in so many places, Brenna wasn't sure if there was any of the original material left. He wore a hat with a wide, droopy brim, and there was a large bulky scarf twined around his neck. A white beard spilled over its edge and spread out to cover most of his chest and stomach. Brenna thought he was probably an old miner, and might not have the best memory anymore, but at least he was sitting in one place and not scurrying around as if he were late for something.

Still, she approached the old man cautiously, walking slowly toward him and being sure to catch his eye. If he turned away, so would she. When he offered her a toothless grin, she walked over and squatted down next to his barrel.

"You need somethin', boy?"

Brenna glanced over at him before pulling her hat lower on her forehead and fixing her eyes straight ahead. "Ever heard of a US Marshal named Jules?"

The old man leaned forward and rested his elbows on his knees. Brenna could hear them creak in protest.

"Cain't say as I have."

Since finding the marshal was her first choice, Brenna tried again. "Maybe any US Marshal?" She figured there probably wasn't more than one in town.

"Cain't say as I have."

Sighing, she debated between asking about the doctor or the gambling hall. Since the odds were the doctor wasn't seeing any patients at this hour, she settled on the place with the magical name.

"How about The Crimson Rose? You ever heard of it?"

He reached up a hand and stroked a flat palm down the long white fall of his beard. "The place Lillian Smith runs with that husband of hers?" He slowly turned his head to give her a wink. "Used to go to her other place when I first come lookin' fer gold. She called it The Gentleman's Club, and there was always a good meal to be had there. Made everyone feel welcome, Lillian did. But she don't have that place no more." He heaved a sighed. "I miss it."

Brenna had no idea if that was the "Lillian" she was looking for or not, and had never heard of a place called The Gentleman's Club, but at least it seemed the old miner did know about The Crimson Rose. "So you've heard of it? The Crimson Rose, I mean."

"Yep. Don't know anything about no marshal, but I've heard of that place."

"Can you tell me where it is?"

He pointed to a street radiating off the far side of the square. "You go right down there a couple of blocks and you cain't miss it." He frowned. "It ain't too far into the Barbary Coast. You jest make sure you don't go no further than that."

"Yes, sir," Brenna answered automatically, leaning over to look at the street he was pointing to. She knew about the infamous area of the city with its gaming halls, saloons, and whore houses.

Anyone who'd been to San Francisco knew about the Barbary Coast.

Raising a gnarled hand, the miner slowly unraveled a scarf from his neck, revealing a second one underneath it. He held the one he'd removed out to Brenna. "Here. You take this."

She immediately shook her head and gently pushed his hand away. "I won't take that. I have nothing to give you in return."

"Don't want nothin'.." He held the scarf out again. "If'n you're set on goin' into the Barbary Coast, then you take this and wrap it around that long neck of yours. Use it to cover up your mouth and chin. And pull that hat down lower over your face. I may be old, but I ain't blind." He chuckled. "At least not yet. And if I can see plain as day that you ain't no boy, then anyone else can too."

"Oh." Brenna looked from his amused gaze down at the scarf. She slowly reached out and took it from his shaking hand, wrapping it around her neck the way he'd told her to.

"Thank you," she said softly. "I'll return it to you."

"Don't want it back, and don't want you to do any talkin'," the miner said. "It's a dead giveaway whenever you open yer mouth." He shook his head, sending his beard drifting back and forth across his chest. "Don't you worry about that scarf. I don't need it."

She nodded and got to her feet. Placing a hand on his thin shoulder, she gave it a firm squeeze before turning away and heading over to the street where she'd find The Crimson Rose, and hopefully someone who could tell her where Dorrie lived.

The old miner had certainly been right when he said she wouldn't miss the gaming hall. It stood three stories high, all made with a deep-brown rock and accented with dark wrought-iron railings and huge double doors that must have been at least ten feet high and stood wide open.

A steady stream of people went in and out of the establishment, and from her position right across the street, Brenna could see that everything inside gleamed with dark wood and deep reds, with gold accents everywhere. Next to Brenna's experience of spending most of her days with only an elderly couple for company, the place was completely mobbed with people. How was she ever going to find someone who might know Dorrie?

Curiosity alone made her want a closer look, so she walked across the street and stopped on the wooden walkway just outside the door. She'd barely had a chance to glance inside when she was shoved from behind.

"You're blocking the door."

Brenna looked over her shoulder and her eyes widened. The man growling at her was huge! When he gave her another hard push, it sent her right through the front doors. She stumbled and had to do a quick step to catch her balance, barely keeping on her feet before there was an even a harder push that spun her around. Flailing her arms out to break what was sure to be a hard fall to the ground, Brenna was suddenly caught by the back of her coat and almost lifted right off her feet before she was set down. She'd almost managed to catch her breath when a broad back appeared in front of her nose, coming between her and the mountain of a man who seemed determined to run right over her.

"You're inside. There's no need to keep shoving people around."

Brenna blinked and stared at the wide shoulders and sunlit hair sitting in thick waves on the back of her rescuer's head. He was too tall for her to peek around and get a look at him, but she could sure see the frown on the face of the big man he was facing.

"You looking for trouble, mister?"

"Nope." The response was slow and drawn out despite the threat in the mountain man's voice. "I just don't like stepping over bodies littering the floor is all. Makes me stumble around like I've had too much to drink." The man with the broad back and light hair clapped a friendly hand on the bigger man's shoulder. "Besides, he's too short and skinny for us to get into a brawl over. If you want to fight, you'll have to pick out someone that doesn't have to jump around to get wet in the rain."

The bark of laughter had the tension around the two men drop several degrees. "He's a puny one, all right." The big man nodded, giving Brenna's rescuer a return slap on the shoulder before moving off, completely ignoring Brenna by simply looking over her head.

Her rescuer turned around and smiled at her.

Brenna completely froze. She'd never seen such a wonderful smile, or handsome face. He looked perfect, and she couldn't stop staring as his blue eyes crinkled at the corners.

"Are you all right, kid?"

She managed a nod then quickly ducked her head when his eyes narrowed.

"Robbie? What's going on?"

A woman with hair the color of rich sable stepped up next to the man who was still staring at Brenna. Of course he'd be with someone like that. She was the most beautiful woman Brenna had ever laid eyes on. Realizing she had to get out of there before she was caught with her mouth open, gaping at both of them, Brenna jumped backwards, putting another foot between herself and the man called "Robbie".

"I was just trying to keep this kid from becoming a floor decoration."

"Are you all right? What's your name?"

The soft feminine voice made Brenna even more aware of her baggy britches and old woolen cap. Backing up another step, she kept her eyes down and her voice low as she bobbed her head. "I'm fine. Thank you for your help."

Before she got any response, Brenna ducked around the couple and practically dove out the door in her hurry to get away. Once she'd gained the walkway, she sprinted for the side of the building, quickly ducking into a narrow alley and peeking around the wall. Sure enough, the far-too-curious Robbie had stepped outside as well. Brenna faded into the deep shadows at the very back of her little hiding place until she was invisible to the street beyond. She held her breath when Robbie walked by, his head turning to look up and down the walkway. When he finally disappeared back in the direction of the gaming hall, Brenna counted off the seconds, waiting for a good five minutes before she left the alley.

Since she couldn't go back into the place to inquire about Dorrie, Brenna decided to find somewhere safe tonight to sleep and then try looking for Doctor Abby in the morning. Pulling her large coat closer around her, Brenna slowly walked back toward Portsmouth Square.

CHAPTER FIVE

"If it bothers you so much, you can always go back to The Crimson Rose tonight and look for the boy." Amelia Jamison raised her teacup to her lips and regarded her childhood friend over its rim.

"Why would he be bothered by a boy in Charles' gaming hall?" Dressed from head to toe in her signature pink, Charlotte was the oldest of the Jamison siblings, and the sister of Ammie's father. Ever since his murder nineteen years ago, followed by Ammie's mother abandoning her and returning to her high-society life back East, Charlotte had taken over raising her niece. Although everyone in their sprawled-out family, including Charlotte's younger brother, Charles, and his wife Lillian, had wondered over the years just who was raising whom.

"After Robbie rescued the poor child from being flattened by a giant of a man, the boy barely said two words to him before bolting out the door like a skittish colt." Ammie lowered her teacup and batted her eyes at the lone male in the room. "I think Robbie felt quite snubbed by the whole affair." She turned toward her aunt and added in a loud conspiratorial whisper, "he went chasing after the boy just to get a proper thank you. Only he couldn't catch him."

Robbie rolled his eyes when he saw her lips twitch. He knew good and well that Ammie had been very entertained last night by his whole reaction to the boy disappearing out the doors of The Crimson Rose. It seemed her amusement hadn't lessened any since then, either.

"You most likely scared that child to death, chasing after him that way," Charlotte declared. She pushed a gray curl away from her face. "You should let that poor boy alone."

"Why yes, Robbie. You should do that, just leave him alone," Ammie chimed in.

Robbie narrowed his eyes on Ammie in warning and only received a cheeky smile in return. He wondered if trying to get a rise out of Ethan was worth putting up with Ammie's teasing, not to mention staying in a house where the predominant color used in all the decor was pink. Deciding two could play at this game, he grinned at his honorary cousin.

"Well, I had to find something to do while you were entertaining that suitor of yours." He gave Ammie a wide smile when her aunt immediately pounced on her niece.

"Amelia Jamison! What suitor? We should have Helen come in here immediately."

Charlotte did an uncharacteristic leap from her chair and scurried off toward the kitchen. Helen was their cook and housekeeper, although a younger girl came in every day to help her. She also had what Charlotte called "the sight", which made her extremely popular among Charlotte's tight little gossip group of local matrons.

"Unfair, Robbie Smith," Ammie shot at him. "You know there wasn't any suitor last night, and now I'll be stuck for at least an hour trying to convince Charlotte and Helen of that."

"You've been listening to Charlotte trying to talk Helen into conjuring up your future husband ever since you turned ten. What's one more time? It certainly won't be the last." Robbie leaned back against the pink brocade pillow on the divan and stretched out his long legs.

"And now you'll have the privilege of listening to it too." Ammie nodded as footsteps sounded in the foyer just outside the parlor.

Robbie laughed as he shook his head. "Afraid not, darlin'. Abby's expecting me this morning so she can have a look at my leg."

"There isn't anything wrong with your leg," Amelia hissed as the footsteps drew closer.

He stood and made a show of rubbing his upper thigh just as Charlotte entered the room, dragging a clearly annoyed Helen behind her. "Sure there is." He turned his most charming smile on the two older women who were watching him as he continued to rub his leg. "I'm supposed to see Abby this morning about my leg." He threw in a mournful sigh. "It's still bothering me some."

Helen only raised an eyebrow, but Charlotte quickly bobbed her head. "Of course you should. We don't want you to be in pain, do we Ammie?"

"Oh no," Ammie quickly agreed, her voice positively dripping sugar, which only made Robbie's grin grow wider. "You should definitely have Abby look at it. As a matter of fact, I'd be happy to drive you in the carriage if you're in too much pain."

"I can manage, thanks." Robbie gave her a wink and walked over to hug Charlotte, making sure he added an exaggerated limp to his step. He repeated the hug with Helen, who'd been with the family ever since he could remember, and strolled out of the room, whistling under his breath. He could just imagine how that made Ammie grind her teeth in annoyance.

It didn't take him long to reach the house where Abby had set up her practice. It had a quiet but charming sense of home about it, with a wide porch and tall oak door. A young woman, who acted as Abby's receptionist and nurse, greeted him from her desk.

"Hello, Robbie. Doctor Abby told me you'd be in today." She glanced at his leg. "Something about being attacked by a cougar?"

He removed his hat and walked quietly across the wooden floors. "Good day, Mrs. Frankle." Since the matronly woman with the pleasant smile had only been working for Abby for a short time, Robbie didn't know her very well, which had him minding his manners to keep him on the better side of Abby and the rest of his honorary aunts.

He shifted his hat to one hand and held it down by his side. "Yes, ma'am. It was a cougar, but it didn't do any damage. At least not to me. Can't say the same for a couple of head of cattle."

The nurse frowned. "I see. Then how did you hurt your leg?"

"I fell on a pile of rocks when Hayseed threw me."

"Hayseed?"

"My horse, ma'am."

Mrs. Frankle's mouth curved upward as she nodded her understanding. "The doctor is with a patient, but she should be able to see you shortly. Please take a seat."

"Thank you, ma'am." Robbie turned toward the waiting area. Five of the half-dozen chairs were occupied. It looked as if Mrs. Frankle's declaration that Abby would be with him shortly had been a bit on the optimistic side.

Resigned to a longer wait than he'd anticipated, Robbie took the only empty seat which was in the far corner of the room. He crossed one booted foot over the opposite knee and slouched down in the chair as he set his hat on his head and tipped it forward until it covered his eyes. He was tired and might as well get a little shut-eye. It had been a long ride yesterday, and a full night escorting Ammie over to The Crimson Rose so they could drop in on Lillian and Charles.

He ignored the sounds around him as he started to drift off. He was almost asleep when a low voice had his eyes snapping open behind the brim of his hat.

"Is this Doctor Abby's place?"

The nurse nodded. "Yes, it is."

Robbie didn't move a muscle as Mrs. Frankle went through her welcoming routine. He couldn't see the newcomer, but he knew that voice. It had a more husky, feminine note to it, but it was definitely the boy who'd run away from him the night before. Robbie would bet his entire stake in his new ranch that it was the same voice.

He slowly moved his hand to set one finger under the brim of his hat and tip it up. He couldn't see much more than the boy's back, but he recognized the ill-fitting familiar coat, ugly scarf, and dull wool cap. It was him all right.

Slowly getting to his feet, Robbie walked quietly across the room until he was standing directly behind the boy. Even when Mrs. Frankle looked over and frowned at him, Robbie didn't take his gaze off the young man standing in front of him.

"Did you need something, Robbie?"

The boy's shoulders instantly tensed beneath the floppy coat he was wearing. Robbie raised one eyebrow as he clamped a firm hand around shoulders that were almost too delicate, even for a boy. He frowned. The kid must not be getting enough to eat.

"I have to go." The boy did a quick twist, taking Robbie by surprise and dislodging his hand.

Not about to let him pull a disappearing act for the second time, Robbie quickly grabbed onto a handful of coat and held on as his captive strained against the fabric.

"I need to go." The voice was higher and had taken on a desperate quality.

"I'm not going to hurt you, I just want to be sure that you're all right. That was quite a shove you took last night."

"I'm fine. Please let me go."

Robbie frowned and tightened his grip. Something here wasn't right, but he couldn't quite put his finger on it. And he wasn't letting go until he knew what it was that was bothering him. He looked over at Mrs. Frankle who was staring, open-mouthed, at both of them. "We don't want to disturb Doctor Abby's other patients, so we'll go have our little conversation out on the porch."

He didn't wait for a response, but simply dragged his captive back wards out the door, and continued until they'd reached the corner farthest away from any prying eyes or ears. He deliberately switched his grip to the boy's shoulders and spun him around so he could finally get a good look at the kid. But the motion caused the boy's wool cap to fly off his head. Robbie froze, and his mouth dropped to his chest, when a long fall of dark, silky hair brushed across his hands.

"You're a girl."

Deep blue eyes looked back at him, causing his breath to catch in his throat.

"That's very perceptive of you, sir. Now if you'd kindly let go of me?"

Her words didn't register as Robbie's gaze roamed over a flawless complexion tinted slightly from the sun, was a perfect complement to the rose color of her full lips. She was a beauty, despite the way she was dressed. Hell, that face wouldn't be diminished if she was walking around in a burlap sack.

He blinked when he realized she'd said something to him. "What?"

"Please let go of me."

Embarrassed that he was still touching her when clearly she didn't want him to, Robbie lifted his hands and took a quick step back. He felt the heat rising up the back of his neck. He wasn't used to being awkward around a woman and didn't like it one bit. When she turned as if she was going to leave, he blurted out the first thing that came into his mind.

"I know Doctor Abby pretty well. If you're sick, she'll be glad to help you." He felt a twinge of anxiety as she slowly turned back and faced him. "You aren't sick, are you?"

She shook her head. "No. Do you know anyone else in her family?"

That made Robbie grin. "I know everyone in her family."

Her eyes brightened and a hint of a smile crossed her lips. "Do you know Dorrie?"

"Dorrie McKenzie?"

When she deflated, he had to clasp his hands behind his back to keep from reaching out and consoling her.

"No," the dark-haired beauty said slowly. "I'm looking for Dorrie Dolan."

Robbie grinned. "They're one and the same. Dorrie married Marshal McKenzie." He was completely caught up in the spell of the smile that bloomed on her face.

"She did? She married Jules?"

"That would be him."

"When?"

"About a month ago."

Tears sparkled in her eyes. "I'm so glad. He's such a nice man." She surprised him with a deep sigh. "And very handsome. She's been in love with him for a long time."

He didn't much like hearing her give so much praise to another man, even if it was one of his best friends. Thinking to change the subject, and get to the bottom of just who this mysterious woman was, Robbie crossed his arms over his chest and leaned against the porch railing.

"I'm Robbie Smith, by the way. One of Dorrie and Jules' many cousins, after a fashion. And who are you?"

She had the grace to blush as if she'd just realized they hadn't had a proper introduction. "I'm Brenna. Brenna Roberts."

Robbie dropped his arms to his side and straightened back up. "Brenna? Dorrie's friend from the market?"

Brenna's eyes opened wide. "Yes."

"Dorrie said you were missing." He blinked when she ducked her head and looked away.

"I had visitors at the farm."

From the tone of her voice, Robbie gathered she wasn't any too pleased with whoever had come by her farm. "Did you invite these people for a visit?"

All he got for an answer was a shrug.

"I was hoping to talk to Dorrie, but if she's newly married..."

Brenna trailed off when Robbie reached over and took her

hand in his. He drew it through the crook of his elbow and smiled at her confounded look. It was the most proper way he could think of to keep her from bolting. He told himself that Dorrie would never forgive him if he let her friend slip away. And it saved Jules a trip out to wherever this farm of Brenna's was located.

He didn't know where it was, and he didn't care. If there were unwanted visitors there, she needed to stay in town while he dealt with it. And Jules too, of course, he silently added. After all, his friend was a US Marshal.

"I happen to know Dorrie is home right now. I'll be happy to escort you there. She'll be relieved to see you."

"I'm not sure I should drop in on her without telling her first that I'm coming." Brenna wrinkled her nose and looked out at the busy street. "It doesn't seem right to disturb a newly married couple."

Remembering that Jules had spent his wedding night camping out with Ethan rather than with his bride, Robbie grinned and gave her hand a quick pat. "Don't you worry about that, darlin'. It won't bother either of them"

He ignored her puzzled look as he led her across the porch. He did remember to open the front door and call out to Mrs. Frankle that he'd see Doctor Abby later at home, before he turned them both toward the side of the house. He sent up a small prayer of thanks that he'd borrowed a horse and carriage from Ammie's stable. He might have had a difficult time explaining to Brenna why they'd have to share the same saddle on Hayseed, although the image that came to mind made him smile.

It wasn't such a bad idea. The fact was, he'd likely enjoy that.

CHAPTER SIX

"HERE WE ARE." ROBBIE PULLED THE CARRIAGE HORSE UP IN front of the McKenzie home. He made a quick exit then turned and held his hand out before Brenna had a chance to climb out on her own.

She gave his hand a wary look. It took some effort on his part not to grin at his passenger's obvious reluctance to touch him. He could almost hear her trying to think of a way not to put her hand in his. He waited patiently until Brenna finally gave in. He closed his long fingers around her much more delicate ones, enjoying the feel of her skin on his. When her feet were on the ground she immediately withdrew her hand and stuck it in the pocket of her coat so he had no chance to recapture it.

Robbie had taken several steps forward before he realized he was walking by himself. He turned his head to look back at Brenna. She was staring at the house as if it were a two-headed monster that she was afraid to go approach. Her eyes were huge, and he doubted she was even aware that she was shaking her head. His brow wrinkled as he glanced over at the house. He didn't see anything unusual about the place. When his gaze returned to

Brenna, her head was down and there was a definite stain of red splashing across her cheeks.

He felt his temper stir. Did she think she wasn't good enough to walk into Dorrie's house? He opened his mouth and then closed it again as he studied her. Women could get some peculiar ideas sometimes. Especially about clothes.

He was eight when he'd gone to live on Lillian Jamison's orphan ranch, and there had been enough girls there during his growing years that he'd seen for himself how odd they could be about what they put on their bodies. Given his experience with that, it was probably likely Brenna wished she was in a fancy dress to go calling at her friend's house, rather than a pair of boy's britches. He thought she looked just fine, but females didn't always see things the same way.

Even though he thought that kind of notion was foolish, he didn't want her to refuse to go inside. She worried him. He still had no idea where she'd gone after she'd disappeared from The Crimson Rose the night before, but where ever it was, she hadn't gotten much sleep. Robbie could see the shadows under her eyes, and was sure she was probably hungry too. None of that sat well in his gut. He needed to get her into that house so Dina and Dorrie could get some food into her and make her rest, and Abby could even take a look at her.

He glanced toward the side of the house. "I need to take Ginger over to the stable." When Brenna raised her head and looked his way, he smiled as he jerked a thumb toward the placid horse at the front of the carriage. "She can be stubborn at times. Dorrie's mentioned that you grew up on a farm. Would you mind giving me a hand?"

Brenna's head turned toward the horse and then back to him. She hadn't said a word on the entire ride to Dorrie's house, and didn't say one now, but she did nod her agreement, and that was good enough.

Robbie waited until she'd taken up a spot on the opposite side of Ginger, and together they walked the unresisting horse into the stable. When Brenna automatically began to unhitch the horse from the carriage, Robbie simply worked beside her. Once Ginger was taken care of, he pointed toward a door at the rear of the house.

"Let's go in through the kitchen. It's closer than walking back out to the front porch."

This time Brenna only hesitated for a moment before she fell into step beside him. Breathing a sigh of relief that at least he'd get her into the house, Robbie opened the door and moved aside so she could step in ahead of him.

The heavenly aroma that filled the kitchen left no doubt that Dina was making bread. He took in a deep, audible sniff of the air, and felt a good dose of satisfaction when he heard the same sound come from Brenna. He lifted a hand in greeting when Dina turned around from stirring a pot bubbling away on top of the stove. The stocky woman gave a friendly smile to Brenna before pointing the spoon she was holding in her hand at Robbie.

"Robbie Smith. You've been taught better manners than to bring guests through the kitchen door." She shook her head at him before shifting her gaze back to the silent Brenna. "Hello. I'm Dina McKenzie."

When Brenna still didn't say a word but looked at the floor, Robbie sighed. "Dorrie says she's more family than guest."

He smiled when Brenna's head snapped up. That certainly got her attention, which is what he'd intended to do. "This is Brenna."

Dina gasped and then hurried forward, her arms extended and the spoon still in her hand. "Brenna? Of course, of course. How wonderful Robbie found you. Dorrie will be so relieved to see you."

When the much shorter Dina engulfed her visitor in a hug, Brenna looked over her head and shot a confused look at Robbie who only grinned back at her.

"Dina? I thought I saw Robbie walking with someone toward the stables. Have you seen...?" Dorrie stopped in mid-sentence when she caught sight of Brenna. Letting out a small shriek, she leaped forward as Dina stepped back, beaming at both of them.

Dorrie had no sooner wrapped her arms around her friend when Brenna dropped her head onto Dorrie's shoulder and burst into tears.

Robbie froze in place. Brenna's sobs tore into his nerves, and the overwhelming need to protect her had him stepping forward. But he was blocked by Dina who suddenly appeared in front of him.

Her hands were on her hips and her eyes were narrowed into a glare. It was the same look she always gave him whenever he'd done something she wholeheartedly disapproved of. And right now, Dorrie was giving him that exact same look that women had perfected so well.

"What did you say to Brenna, Robbie Smith?"

His back went stiff, and he glared right back at Dorrie. "I didn't say anything to make her cry."

Dorrie only sniffed at that and so did Dina, who raised one arm straight out and pointed a finger at the door leading into the back hallway. "Robbie, you get yourself into the parlor while we sort this out."

Indignant over the unfair accusations from both women, he still couldn't disobey Dina. Once Brenna had set them both straight, he was going to demand an apology. In the meantime, he had no choice but to make a retreat. But he sure didn't have to like it.

Stomping his way across the kitchen, he gave the door into the hallway a hard shove that sent it banging against the wall. Not feeling the least contrite over the show of temper, he marched into the parlor, ignoring the startled looks from Ammie and Jules.

"What's gotten into you?" Jules demanded. He looked past Robbie. "And where's my wife?"

"Your wife is what's gotten into me, and she's in the kitchen trying to console a crying Brenna." Robbie blinked when Ammie flew off her seat on the divan and faced him with her hands on her hips.

"Brenna? She's in the kitchen with Dorrie? And she's crying?"

Confronted with another woman who was glaring at him for no good reason, Robbie let out an exasperated snort. "Yes, she is. I ran into her at Doctor Abby's and brought her here. It seemed like a good idea, but all it's done is make her cry."

"What did you say to her?" Ammie demanded.

Robbie rolled his eyes and threw up his hands. "I didn't say anything to her."

"You just dragged her over here without saying a word? No wonder she's crying."

"That's not what I..." He couldn't believe it when Ammie walked right past him and out the parlor doors.

There was a long silence as the two men stared at the empty doorway. Jules finally raised one eyebrow and looked over at his friend.

"Care to explain to me what just happened here?"

"I'd be happy to if I had any idea myself." Shaking his head in disbelief, Robbie walked over to the divan that Ammie had deserted and flopped down.

"What's going on?" Ethan stood in the doorway. "I came into the kitchen and I hear a woman crying, and then Ammie points a finger at me and orders me to go to the parlor with the rest of the idiots." He frowned at Jules. "What the hell was she talking about?"

Jules shrugged. "Apparently either all men are idiots or just the one over there." He jerked his head at Robbie.

Ethan's mouth dropped open. "You made a woman cry?"

"I didn't make anyone cry." Robbie had had his fill of hearing that. He'd never make Brenna cry. "She was fine until I brought her here. Just seeing Dorrie made her burst into tears."

"That doesn't make any sense." Ethan frowned. "Dorrie's her friend."

"We need to hear the whole story." Jules walked over and took a seat one of the chairs next to the fireplace and pointed to the empty one next to him. "Take a seat, Ethan. Robbie has some explaining to do."

As Ethan walked across the room, Robbie rubbed a hand across his chin. He wished he knew what had upset Brenna so suddenly.

"Well?" Ethan demanded when Robbie stayed silent. "How is it that you happened to bring Brenna here?"

"I sort of ran into her last night at The Crimson Rose."

"Sort of?" Jules frowned.

Robbie shrugged. "I didn't know it was her. I thought she was a boy some big man was being too rough with."

Jules' eyebrows shot straight up. "You thought Brenna was a boy? With that face of hers?" He shot Ethan a grin. "I've met the woman. The only way any male would think she was a boy is if it were pitch black and he couldn't see his hand in front of his face."

Robbie gave a mental groan when Ethan laughed. "I didn't get a good look at her. I was keeping my eye on the man who was pushing her around."

Ethan made a tsking sound in the back of his throat. "You let a man put his hands on a woman that way?"

"No. I told you, I was trying to keep his hands off of her, and I didn't know he was a woman." Robbie took a deep breath. "I mean I didn't know the boy I thought he was shoving was actually a 'she'."

The marshal gave a solemn nod. "All right. You had trouble recognizing a woman." Jules grinned when Robbie glared at him. "I gather you did manage to keep her from getting a beating?"

"Yes. And while I was doing that, she ran out the door."

"Didn't you follow her?" Ethan asked.

Robbie nodded. "I did. But she'd vanished." He gritted his teeth when Ethan started laughing again.

"You couldn't chase down a woman?" When Robbie glared at him, Ethan only laughed harder.

The marshal reached over and gave Ethan's arm a sharp slap.

"Let him finish. I want to hear how he happened to find Brenna again."

"I didn't. She found me." Robbie slumped further down in the divan when both his friends rolled their eyes. "I went to see Abby this morning about my leg, and Brenna walked in. I wasn't about to lose her a second time. That's when she told me her name, and that she was looking for Dorrie. So I told her I could take her to see Dorrie."

"And that's all you said to her?" Jules asked.

"Pretty much. She didn't say a word on the ride over here, so I didn't either."

"So then you brought her here and she started crying?" Ethan shook his head. "Sounds like a female thing to do."

Glad to finally get some male understanding of the situation, Robbie smiled. "I think she's just tired and hungry. I don't know where she went after she left The Crimson Rose, but I don't think she slept much." He glanced over at Jules. "Maybe we should send for Abby to take a look at her."

"Dorrie will see to whatever she needs," Jules assured him. He looked at Robbie's leg. "Did Abby get a chance to look at your leg?"

Robbie shook his head. "No, but it doesn't matter. I just wanted an excuse to get away from Ammie's house."

Ethan's eyes narrowed on Robbie's face. "You're staying with Ammie?"

Before Robbie could say a word, Dina appeared in the doorway. She directed a stern look at Ethan.

"Don't you start in on that, Ethan Mayes. We have bigger problems."

"Such as?" Ethan said, not taking his eyes off of Robbie.

"Right now, Brenna's needs come first," Dina declared, drawing the attention of all three men.

Robbie rose to his feet, his shoulders tensed. "What's wrong? Should I get Abby?"

"She isn't sick, Robbie. She needs food and rest is all. And to know she has friends to help her. Brenna's had a very hard time of it." Dina's eyes softened and her mouth turned down at the corners. "She was put out of her home."

"Who put Brenna out?" Robbie demanded.

"The son of the people she thought of as her grandparents." Dina clasped her hands in front of her and sighed. "It seems her meemaw and gramps died within days of each other, and their son came to claim the farm. He took Brenna as far as the edge of town and left her there." Dina wiped away the single tear rolling down her cheek. "The poor thing had to change into her boy's garb behind a shack and leave the rest of her belongings under a pile of leaves." She looked over at Jules. "After Brenna's rested up, Dorrie intends to go back there with her and fetch them."

"I'll get them for her," Robbie spoke up. He didn't notice the surprised looks from both his friends. He glanced over toward the doorway. "Is she upstairs resting now?"

"That's what I came to talk to you about, Robbie. Brenna has gone home with Ammie, and Dorrie went along to be sure she got all settled in there."

"What?"

"You'll be staying here," Dina continued on. "It wouldn't be right for you to stay with Ammie while Brenna is there."

"What?" Robbie didn't know why not. Aunt Charlotte, Helen, and even Ammie should be enough to satisfy any gossiping busybodies.

"Ammie said she'd let you know if there was anything more you could do for Brenna."

"What?" Robbie couldn't believe that Ammie really thought he'd meekly go along with not helping Brenna.

"Has your hearing suddenly gone bad?" Ethan asked. He grinned at Jules. "Did you understand what Dina said? Because Robbie sure doesn't."

"Perfectly." Jules turned a bland look on Robbie. "But I'll be happy to explain. You'll no longer be staying at Ammie's place, and you aren't to go near Brenna unless the women say you can."

"I heard her," Robbie snapped at his friend. "But I'm not staying here."

"That's fine then," Dina said loudly, her voice carrying clearly through the entire parlor. "You can sweet-talk your Uncle Charles into giving you one of the family rooms at The Crimson Rose, along with the one's he's already given to Ethan. Now, I have work to do." She gave a parental stare to each of the men she'd known since they were boys wrestling each other on her kitchen floor, finally settling her gaze on Jules. "You make sure the two of them behave."

Jules laughed. "How do you suggest I do that?"

"You're a US Marshal, Jules McKenzie. You just figure it out." Dina gave them all one last warning look before leaving them alone.

"So," Jules drawled with a glance at Robbie. "Are you going to behave and stay away from Brenna, or do I have to arrest you?"

Robbie cocked an eyebrow at him. "Don't you have a dozen or so outlaws you have to go chasing after? Maybe somewhere outside of town?"

The marshal grinned. "No. And unlike you, I'm going to sleep just fine tonight. In a nice warm bed, with my wife, while you two go find a bed at the gaming hall." He glanced over at Ethan. "Either one of you have a problem with that?"

"Shut up, Jules," both his friends said in unison.

CHAPTER SEVEN

"I didn't have any way to prove that MeeMaw and Gramps wanted to leave the farm to me." Brenna lifted her shoulders in a resigned shrug.

After she'd practically inhaled the food the very kind Helen had set in front of her last night, Brenna had been awe-struck when Ammie had not only had a hot bath ready for her, but had handed her a silk nightgown and left her in a bedchamber that was larger than any Brenna had ever imagined. It was only the second time she'd ever touched silk, much less worn something made from it, and the very first time she'd ever slept on a feather mattress, or any mattress that wasn't made from a pile of straw.

As exhausted as she'd been, she hadn't stayed awake long enough to enjoy the soft bed, or the feel of silk against her skin. But when she'd opened her eyes just before dawn as was her habit from many years of tending to farm animals, and hadn't heard anyone else stirring in the house, she'd lain in that soft bed for a good half-hour, enjoying a luxury she was certain she'd never have again.

"But after all the years of work you'd done, surely he must have considered that it would have been a reasonable thing for his parents to do?" Dorrie's question brought Brenna back to the very real problems she was facing, now that the morning sun was well over the horizon.

She was once again back in her britches, having ignored the fancy skirt and blouse left draped over a chair in the bedchamber. Those weren't for her. She'd have to make do with what she had.

"Daniel had already made up his mind to give the farm to his daughter and her husband." Brenna had no problem remembering the smug look on Roberta's face when her father had made that announcement. "I could have had a hundred pieces of paper saying the farm was mine and he still wouldn't have believed it." Her lips curved up into a rueful smile. "Daniel's wife, Lizzie, told me that he wanted Roberta and what she called her daughter's 'useless husband', out of his house, and the farm was the way to do that, I guess."

"It still wasn't fair to you," Ammie declared.

The three women were sitting in the pink parlor of the home Ammie shared with her Aunt Charlotte. Brenna had blinked when she first saw the room, but having no experience with large houses in the city, she'd figured that was just the way the rooms were decorated, with pink everywhere.

She was sitting on the edge of a dainty chair with a pretty cushion boasting a whole bouquet of embroidered flowers on its top. She wasn't entirely sure if you were supposed to sit on all those flowers, so she carefully kept to the very edge.

"Fair or not, we have to deal with the way it is," Dorrie said. She smiled at her friend. "First, we need to decide on where you want to stay."

Brenna nodded her agreement. She couldn't do anything to change what had happened at the farm. All she could do was look to the future. And she'd given it some thought while she'd lain in that soft bed, enjoying the cool touch of the silk nightgown.

"I was hoping you might let me stay in your stable." She wasn't used to asking for favors, but didn't have a lot of choices left to her. "I can help with the horses, and I can pay a little too. Lizzie Tolan gave me a five-dollar gold piece."

"Brenna Roberts, don't insult our friendship," Dorrie said quietly. "I would have been devastated if I'd discovered what had happened to you and you hadn't come to me straightaway."

The hurt look in Dorrie's eyes made Brenna ashamed and grateful all at the same time. She'd never meant to injure her friend's feelings, but felt a warmth at the sincerity in Dorrie's voice. She was the only friend Brenna had ever had, and the very best one any person could ask for.

"You can count me as one of your friends too, Brenna," Ammie declared.

Brenna blushed as she sent a sideways glance at the stunning brunette who had shown her so much generosity. No wonder Robbie Smith was courting her. It was a puzzle to her why every eligible man in the city wasn't at her doorstep. But the fact was that Brenna could still remember the spurt of pleasure she'd felt when Robbie had drawn her hand through the crook of his elbow, and she was feeling guilty about it.

He belonged with this beautiful woman sitting across from her, and Brenna shouldn't be attracted to him. It was wrong. Wanting to atone for her errant thoughts about Ammie's beau, Brenna found the courage to face her hostess, and even managed a smile.

"Thank you. That's very kind of you." Having gotten those words out, Brenna was at a loss at to what to say next.

"Now that we have that settled, all you have to do is decide where you want to stay," Ammie declared, seemingly oblivious to Brenna's abrupt silence. "Since Dorrie and Jules are newly married, staying with me is the better choice." She gave Brenna an exaggerated wink. "Even Jules' brother, Cade, and his wife, Abby, don't spend much time in the house whenever Dorrie and Jules are around."

Dorrie lifted her chin and wrinkled her nose. "That isn't true at all, Amelia Jamison, and stop saying such things. You're embarrassing Brenna."

"Since she grew up on a farm, I doubt that very much." Amelia's bright laugh had Brenna smiling.

"Oh, Ammie, dear?" The tall woman with the sausage-sized curls stuck her head around the doorway. "Can you please come talk to Helen? She's insisting there's a dark shadow coming, but isn't making any sense about it at all."

"Of course, Aunt Charlotte. I'll be right there." As Charlotte's head disappeared, Ammie stood and shook out the skirts of her deep-blue gown. "Oh bother. Helen's been going on about this dark shadow for the last two months." She gave Brenna an apologetic smile. "Please excuse me for a moment and think about staying here with us. I'd truly love the company."

As Brenna turned a questioning look on Dorrie, her friend let out a long sigh. "Helen has what Aunt Charlotte and Dorrie's mam call 'the sight'."

Brenna wasn't entirely sure what "the sight" meant, but it didn't sound like it was anything good. "Is it some kind of sickness?"

Dorrie laughed. "Heavens, no. Helen can see things that might happen in the future."

And she was seeing a dark shadow? Brenna's eyes grew wide. Now that was something to worry about! She chewed on her lower lip and considered the possibilities. "Do you think the dark shadow Helen sees is me?"

Her friend smiled as she gave her head a decisive shake. "Of course not. Most of the time even Helen doesn't know what her dark shadows are." Dorrie shook her head again. "Helen's been talking about a 'dark shadow' ever since I can remember."

"Oh." Brenna didn't quite understand it all, but since Dorrie didn't seem concerned, she decided there was no need for her to be either. But there was something she wanted to tell Dorrie before Ammie returned to the parlor. Keeping one eye on the doorway, Brenna leaned forward and lowered her voice. "I'm very grateful for Ammie's offer to stay here, but I don't think her beau would like that."

"Her beau? When did you meet Ethan?"

"Who?" Brenna frowned. Ethan? Did Ammie have two men courting her?

Dorrie cleared her throat. "Never mind. Who do you think is Ammie's beau?"

"Well, Robbie, of course. I saw them together at that gambling hall." Brenna cut her words off as Ammie strolled back into the room.

Once she was seated, Ammie looked from Brenna's downcast eyes to Dorrie's amused grin. "Did I miss something?"

Brenna shook her head while Dorrie nodded hers.

"Brenna doesn't think your beau will approve of her staying here with you."

"My beau?" Ammie's wide-eyed gaze shifted to Brenna. "What beau?"

"Robbie," Brenna said in a small voice. "You were with him at the gambling hall."

"Robbie?" Ammie's stunned expression quickly gave way to a peal of laughter. "Robbie Smith?"

At Brenna's nod, Ammie laughed even harder and Dorrie joined in, while Brenna wondered what the two of them found to be so funny. Robbie Smith was a good-looking man. Any woman would be proud to have him as her beau.

When she'd finally wound down into a few giggles, Ammie looked over at her childhood friend. "Did I tell you what that idiot told Aunt Charlotte yesterday? He told her that he'd been my chaperon at The Crimson Rose while I was entertaining a suitor."

"He didn't?"

Ammie's confirming nod set Dorrie off into another round of laughter while Brenna tried to make sense of the whole exchange.

"Robbie isn't your suitor?" She finally asked. When Ammie shook her head, Brenna smiled. "So this Ethan is your beau?"

"What?" Anmie's eyes shot wide open as Dorrie's laughter dissolved into a fit of coughing.

"No, no," Dorrie choked out. "Ammie doesn't have a suitor. At least not one she's willing to acknowledge."

"Oh." Brenna had no idea why Ammie was suddenly glaring at Dorrie, but she was cheered by the fact that Robbie and Ammie weren't interested in each other that way. Well, at least *she* isn't interested in Robbie. Brenna wondered how the tall rancher felt about Ammie.

"So it's settled then," her hostess finally said. "You'll stay here and save me from Aunt Charlotte constantly bringing around women who have eligible sons."

Brenna gave her an uncertain look. "I don't want to be a bother. I could help out with the chores."

"We have more than enough help," Ammie assured her. "Maybe you'd like to help me with my inquiries."

"Inquiries?" Brenna didn't have any idea what that might be.

"Ammie, you are not going to teach Brenna how to follow people around without them knowing it." Dorrie's firm voice left no doubt what she thought of Ammie's idea.

"You spy on people?" Brenna was not only astonished at such a notion, but fascinated too. She never would have thought the refined and elegant Ammie would do such a thing.

"Not spy, exactly. I have clients who are worried about other family members, or maybe business associates, and I help put those worries to rest."

"Or maybe she could help with the new sweets shop I'm planning." Dorrie smiled at Brenna. "I know you like to cook, you told me so yourself. And Dina's husband is one of the best cooks in the city. He said he'd help me with the baked goods. I intend to get it open before the end of the year."

Brenna's hopes fell back to the pit of her stomach. She couldn't live off her friends for that long. She'd love to help Dorrie with her shop, but she'd need to find other work until then. And besides cooking and tending to animals, the only other thing she knew how to do was a little sewing and how to take care of a farm. She hadn't seen any farms when she'd been wandering around the city. But she still smiled at her friend.

"I'd love to help you. But until then, I'll start looking for other work to tide me over." Taking a deep breath, and swallowing a bit of her pride, she turned her smile on Ammie. "And I'd be happy to stay here with you, and thank you for that kindness."

"Wonderful," Dorrie smiled. "I thought you would, so I've already asked Helen to pack up Robbie's things. I'll take them with me."

"Robbie's things?" Brenna wondered why Robbie had his belongings at Ammie's house.

"Oh, don't start with that again," Ammie scolded. Apparently she'd seen the questioning look on Brenna's face. "Robbie's family. Just like Dorrie's a sister to me, our Robbie is more like a very annoying brother. He only stayed here because he refused to be in the same house with two newlyweds."

"Honestly. From the way everyone talks, you'd think Jules and I do nothing but kiss all day," Dorrie complained.

Ammie smiled sweetly and batted her long eyelashes. "Or something like that."

Red bloomed along Dorrie's cheeks. "Oh, do be quiet."

Brenna laughed. The two of them really did act like sisters. "Why don't we find something else to talk about?" she offered, hoping a change of subject would keep Dorrie's face from going completely red.

"Excellent!" Ammie clapped her hands together. "Let's talk about *your* beau."

Dorrie grinned. "Yes, let's do that."

Both women turned and raised an eyebrow at Brenna, who stared back at them in astonishment. "My beau? I don't have a beau."

"Oh really?" Dorrie's eyes crinkled at the corners. "Then who was that man who you said wouldn't let go of you once he saw you at Abby's practice?"

Ammie tapped a slim finger against her lower lip. "Why I

believe it was the same one who went charging after you when you ran out of The Crimson Rose, then spent the entire night worrying about where you'd disappeared to."

Dorrie glanced over at Ammie and nodded. "And he almost fell apart when Brenna started crying in the kitchen. I've never seen that look on his face before."

Brenna, who was about to deny the whole ridiculous conversation, was brought up short by Dorrie's comment. "What look?"

"As if he wanted to rip apart whoever it was who'd made you cry."

Blue eyes blinked back at Dorrie. "Oh, he did not."

"Yes, he did," Dorrie stated.

"This is all fascinating," Ammie declared. "Is there anything else unusual our Robbie did?"

Ignoring Brenna, Dorrie smiled at Ammie. "If Dina hadn't been blocking his path when Brenna started crying, I swear Robbie would have grabbed her and carried her away."

Brenna's mouth dropped open. She was completely dumbfounded. Robbie Smith may have been a little high-handed in how he'd gotten her to Dorrie's house, but it wasn't because he was smitten with her. She would have known something like that. After all, she wasn't completely naïve. Quite a few of the men who'd come to sell their produce at the market had approached her. Both the single and the married ones.

"Brenna, what is it you said happened to the rest of your things?" Ammie smiled when Brenna glanced over at her.

Glad not to talk about a certain rancher anymore, Brenna shrugged. "I had to leave them behind a deserted shed. I thought it would make the walk into town a bit easier, and if I wasn't carrying anything, no one would have any reason to try to rob me."

"Very clever of you." Her hostess nodded her approval. "How long did it take you to walk from the shed to the square? That was where you met that miner you told us about last night, wasn't it?"

"Yes. He was a nice old man." Brenna's forehead wrinkled as

she considered Ammie's question. "It took me a little more than an hour, I think."

"A little more than an hour? That's a long way to walk." Ammie leaned against the divan's cushioned back and tilted her head to one side. "Do you remember what the shack looked like? Or anything about its surroundings?"

CHAPTER EIGHT

"So, we're agreed?"

Robbie stared back at Ethan, wondering how many times he was going to have to repeat himself before his friend believed him. "I said I wouldn't stay at Ammie's place again if you'd find out from Dina what else Brenna told the women last night."

Ethan stuck out his hand. "Then we have a bargain."

Exasperated, Robbie took the offered hand and gave it one, hard shake. "There. Are you satisfied now?"

"All right. But you have to keep your word even if you don't like what I have to tell you."

"Fine," Robbie agreed. "And by the way, that's more than just a friendly concern you have over who's staying with Ammie."

"You're imagining things, Robbie. I'm just being a gentleman." Ethan narrowed his gaze on his friend. "And making sure that you're being one too."

"Uh huh."

"Do you want to hear what I found out from Dina or not?"

Robbie let Ethan's secret obsession with Ammie go, and got back to the business at hand. "I said I did. So, what did Dina say?"

Ethan leaned back in the comfortable chair set at the far end of the second floor of The Crimson Rose. A long bar made of a rich mahogany spanned one entire side of the room, and most of the tables clustered around it were occupied by small groups of men. Ethan pointed at the half-filled whiskey glass sitting in front of Robbie.

"You might need that." When the rancher started to tap his fingers on the tabletop, Ethan grinned. "Dina said Brenna was left outside of town and had to abandon her belongings behind a shack."

Robbie rolled his eyes. He'd already heard that part of the story. He began to tap louder on the tabletop.

"I'm working up to it," Ethan said. "She walked into town and an old miner told her how to get to The Crimson Rose."

Robbie's fingers stopped tapping and his hand clenched into a fist. "She walked into the Barbary Coast by herself?"

Ethan raised one eyebrow. "How did you *think* she got to The Crimson Rose?"

Robbie ignored the question and asked one of his own. "Where did she go that night?"

"Dina said she found a deserted street where there were shops closed up for the night and slept in one of the alleys there."

"All night? In an alley by herself?" Robbie sat straight up and his fist came down on the table with a hard thump. "She could have been killed!"

"But she wasn't," Ethan pointed out. "So there's no use getting mad about it now."

Since his blood had already started to boil, Robbie thought that piece of advice was too late. "What else?"

Ethan shrugged. "Not much else to tell that you already don't know. She found out where Doctor Abby's practice was, and walked in there intending to ask Abby how to find Dorrie. But she ran into you instead." Ethan grinned. "Or rather Dina said you grabbed onto her and wouldn't let go."

"I didn't want her running off again."

"Uh huh," Ethan said, in a perfect imitation of his friend.

"She got herself into trouble the night before, and it was my gentlemanly duty to be sure she didn't stumble into any more of it."

"Uh huh."

"And Dorrie had already said she was worried about her friend, Brenna, and I sure didn't want Dorrie worrying when she didn't have to."

"Uh huh."

Robbie glared at his friend. "Don't you have anything else to say?"

Ethan's grin got wider. "Nope."

"Fine." Robbie forced himself to relax back into his chair. He figured there was no use in giving his friend anything else to add to that smug smile of his, so he deliberately switched his conversation to another topic. "I've almost got enough to finish paying for that land up north. Another few months should do it."

"You figure on leaving sometime at the end of the summer?"

Robbie nodded. "I've already talked to Lillian. She's fine with it. She thinks since all the hands want to come with me to start the new place, she might sell The Orphan Ranch." Robbie sighed and looked down at his hands wrapped around the whiskey glass. "I'll miss the place."

Ethan nodded his understanding. "You grew up there after your ma died. It's home to you. Hard to see your home sold off to someone else."

His friend was right about that. Robbie had a lot of good memories there, and he liked managing the place for Lillian. But he'd dreamed for years of having a ranch he'd built on his own, and he'd worked hard and saved every penny he could to make that happen.

"Is Shue going with you?"

Since Shue was an old friend of Ethan's sister, Shannon, he had a natural interest in what the woman's plans were. Robbie knew that Shannon was hoping the crusty former miner would come live out her days in the cabin Shannon had built for her on their land.

From the rather broad hints, and outright declarations, that Shue had been making over the past six months, Robbie was certain Shannon was going to get her wish.

"Shue won't be coming, so she'll be headed back to your place sometime this summer."

"Shannon will be happy to hear that." Ethan smiled.

Even though the expert tracker and Shannon weren't blood related, Shannon had taken Ethan in and had had a legal paper drawn up declaring him as her brother. As far as the two of them were concerned, they were family. And Robbie thought of him the same way. In his mind, Ethan was a brother exactly the same way he felt about Jules.

"Shue came into town with me to see to the supplies. I guess the last time I forgot to get saffron." Robbie shrugged. "I don't even know what that is."

Ethan held up a hand with the palm out. "I don't either. What is it?"

"Something you cook with, I guess." Feeling restless, Robbie shoved his chair back and stood up. "I've got to take a ride out to the southern edge of town. Do you want to come along?"

Ethan got to his feet as well. "Depends on why you're going. There's nothing out there but trees and shacks."

"Ammie sent me a note describing the shack where Brenna had to leave her things."

His friend rolled his eyes to the ceiling. "You're going to go searching behind every shack on the road leading out of town? They're spread out over a couple of miles."

Robbie shrugged his broad shoulders. "Ammie's note said it took Brenna just over an hour to walk to Portsmouth Square. That narrows it down some."

"Uh huh."

"Don't start on that again," Robbie warned. "She can't go running around in britches all the time. She needs the rest of her things."

"Uh huh." At Robbie's hard stare, Ethan grinned and held up

his hands. "All right. She needs the rest of her things. But I'd like to point out that she's staying at Ammie's, and that woman probably has wardrobes full of clothes she's never even worn. She won't mind sharing with Brenna."

"What's that got to do with Brenna getting back her own things?"

Ethan shrugged. "It would save you a long afternoon of searching for something you're not likely to find."

"Well, at least I could tell her I tried."

"You can find something else to be her hero about."

Robbie was back to glaring at his friend. "I'm not trying to be anyone's hero."

Ethan crossed his arms over his chest. "Uh huh."

The rancher mimicked Ethan's stance and stared back at him. "I don't like to see people treated so poorly for no reason at all." He cocked an eyebrow at Ethan. "How would you feel if you'd been tossed out of the only home you had, and dropped off miles away from it in the middle of the night?"

Shifting from one foot to the other, Ethan dropped his arms. "Hard thing to have happen."

"I think I can spare a couple of hours of my time to look for Brenna's things. It might help ease some of the hurt." Robbie also unwound his arms and passed a hand across his chin. "I don't like to hear that anyone was treated that way."

Ethan nodded. "It does make you want to go out and give the person who did that to her a good talking to."

"Or maybe something else if talking doesn't work." Robbie had considered doing exactly that, but knew the two marshals in the family wouldn't approve. Not to mention all the women. And from what little he knew of her, he was pretty sure Brenna wouldn't either. So the next best thing he could do was to fetch her belongings for her.

"Fine." Ethan let out a sigh. "If we're going to go on this fool's errand, we may as well get started before we lose any more daylight."

———

"THIS ONE LOOKS RIGHT," Robbie called out, glancing away from the heavily leaning shack to Ammie's note that he held in his hand.

"More than the last ten or so we've already searched?" Ethan grumbled.

"She walked faster than I figured. Must be those long legs, I guess."

"Not surprised you noticed those." Ethan looked around before he dismounted. He walked slowly, searching the ground between the road and the sagging structure set back on the edge of a thick patch of weeds. "Hard to tell, but it looks like someone came through here not too long ago." He looked up and pointed to the edge of the shack. "Whoever it was, was headed in that direction."

Robbie slid off his saddle and gave Hayseed a pat on the neck as he walked around his horse. "Brenna said she left her things in back."

Nodding, Ethan kept his head down as he walked slowly toward the shack, skirting around its side toward the rear. Robbie followed him, stopping when Ethan did. Now that they were standing behind the sad-looking building, the signs that someone had recently been there were more obvious. So was the slight mound of leaves that had been scraped into a pile next to the rotting boards along the bottom of the shack. Robbie stepped forward and knelt down, pushing aside the leaves to uncover a small burlap sack. He picked it up and shook it, frowning at how light it was. Whatever was in it, there wasn't much of it. He held it out so Ethan could see it.

"Do you think someone else got here first?"

Ethan glanced at the limp-looking sack and then at the ground around them before he shook his head. "Doesn't look like it." He pushed his broad-brimmed hat further back on his head and frowned. "Could be that's all she has."

The slow simmer that started in Robbie's veins had already become such a familiar feeling when it came to Brenna, that he hardly noticed it. "They didn't let her leave with much for all those years she spent working on that farm."

His friend gave him a solemn nod. "Something else for you to talk over with the man who did that to her."

"Amen to that," Robbie said under his breath.

Now *there* was a discussion he was looking forward to having one day soon.

CHAPTER NINE

"AND THIS ONE, I THINK." AMMIE HELD UP A DEEP-BLUE SKIRT. "It's the same color as your eyes, and I have a matching ribbon."

Brenna thought the skirt, and the lace-trimmed white blouse Ammie had brought in with it, was beautiful. But as much as she appreciated her newest friend's unfailing generosity, she was going to have to put her foot down. Ammie had already given her three dresses and a half-dozen skirts. Brenna had no idea why she would need so many clothes. Her hand ran down the soft muslin of the pale-yellow dress lying next to her on the bed. Although they certainly were beautiful.

Stiffening her resolve, Brenna shook her head. "No more." When Ammie wrinkled her nose, Brenna laughed but held her ground. "No more, Amelia Jamison. If I need anything else, I'll just go into your wardrobe and help myself. I doubt if you'd miss it."

Ammie gave a careless shrug. "My Uncle Charles bought most of them for me. Even Aunt Lillian thinks he was far too indulgent. But Aunt Charlotte is convinced that every young lady needs what she refers to as 'a proper wardrobe', and all she had to do was mention that she was going to go out and buy me a gown and suddenly Dorrie's mam would show up at the house, measuring me." Amelia grinned. "It was Uncle Charles' way of being sure I didn't end up drowning in an endless sea of pink satin."

"You have a wonderful family."

The brunette beauty shrugged. "Most of them are."

Since they'd stayed up late into the night exchanging confidences, Brenna didn't have to ask why Ammie had said that. Sometime around midnight, the two women discovered they had something in common. Both of them had lost their parents. And although Brenna's had both died in a terrible fire, she at least knew what had happened to her mama and her papa. All Ammie knew was that her father had been murdered, and her mother had returned to her high-society lifestyle in New York without her very young daughter. And although Charles and Charlotte were her real uncle and aunt, Brenna still wouldn't trade her own story for Ammie's, no matter how privileged her friend's life might seem.

The two striking brunettes exchanged a knowing look.

"Someday I'm going to find them both," Ammie said quietly. "My mother, and the man who killed my father."

Staring at the fierce determination in Ammie's eyes, Brenna wondered if that was why she'd started her "inquiries" business, where she followed people around to discover what they were up to. Maybe Ammie's next step was to learn how to find someone who had disappeared. The way the man who'd murdered her father had.

"Revenge isn't always a good thing," Brenna said in the same quiet tone. "People with secrets don't like to have them revealed. You could get hurt."

Ammie shrugged as she leaned over and picked up Brenna's old coat that had fallen to the floor. "We should get this washed. And your britches too. And we need to have Dorrie's mam make you at least one more pair." She wiggled her eyebrows. "I have four pairs myself."

Brenna laughed. "You're funning with me." She simply could not picture the very elegant Amelia Jamison in a pair of britches.

"I most certainly do," Ammie insisted. "So does Aunt Lillian."

She frowned at the crackling noise coming from the coat pocket. "What's that?"

"Here. Give it to me and I'll show you." Brenna held out her hand. Once Ammie had relinquished her ragged coat, Brenna reached into the pocket and pulled out a sheaf of papers. "It's letters to my papa. He kept them in a tin box that Gramps found after the fire."

"Really?" Ammie looked fascinated. "Who are they from?"

"Papa's family, I think. I'm not positive though," Brenna admitted.

"Why not? Haven't you read them?"

Biting her lower lip, Brenna dropped her gaze to the neatly stacked and tied letters she held in her hand. "Did you mean it when you said that friends never tell each other's secrets?"

"Of course I did." Ammie walked over to the bed and sat next to Brenna. "Are the letters a secret?"

Making up her mind, Brenna took a deep breath. "I don't know. Because I can't read them."

"Why not? I don't think your papa would mind."

"No," Brenna said slowly. "I mean I *can't* read them. I don't know how to read." She looked up, relieved to see astonishment in Ammie's gaze, but no ridicule. "My papa was going to teach me, but there was so much work on the farm he never had the chance."

"And your mama couldn't read either, otherwise she would have taught you," Ammie guessed.

"Mama never said. But I figured as much."

There were several long moments of silence before Ammie reached over and took one of Brenna's hands in hers. "I can read them to you, if you'd like."

Brenna's head snapped up and a frission of excitement sent a shiver up her spine before caution whispered in her ear. Maybe there was something in them she didn't want to hear, or have anyone else hear either. She looked down at the letters again. But it would fill a hole in her life to finally know what they said. And both her parents were gone, and had been for eighteen years. What could be in those letters that could hurt her now?

She held the packet out to Ammie. "I'd like that."

Ammie carefully untied the twine binding them together. Gently lifting the top envelope, she slid the single sheet of paper out and opened it up. Before she'd read a word, she looked up at Brenna and smiled.

"This says 'Dear John, Mary and Brenna'.

"Really?" Brenna leaned over to gaze at the words. "My name is on there?"

"Yes, it is," Ammie laughed, pointing it out to Brenna. She looked down at the envelope lying face-up in her lap. "It's from a Mathias Roberts." She smiled at Brenna. "One of your father's relatives then."

Brenna nodded. "His brother. Papa used to talk about him. He lives in St. Louis. Or at least he used to." Brenna's forehead wrinkled in thought. "I think he owned a mercantile there."

"St. Louis is the address on the envelope, so it must be the same one. All right. Are you ready to hear what he has to say?"

An hour later, Brenna's smile was brilliant despite the sheen of tears in her eyes. "Did he really ask if I had freckles?" When Ammie nodded, Brenna laughed. "My uncle would have been disappointed then."

"You never had freckles?"

"Not a one," Brenna confirmed, her smile still in place. It had been a wonderfully unexpected gift to discover her papa's brother had asked about her in every single letter he'd written. It made her heart glow to think that there had been a relative somewhere who'd thought of her. Maybe he still did now and then, even after all these years.

Ammie folded the last letter and eased it back inside its envelope. She set it on top of the others, then watched as Brenna slowly tied the twine around them.

"You know, those letters certainly don't sound like someone who didn't care what happened to you," Ammie said.

"I know." The thought had crossed Brenna's mind too. It had set her to wondering why her uncle had never come for her.

"Maybe he didn't come because he never knew what happened."

Ammie's words mirrored Brenna's thoughts, but even if that were true, eighteen years had passed since her uncle had sent his last letter. It was too late.

"It might not be."

Startled, Brenna frowned at Ammie. "It might not be what?"

"Too late." Ammie tilted her head to one side in a habit Brenna had come to recognize. "That's what you said, isn't it? That it was too late?" She tapped a finger on top of the stack of letters. "You could write to them. We have an address." Ammie looked up and smiled. "I mean that I could write the words for you."

Brenna was silent as she considered it. It was very likely that after so many years had passed, her uncle didn't want to hear from her. Or maybe he had moved and the address on the envelope was no longer his. Another half-dozen reasons for why it would be futile to try to contact someone after more than a decade flitted through her mind. But each one was met with the same response. If she never received an answer, she'd be no worse off than she was today. And what if Ammie was right, and her uncle never knew why his brother had stopped writing to him? Wouldn't she want to know what had happened, even after all these years?

"Do you have a paper and ink?"

Ammie grabbed Brenna's hand and jumped off the bed, pulling her captive with her. "Right over there."

Brenna glanced at the delicate curves of the piece of furniture sitting beneath the window. "Then we'd better get started."

———

BOTH WOMEN SLUMPED down in the overstuffed chairs in the pink parlor Aunt Charlotte was so proud of. Brenna had had no idea it would be so emotionally draining to write a letter to someone who was both a relative and a complete stranger. But it was done and placed inside an envelope that Ammie had sealed shut and penned an address on. It was sitting on the table in the foyer, and Ammie had promised they would take it to the postmaster first thing in the morning.

Charlotte bustled into the parlor, followed by Helen, who was carrying a large tea tray. Tall, with gray hair, a long face, and toothy smile, Helen winked at both the young women who were collapsed in their chairs before she set the tea service down and started to pour out two cups. She handed one to Charlotte and the other to Ammie. She then picked up a steaming mug from the tray and held it out to Brenna.

"Coffee for you. I imagine you've had enough tea by now."

Brenna smiled her gratitude. "How did you know I'd prefer it?"

Helen darted a pitying look at Charlotte and Ammie. "Despite what those two may have led you to believe, most of the members of this family drink coffee." She gave Brenna a huge grin. "You'll fit right in."

"Lillian made a tea-drinker out of me," Charlotte admitted, gesturing toward her niece with the cup in her hand. "And Ammie too." She eyed her niece's sprawled-out form. "Who certainly knows better than to sit like that."

Ammie sighed but dutifully straightened up, smoothing her skirts over her lap while Brenna did the same.

"Hello? Anybody in here?"

The raspy voice boomed across the foyer, causing Charlotte to raise one hand to her throat as she gasped out loud. "Good heavens. We have an intruder."

Helen wagged a finger at her employer and friend. "You know very well that's Shue doing all that shouting, and not some stranger who barged in off the street."

Brenna's eyes widened when the mysterious Shue appeared in the doorway. She was dressed in wool pants, held up at the waist by a thick piece of rope. Her rough cotton shirt looked large enough to fit two of her inside it, and she had a bright-red bandanna tied around her neck. Short and stocky, Shue's hair was cropped off just below her ears, and at first, Brenna had no idea if she was a man or a woman. She blinked several times before turning a questioning look on Ammie.

"She's Robbie's cook," Ammie whispered out the side of her mouth, before she set her teacup aside and rose to greet their visitor with a big smile. "Hello, Shue." Ammie hurried across the room and gave the much shorter woman a quick hug. "I'm so glad to see you."

Shue gave Ammie's back a firm pat. "That's good to know. I'm glad to see you too." She pulled back and used one arm to hold Ammie away. "We'll do all the polite talk in a while. Right now I have a bit of business to take care of." She swept a floppy-brimmed hat off her head and peered around the room as she held out one hand.

"I got this note here from Dina that says you have someone stayin' here and she's lookin' for work." Shue fixed her gaze on Brenna. "Is that you?"

Having no idea what the odd woman had in mind, Brenna shot a glance at Ammie who only shrugged her shoulders. "I guess it is. I mean Dina's right, I am looking for work. I'm Brenna Roberts."

"That's the name in this note." Shue stepped further into the room until she was standing close enough to Brenna to give her a good once-over. "You don't look like you've worked much."

Taking offense at Shue's obvious assumption that she was some kind of weakling, Brenna's back stiffened. "I have a pair of britches, same as you. I needed them to work the farm. Which I did every day, including Sundays."

Shue's eyebrows shot up, but the corners of her mouth began to twitch. "Well, the men gotta eat every day, including Sundays, so that's a good thing. Can you cook? Dina says you can."

Brenna's eyes narrowed, but she gave a brief nod and waited for Shue to get around to stating what type of work she was offering.

"That's good too. Have you ever been on a ranch?"

Brenna shook her head. "Just a farm."

"But you've been around animals?"

"Certainly, Mrs. Shue. I lived on a farm after all."

The older woman grinned, showing two rows of crooked teeth. "No need to sass, girl. And I ain't never been a missus. You can just call me Shue like everyone else does. Can you ride a horse?"

"I've ridden the plow horse a time or two."

"With or without a saddle?"

Brenna snorted. Saddles were expensive, and they'd had no use for one anyway. "No saddle."

Shue pursed her lips. "Can you drive a wagon?"

"Yes. I took one to market almost every week during the summer months. Can hitch one up, too."

"That's good then." Shue smiled. "How about shoot? Can you shoot?"

"Good enough to scare the coyotes away from our chickens."

"That's good enough." Shue nodded. "You've got the job then. You got here late so there's not much time to say your goodbyes. We'll be leavin' tomorrow."

"Leaving?" Brenna was having trouble keeping up with Shue's thoughts. "And a job doing what?"

"Cookin' for the hands. I can't stay on the ranch forever. I need to be headin' home. And it won't be for long. They'll all be pulling up stakes and goin' to the new place at the end of the summer."

Ammie clapped her hands together drawing everyone's attention away from Shue. "I think it's an excellent idea. You can work out at the ranch for a few months, then come back and help Dorrie open her new sweets shop. Don't you think so too, Aunt Charlotte?"

The middle-aged woman blinked several times as she looked between her niece and Shue. "I have no idea." She glanced over at her housekeeper. "What do you think, Helen?"

Helen set her coffee mug down and studied Brenna. "I sense that you have two roads in front of you. It would be best if you walked along this one for a while before deciding which is the better one for you."

Brenna had no idea what Helen was talking about, but she smiled politely. She did need a job. And cooking for a bunch of men couldn't be all that hard. And even if it was, she was used to working long hours. Aunt Charlotte might not know what this Shue person was talking about, but Ammie certainly seemed to, and her friend thought it would be a fine idea. If Ammie approved, then that was good enough for her.

"All right. Where is this ranch?"

"About eight hours on horseback if you go the shortcut. It'll take us two days on the road with the supply wagons." Shue smiled. "It's good you can drive one of them instead of one of the hands havin' to do it. We need them both to keep a sharp eye out instead of drivin' the team. I was gettin' worried about it."

"That's fine." Brenna frowned. "Doesn't the ranch owner have to approve of me before I'm hired?"

"Don't you be worryin' about that. Robbie will be fine with my pick. He told me so before we came into town." Shue nodded then slapped her hat on top of her head. "We'll be meetin' about ten tomorrow mornin' in front of Luke's stables. Ammie can bring you."

Brenna stood with her mouth open. Not a word came out as she watched Shue turn on her heel and stride out of the room. She finally sank slowly back into her chair and stared at the empty spot where Shue had been standing. "Did she say Robbie? Am I going to be cooking on Robbie Smith's ranch?"

"Why yes, dear. Whose ranch did you think Shue was talking about?" Aunt Charlotte asked.

Brenna turned her head and narrowed her eyes as Ammie but her hands behind her back. She looked the very picture of innocence. Brenna wasn't fooled for a moment. But it was too late. She'd given her word, and Shue had already left.

"You make sure you mail that letter, Amelia Jamison."

Ammie's smile grew cheekier. "I'd be happy to, Brenna Roberts."

CHAPTER TEN

ROBBIE RODE INTO THE YARD FLANKING THE STABLES LUKE HAD built on the northern side of the town. The supply wagons were loaded and their horses stood quietly on the far side of the fence. Robbie squinted against the morning sun, trying to find Shue and the two hands who would be making the trip back to the ranch with her. But the yard was bustling with a lot of activity, so he gave up the attempt, turning to look at Ethan who'd pulled his horse up next to him.

"Looks like business is good for your brother-in-law."

Luke had bought the land for the stables before he'd married Shannon, and had expanded it over the years to accommodate the steady growth of customers. The newest building housed additional stalls and gleamed with fresh paint.

Ethan nodded then dismounted, leading his light-colored chestnut through the tangle of carriages and tying him to a fence post. Robbie followed close behind, giving Hayseed a friendly smack on his rump before heading into the stables. They made their way to the back office, expecting to find Jules waiting for them. Instead, they walked into a tea party. Robbie grinned at the sight of Dorrie, Ammie, and Lillian sitting on wooden stools, gathered around an overturned barrel that was serving as a table for their teapot.

He directed a smile at Lillian, who was not only his honorary aunt but also his employer. "I thought we'd said our goodbyes last night."

The breathtaking woman, with the platinum-blond hair and crystal-blue eyes, smiled back at him. "Ammie asked me to accompany her here today."

"And what are *you* doing here?" Ethan demanded, his dark eyes fixed on Ammie.

"Why, hello. It's good to see you too?" Ammie's voice dripped with sweetness. "How long have you been in town?"

From the corner of his eye, Robbie caught the flash of red racing up Ethan's neck. It seemed his friend just couldn't find his footing when it came to Ammie. Ethan never had a problem with any other female. Of course, Robbie had never seen him pay much attention to any other female either.

Giving a mental shake of his head, Robbie nudged Ethan with his elbow. "They probably came to say goodbye to Shue. You know how fond they all are of her."

Ethan only grunted and dropped his gaze to the ground.

Robbie ignored the exasperated glare Ammie shot at him and smiled at Dorrie instead. "We're looking for your husband, assuming the two of you are still married." He let out a deep dramatic sigh. "If you aren't, maybe you'd reconsider coming out to the ranch? We still need a cook."

"Do you?" Dorrie's lips curved upward. "Jules is out by the corral. He said to send you out that way if we happened to see you."

"Well, it's purely our pleasure we ran into all of you." He gave Ethan a good shove to get him started. "We'll go find Jules and meet you over by the wagons to give Shue a good send-off."

"You can be certain we won't miss that," Ammie called out as the two men turned and headed back out the doorway.

It only took them a minute to locate the marshal, who was

leaning against the corral fence, watching the activity in the stable yard. His grin stretched from ear to ear when he spotted them walking toward him. Robbie halted a few feet away and eyed him suspiciously.

"You seem to be in a good mood this morning."

Jules raised an eyebrow. "Any reason why I shouldn't be?"

Robbie shrugged. "None that I can think of." He jerked his head back toward the stable. "I was surprised to see Lillian here. It's a little early for her to be up and about."

Lillian kept late hours, helping her husband run The Crimson Rose.

"I think Ammie wanted her to come along in case there's a problem," Jules said.

"What kind of problem?" Robbie frowned. He couldn't think of anything having to do with the supply wagons that would need Lillian's presence. He'd been dealing on his own with anything that came up concerning the ranch for years.

"They didn't mention anything specific," Jules said cheerfully. "It's just an impression I got, but it can be hard sometimes to figure out the way women think."

"Especially that one," Ethan muttered under his breath.

Both men ignored him as they shifted their attention to the two wagons on the other side of the yard.

Jules shot a grin at Robbie. "You should be in a good mood too. I understand Shue's found you a new cook."

Taken by surprise, Robbie blinked at his friend before shifting his gaze back to the wagons. "She didn't mention it or send me word."

"Shue came by last night to thank Dina. She said this new cook should work out fine."

"Then he's someone Cook must have recommended." Robbie smiled in satisfaction. A recommendation from Dina's husband was better than gold in the bank. The hands were sure to be happy, and that would make his job a whole lot easier. At least he wouldn't have to listen to Toby complaining about the food.

"Maybe he'll be willing to come with us to the new ranch," Robbie mused out loud.

Jules laughed. "That might take a bit of talking on your part."

"Shouldn't be a problem for him," Ethan cut in. "He's used to talking a lot."

"That's better than standing around glaring all the time," Robbie said, but there wasn't any heat in his voice. His thoughts were centered on meeting this new cook Shue had hired.

"Are you planning on riding with the wagons?" Jules asked.

Robbie shook his head. "No. I'll be going over the open country. I need to get back to the ranch. I'll be making a short stop first and then head out."

"That wouldn't be to deliver that burlap sack you have tied behind your saddle, would it?" Ethan grinned when Robbie frowned at him.

Jules' gaze shifted between the two men "What's in the burlap sack?"

When Robbie only snorted, Ethan chuckled. "The rest of Brenna's things that she left behind that shack outside town."

"How did you get hold of that?" Jules asked.

"Well," Ethan drawled. "Our friend here had a general description of where this shack was and he insisted we go out and take a look, since it was the gentlemanly thing to do. Took us the better part of the afternoon to find the right one."

Robbie squirmed under Jules' amused gaze.

"Is that a fact?" Jules' grin didn't fade one bit as the heat crept across Robbie's face.

Having nothing to say that wouldn't give his friends more to laugh at, Robbie went in a different direction. "I'm worried about the water supply this summer. There wasn't much winter up in the mountains this year."

Jules' expression immediately sobered as he nodded. "It was a mild winter for the miners, but not so good for the ranches who depend on that snowmelt for their water."

"Luke thinks water will be scarcer, but it should be enough,"

Ethan volunteered. "I'm not looking forward to finding dead cattle, though, if they have to share a watering hole with the cougars and coyotes."

Robbie rubbed his leg. He didn't want to have any more run-ins with a cougar either. "I think the water will be better on my new place up north."

The other two men nodded their agreement.

"It might be a good thing that Lillian will be selling the place now," Jules observed. "Water and cattle will be two less things she'll need to worry about."

They all smiled at once when Shue came walking across the yard, acting as if she didn't notice all the chaos going on around her. She nodded at Robbie as she drew closer.

"We're about ready to go, if'n you got somethin' more to say to the hands."

"Do you have everything you need?" Robbie asked. He didn't want to have to send anyone back into town.

The old miner nodded, her hat brim flopping up and down with the movement. "Yep. Even the saffron. I made sure of it."

He had a feeling it would be a long time before he heard the end of forgetting that particular spice. Hopefully this new cook didn't use the stuff so he wouldn't have to worry about forgetting it. "I hear you hired a new cook?"

"Yep. Haven't tried her food yet, but Dina and Dorrie said she cooks just fine. And she's used to country life,"

Robbie and Ethan exchanged a look. Did Shue just say "she"? Robbie glanced over at Jules who was busy studying the toes of his boots.

"You hired a woman?"

Shue's thick eyebrows beetled together. "That's what I jest said, didn't I?"

He shot a second look at Jules who held up his hands in denial. "I didn't have anything to do with this."

Still not sure about that, Robbie quickly climbed over the

fence and headed for the wagons. He could hear two pairs of heavy boots hit the ground as Ethan and Jules followed him.

The bench seat on the first wagon was empty so Robbie strode past it, his focus on the figure sitting on the high seat of the next wagon. Her back was to him so he couldn't see her face, but he sure did recognize that coat. Lengthening his stride, Robbie reached the front of the wagon and skidded to a halt as he glared up at Brenna.

"What are you doing?"

Brenna stared back at him from beneath the same type of floppy hat that Shue favored. "Waiting."

"I can see that for myself," Robbie snapped. "I'm talking about the cooking."

Her small shrug didn't do anything to calm his growing temper. "I was offered a job, and I took it."

"The job is for a cook. You can't cook."

She raised an eyebrow at him. "Yes, I can."

Frustrated, Robbie ran a hand across his chin. "I mean that you can't cook for all the hands. It's too much work."

Now she looked surprised. "You know I lived on a farm. I'm used to a lot of work."

"But you've never worked on a cattle ranch." Robbie crossed his arms over his chest. He wasn't going to have her come out to his place and work herself to death.

"Are you saying I can't have the job?"

Shue suddenly appeared beside him and gave Robbie a sharp poke in the ribs. "Now you wait just a minute there, Robbie Smith. You told me it to hire a cook, and I did that. You cain't be raisin' a ruckus about it now." The older woman stuck out her chin. "If'n she doesn't go, then I don't go."

Not willing to give in to that kind of blackmail, Robbie glared at Shue. "Then Hopper can do the cooking."

The short feisty miner snorted at that. "His food tastes like cow droppin's. You won't have a hand left on the place inside a week."

Robbie drew in a sharp breath. She was right. But he still didn't want Brenna working that hard.

"Now that would be a problem."

Robbie turned at the sound of Ammie's clearly amused voice and came face-to-face with Lillian.

"What's wrong, Robbie?" His glamorous aunt gave him a puzzled look. "Maybe I can help."

He glanced up at Brenna and then back at Lillian. "Do you know each other?"

Lillian looked over at the woman sitting quietly on the driver's seat of the wagon before returning her attention to her annoyed ranch manager. "We met over dinner at Ammie and Charlotte's house last night."

Robbie shot Ammie a narrow-eyed look. "Now isn't that a coincidence."

"I don't see why," Lillian said calmly. "We often have dinner together. Weren't you aware that Brenna was staying there?"

"Yes," Robbie was forced to admit, then a new idea struck him. "And she should keep staying with Ammie. It isn't proper for Brenna to stay in the ranch house. And she certainly can't sleep in the bunkhouse." He gave a decisive nod only to get another poke from Shue.

"She's not stayin' in either of those places. She'll be in the casita with me," Shue said. The older woman preferred to bed down in the roomy, one-room cottage Lillian had built away from the main ranch house.

"With Shue there, that seems perfectly proper," Lillian commented. "You did say you needed a cook, didn't you?"

"Yes. But not her," Robbie said through gritted teeth. Why did everyone seem determined for Brenna to work herself to death?

"You don't want me?"

The quiet question floated down from the top of the wagon. Robbie looked up and met Brenna's gaze, instantly feeling guilty at the hurt he saw in her eyes. "Of course I do, it's just that..."

"It's settled then," Lillian declared, cutting his explanation short. "I think it would be best if you were on your way, Shue."

"Good," Shue said. "We've wasted enough time." She tugged on the leg of Brenna's britches. "Are you ready, girl?"

Robbie's mouth gaped open when Brenna picked up the reins for the team of horses hitched to the big wagon. "Wait a minute." He waved his arms back and forth. "She's not driving that wagon all the way to the ranch, is she?"

Shue let out a loud snort. "We aren't goin' through this agin, are we boy?" This time she poked him square in the chest. "The owner of the ranch said it's settled, so there's nothin' more to be discussin'."

He looked up at Brenna who politely smiled back at him.

"If you'll step back, please?"

Frustrated, but knowing there was little he could do about it, Robbie stepped back and stuck his thumbs into his belt. He stood a long time watching the wagons rumble their way down the street. When there was nothing left to see, he walked back across the stable yard, walking over to the fence where all the rest of his family were waiting. Except for Ethan. He'd already disappeared. Probably the minute he'd spotted Ammie walking toward him.

"Guess there was a problem?" Jules asked in a neutral voice as Robbie came to a stop beside him.

Robbie kept silent, not trusting himself to speak. He was still furious, and worried too. Anything could happen to the supply wagons for the two days they'd be on the road, making their way to the ranch. And all they had for protection was a couple of ranch hands. Robbie completely dismissed the fact that Shue was a better shot than any of them.

"Guess you forgot to give her the rest of her things?" Jules asked.

"What?"

"I didn't see you give Brenna the rest of her things that Ethan said were tied to the back of your saddle."

Robbie's hands balled into fists and he had to do a quick mental count to ten to keep from hitting his friend, the US Marshal.

"It doesn't matter," Lillian put in smoothly. "You can give them to her later. The important thing is that you have a cook and Shue will be able to go back to her cabin."

"I'm surprised you're still standing around here, though," Ammie said. "I'd think you'd want to get things ready before the wagons get to the ranch."

Seeing the sparkle in Ammie's gaze, Robbie knew she was up to something, but couldn't help roll his eyes. "What things? There isn't anything that needs doing."

Dorrie tapped a finger against her lower lip. "I don't know. Maybe have the ranch hands clean themselves up a bit? You don't want Brenna to turn around and flee at the sight of them."

Crossing his arms over his chest, Robbie glared at the two women he'd grown up with. "She'll have to take them the way they are. I'm too busy to fool around with that kind of nonsense."

"Well at least someone will have to show her around the ranch," Ammie declared. "If you're so busy, maybe Jonah could do it."

"That's an excellent idea." Dorrie nodded her agreement. Her eyes took on the same mischievous sparkle as Ammie's had. "He's certainly presentable enough."

Jules gave his wife a knowing look. "Isn't that the hand with the pretty face that all the women swoon over whenever he comes to town?"

Ammie hooked one arm through Lillian's and grinned at her aunt. "You've met Jonah, haven't you?"

Lillian nodded. "Of course. He's been on the ranch for several years. He's a very nice man." She looked over at Robbie and smiled. "And a very handsome one."

"And quite charming," Ammie added, not even sparing Robbie a glance.

He glared at all of them, including Jules who looked like he was trying not to laugh. Pulling his hat down lower across his brow, he turned on his heel and stomped toward Hayseed.

CHAPTER ELEVEN

"WHAT'S THE BURR UNDER YER SADDLE?" TOBY SHOOK HIS HEAD. "Cain't you sit down? Or maybe you oughta try doin' a bit of work today?"

Robbie stopped his pacing long enough to glance over at his foreman. "I've been working."

Toby lifted his coffee mug and circled it in a large arc in front of him. "I meant some ranch work. Every time I've come in here to ask you somethin', you've been polishin' or sweepin' or wipin' up the table."

Embarrassed, and irritated that he was, Robbie frowned. "I like a clean place, and someone has to keep it that way when Shue isn't around. You don't even comb your hair, much less sweep up a floor."

"Don't have much hair left to comb," Toby said. "And does that sweepin' include the casita? 'Cause I could have sworn I saw you carryin' a broom out that way." He stroked along the side of his jaw, his calloused hand making a rasping sound against the perpetual bristle on his chin. "Don't know of anythin' different around here exceptin' that new cook you said would be comin' with Shue. Is there somethin' you need to tell me about her before she gits here? I don't like surprises, boss."

"She's just here to cook." Robbie heard the snap in his voice and took a deep breath to get it under control. "That's all she signed up to do. So we'll have to divvy up some of the other chores Shue did."

Toby dropped his hand back to the table. "Weren't that many. Is this new cook the puny sort?"

Exasperated, and not wanting to get into the subject of Brenna with his far-too-observant foreman, Robbie kept his answer short. "She's only going to cook, there isn't anything more to say about it."

When Toby picked up his coffee mug and took a long sip, Robbie resumed his pacing, glancing out the window to gauge how much daylight was left. If the supply wagons didn't show up in another hour, he had every intention of saddling up Hayseed and tracking them down.

"Maybe you should have gone with Jonah and Pete to round up those strays off the northern pastures. A hard day's work and a night under the stars might have helped corral some of that energy of yers." Toby scratched his head. "Though I'm not real clear on why you sent them out there. I thought we were goin' to work closer to the ranch for a spell?"

A shout sounded from outside, sparing Robbie having to come up with a response which he might have been hard-pressed to do. Dismissing the subject from his mind, he stepped out onto the wide porch that spanned the entire front of the ranch house. From there he had a clear view of the road that wound through the hills, ending in the large flat yard between the house and the stable.

The wagons had cleared the last bend and were making their way slowly toward the ranch with the two hands riding in front of them. Robbie couldn't blame them much. Even this early in the spring the land was dry, and the wagons were kicking up a small cloud of dust. They'd drawn close enough that he could see Shue was driving the lead wagon, with Brenna following. She'd pulled a bandanna up to cover the lower half of her face.

Toby joined him on the porch and leaned over the rail, his gaze fixed on the young boy jumping about the yard as he shouted and pointed at the wagons. Robbie grinned. Steph was twelve years old and still had a good dose of child in him. Tall for his age, wiry and quick, he darted around the yard as if he'd been thrown from a sling-shot.

"Do you see the wagons, Toby? Miss Shue is back. We're sure to have cornbread tonight, and she promised to bring me a licorice stick."

Toby aimed a crooked finger at the boy. "We can see them plain enough. You can quit yellin' and jumpin' about like a jackrabbit." He shifted his finger, so it was pointed at the large barn on the opposite side of the yard. "Go'n git Hopper so he can help with the teams, and both of you start unloadin' those wagons once Miss Shue gits them here."

Steph did a few quick steps backward as he waved at Toby before turning about and breaking into a full-out run toward the barn.

Toby chuckled. "That boy don't know how to stand still."

"He's a happy kid, and that's all that matters," Robbie said, knowing the young boy hadn't had the best start in life. Descending the porch steps two at a time, Robbie strolled across the yard as the two hands he'd sent with the wagons pulled their horses up and quickly dismounted, each of them stretching their arms out.

"Joe, Miguel," Robbie greeted the two men. The both grinned at him from dust-smudged faces.

"Boss." Joe spoke with a heavy lisp since both his front teeth were missing. "It was a long ride, but nothing much happened."

"The new cook did a good job," Miguel put in. He removed his hat and slapped it against his leg, starting a small dust storm that reached all the way to his feet. "I thought maybe you hired her

because she's a fine-lookin' woman, but her cookin' is good. The
rest of the boys will be happy with it."

"I didn't hire her," Robbie corrected. "Shue and Lillian did."

"Lillian always did look after us," Miguel said. "Is she one of
those orphan girls that Lillian is always rescuin'? Because if Lillian
sent her out here to find a husband, I'd be happy to marry her if
the girl I already got my eye on turns me down."

"Me too," Joe chimed in just as Toby came up behind him.

He looked from one man the other. "You already got a wife,
Joe, and you sure don't need another one. Who's gittin' married?"

"No one is," Robbie said. He'd been so concerned about the
amount of work Brenna would be taking on, that he hadn't even
considered what might happen when a pretty woman was put
down in the middle of a bunch of men. Well, except for Jonah.

"You all goin' to stand there jawin' all day, or are you gonna help
Steph unload these wagons?" Shue tied off the reins then crossed
her arms and stared at them.

"Go put your horses away, then come out and help with the
unloading." Robbie waited until the men had moved off before he
went to greet Shue. He knew better than to offer her a hand down
off her perch, but stood close just in case. He'd noticed lately that
Shue was taking more time to climb on and off wagons. Her feet
were barely on the ground when young Steph's voice sailed across
the yard.

"Holy bejebees! Who are you?"

Robbie leaned to the side just in time to see Brenna step onto
the ground. She turned around to face Steph, who was staring up
at her as if he were seeing something magical. When she smiled at
him, Robbie thought the young boy was going to melt into a
puddle at her feet. He rolled his eyes and then closed them as Toby
walked up and grabbed Steph by the collar.

"You look like yer about to fall over. What's wrong with
you, boy?"

Steph raised a hand and pointed a finger at Brenna. "She's the new cook." His forehead wrinkled for a moment. "You are, aren't you?"

Brenna laughed. "Yes, I am. That is if Shue is satisfied with my food." She smiled and nodded at Robbie and then Toby. "And both of you too, of course. I'm Brenna."

"Pleased to meet you," Toby's voice was even more gruff than usual. "This here is Steph and I'm Toby."

Robbie knew the long moment of silence that followed the introduction was not a good sign at all. It took a lot for Toby to be jolted into silence.

"If'n you'll excuse me, Steph here will start unloadin' the wagon. I got something I need to do."

Having a pretty good idea exactly what Toby needed to do, Robbie moved off so he and the foreman could talk without everyone else in the yard hearing them. He waited, with his arms crossed and legs braced apart, as Toby came marching over to where he was standing.

"I need to have a word with you, boss."

"I figured as much." Robbie sighed. "What is it, Toby?"

"I thought you said there was nothin' you needed to tell me about the new cook?"

Robbie shrugged. "Miguel and Joe said her cooking was fine."

Toby gaped at him. "Did you lose yer mind somewhere between here and town? Bringin' a woman who looks like that to the ranch is just plain foolish. We'll be breakin' up fights between the men all the time." He stuck his chin out when Robbie shook his head. "Don't you stand there and tell me you didn't notice how purty she is. You ain't blind."

"I noticed," Robbie conceded. "But I told you, Shue and Lillian hired her. There wasn't much I could do about it."

The foreman made a frustrated sound deep in his throat. "So now yer gonna be stayin' in the bunkhouse? You cain't stay in the ranch house with her in it. That jest ain't right."

"She's going to stay in the casita with Shue." Robbie rubbed a hand along his jaw. "That was Shue's idea."

"Well at least git her to put on somethin' besides those britches. That ain't right either."

Robbie raised an eyebrow. "Shue's a female and *she* wears britches."

Toby glared at him. "It ain't the same thing, and yer too old for me to have to explain to you why." He peered around Robbie for a quick look in Brenna's direction. "I don't think Shue's got any of those dresses females usually wear. Do you think that new cook brought any with her?"

His boss certainly hoped so. He'd left the burlap bag on the bed when he'd gone to sweep out the casita. He swiveled around when he felt a hard tap on his shoulder. Shue stood with her hands on her hips.

"You'd better go do yer hello's to that girl, or she's gonna think you don't want her here and have second thoughts about stayin." She cocked her head to the side. "And that won't make anyone very happy. She did the cookin' on the way here, and those two hands of yers were as happy as pigs in a mud hole. Acted like them too." Shue's thin lips turned up into a smug smile. "I thought a farm girl would know how to cook, and I was sure right about that."

Thinking Shue was also right about his delay in greeting Brenna being rude, Robbie jerked his head at Toby. "Get the wagons unloaded."

"And take care of what I told you," Toby called out to Robbie's back as his boss walked away.

Wondering what he'd done to get into a mess that called for him to tell a woman what she could and couldn't wear, Robbie made his way to the second wagon where Brenna was leaning against the wheel, watching him.

He stuck his thumbs in his belt and nodded at her. "Glad you made it."

She smiled. "I am too. It wasn't a bad trip." She untied the bandanna from her neck and shook it out. "Just a bit dusty."

"We need rain." Robbie inwardly winced. Why was talking to her so hard all of a sudden? He was the manager of this ranch, and her boss. All he had to do was tell her what he expected and let her go get settled in with Shue. Clearing his throat, he tried again. "I left your things in the casita." He pointed to the small adobe building that sat apart from the main house.

"My things?"

He frowned. "In that burlap bag you left behind the shack at the edge of town."

Brenna's large blue eyes blinked several times as if she hadn't understood what he had said. "You found my bag?"

"Ethan and I did."

He drew in a quick breath when a smile lit up her whole face. Even covered with dust she was beautiful.

"Thank you," Brenna said. "That was very kind of you to go to all that trouble."

"It wasn't any trouble." Robbie was glad Ethan wasn't standing there to hear that whopper. "The men will unload the wagon if you want to go lie down for a spell."

"I should help Shue store the supplies away."

When he made a sound of protest, she held up her hand. "I'm not made out of glass, Robbie. I can earn my way."

"Is that so?" Before he could stop himself, Robbie reached out and snagged one of her hands and flipped it over. He stared down at the blisters and several cuts on them. "You should have worn gloves."

"I will next time," Brenna said. "Shue is going to find an extra pair for me."

Kicking himself for not realizing she wouldn't have any, Robbie dropped her hand and looked away for a moment. "Do you have a dress or a skirt you can wear?"

"Yes."

He shifted his gaze back to her, grateful that she didn't look angry at his bald question about her clothes. "When we're on the trail, wearing britches is fine. But it might be best if you wore a dress when you're at the ranch house."

"All right."

"Brenna? You done talkin' to Robbie? 'Cause we got work to do." Shue's shout had them both turning in the older woman's direction.

"I'm coming," Brenna called out. She glanced back at Robbie. "Please excuse me."

He couldn't do anything but nod and watch her walk away. Shue started talking the minute Brenna reached her side, and the two women moved off toward the casita together. Seeing the slight feminine sway of Brenna's hips, Robbie couldn't decide if he was glad or annoyed that she was at the ranch.

"If yer through gawkin', don't you got any work that needs doin'? Or are you fixin' on sweepin' some more floors?"

Robbie didn't even bother to turn around. "Shut up, Toby."

CHAPTER TWELVE

AFTER A RESTLESS NIGHT, ROBBIE WOKE TO THE SMELLS OF coffee and freshly baked bread. A quick look out the window showed the sun barely clearing the horizon in its daily climb across the sky. Grateful Shue had gotten an early start on the day, and he'd be able to have some coffee before he put in a few hours' work, Robbie quickly pulled on his clothes and boots. He was still buckling his belt when he walked into the large room at the front of the ranch house where he stopped dead just over the threshold. The tall slender frame and dark hair of the woman sitting at the long table in front of the cookstove clearly wasn't Shue's.

Brenna's dark head was bent over her task, as she pulled a needle and thread through the cloth she was holding in her hand. Not sure whether he should retreat out the back door, the smell of coffee finally made Robbie's decision for him. He started across the room and the sound of his boot steps drew Brenna's attention.

"Good morning."

Robbie thought her smile would be enough to make a man glad to get up every day, then quickly shook the thought off. She was the new cook, nothing more. And he'd better start treating her that way as an example for the hands. Otherwise, fistfights breaking out over who was entitled to the new cook's attention would become a fact, and not just one of Toby's dire predictions.

"'Morning." He gave her a polite nod before carefully switching his gaze over to the stove. "Is that coffee I smell?" He took another appreciative sniff of the air. "And bread?"

Brenna set her sewing aside and disappeared into the kitchen, quickly returning with a large mug, steam curling out of its top. She set it on the table, opposite from where she'd been sitting, then stood waiting for him to take a seat. Since she was still standing, Robbie wasn't sure what the proper thing to do was, so he simply picked up the mug and took a sip of the hot brew, raising an eyebrow when it hit his mouth and tongue.

"This is good." He looked down into his cup and then back up at her. "Really good."

"I don't know whether to thank you for the compliment, or be annoyed that you sound so surprised," Brenna laughed. "The bread won't be done for a while yet, but I have eggs ready to fry up if you'd like some."

"Eggs?" Robbie looked around as if he expected to see laying hens in the middle of the room. "Where did you get eggs?"

"Um." Brenna followed his gaze around the room before giving him a puzzled look. "There's a coop out back. Didn't you know there were chickens in it?"

Feeling more than a little foolish, Robbie nodded. "Of course I do. But I have to wonder how the eggs got from there into the kitchen? You haven't already been out to the coop, have you?"

"Why wouldn't I have already been out there?"

"It's early, Brenna."

She shrugged that off. "I'd have milked the cow by this time if I were still on the farm."

He set his coffee mug down and took a seat at the table, waving his hand to indicate that she should too. Once she was sitting across from him, her hands folded primly in front of her, he put his elbows down and leaned forward.

"That's my point. This isn't the farm. We're in the middle of open range and it would've still been dark an hour ago." He glanced out one of the three windows that faced the front porch. "All kinds of hunters would have been out and could have taken you by surprise."

"We had coyotes raid our chicken coop on the farm too, Robbie."

He ran a hand over his chin as he studied her for a moment. "It's the first of spring, and water's already scarce. They aren't just after some easy food. They're looking for water too. Hungry and thirsty animals are desperate ones. It isn't safe to be out by yourself in the dark."

She nodded. "I'll remember that. I don't want to cause any problems." She hesitated for a moment. "Shue said that's what happened to your leg. That a cougar attacked you." He could see the sympathy in her eyes. "I noticed you limping a bit yesterday. Does it still bother you?"

"Only when I'm aggravated," Robbie said. He grinned at the unspoken question in her eyes. "Toby enjoys aggravating me."

His grin grew into a smile when she laughed. "I'm guessing that's common enough when you're the boss."

Reminded of the relationship between them, he drew in a breath. "I see you're still wearing those britches."

Brenna picked up the cloth she'd been sewing. "I only have a little to finish the patching and then I'll change." She held up the garment that was clearly a plain cotton skirt in a drab brown. Robbie could also see it wasn't the first patch she'd had to make to it.

"That the only one you have?" He winced at the terse question that had come blurting out. It didn't make him feel any better when a stain of red appeared on Brenna's cheeks as she ducked her head.

"I can only wear one at a time, so this one's enough."

"Ammie didn't lend you any of hers?"

"Ammie gave me a whole pile of skirts and dresses. None of them were fit for ranch work, so I left them with her."

He forced his shoulders to relax as he picked up his coffee mug. "I guess that one will do." He gestured over to the desk in the far corner of the room. "I have a tin full of receipts that Carrie Cowan left behind. The men had a particular liking for her biscuits." He smiled. "I think she got that particular receipt from Cook."

She bit her lower lip as she looked over at the desk. "Carrie?"

"She was the mistress in this house for a lot of years," Robbie said. "She passed away two winters ago. That's how Shue came to be here."

Brenna smiled. "Shue said this used to be an orphanage?"

He chuckled. "I guess it was, but we didn't think of it that way. To us, it was a great place to grow up."

"Us?" Brenna stared at him. "You grew up on the ranch?"

"I did."

"You've lost both of your parents too?" she asked softly.

"One of them anyway." Robbie's tone made it clear that particular subject was closed. He didn't discuss his birth family with anyone. Even Jules and Ethan knew very little about his life before he came to Lillian's orphan ranch. Of course, neither did he.

He got to his feet and went over to the desk, picking up a tin box sitting off to one side. Bringing it back to the table, he handed it to Brenna. "Carrie kept all her receipts in here. Most of them she wrote down after she started feeling poorly."

Brenna took the box in both her hands, holding it gingerly as if she thought it might break. She finally looked up at him and nodded her thanks. "I'll read them later."

The front door suddenly opened and two men stepped into the room. One was short and stocky with black hair, dark eyes, and a long, thick mustache that hung down to the edge of his chin, but it was the second one who had Robbie giving an inward groan. Resigned to what couldn't be put off forever, he raised one hand in greeting.

"Pete, Jonah. Did you get the strays brought closer in?"

The short man grinned and nodded. "Sure did. At least a half-dozen of them, anyway. Got an early start this morning hoping

Shue would be back and we could get something besides hard tack and bad coffee." He stuck his nose up and gave a loud audible sniff. "That doesn't smell like bad coffee."

"The coffee's fine," Robbie grudgingly admitted. "Help yourself."

Both men took one more step into the room before stopping dead. Robbie didn't need to look over to know they were staring at Brenna, who'd quietly slipped the skirt she'd been mending out of sight.

"Who are you?" Pete didn't wait for a response before turning a huge smile on his boss. "Did you get married while you were in town, Robbie?" He beamed at Brenna. "She sure is a pretty one."

"No, I didn't get married." Robbie glared at Pete. "This is Brenna. She's working with Shue to learn how to be our new cook." He intensified his glare. "Temporarily, until we head for the new place."

"She can cook too?" Pete turned an amazed look on Brenna before he snatched his hat off his head. "Howdy, ma'am. I'm Pete, and this here is Jonah."

The handsome cowboy with hair the color or honey to go along with warm, brown eyes, moved closer to the table. "I can speak for myself, Pete."

Robbie's eyes narrowed as Jonah placed his hat on the end of the table and took a seat on the bench right next to Brenna.

"And what name do you go by?"

"I'm Brenna."

Robbie's shoulders tensed up even more when she smiled back at Jonah.

"Calling me Brenna is fine. That may not be proper if we were in the city, but out here I'm just another hired hand." She nodded at Jonah's skeptical look. "Only I cook rather than chase cows all day."

"Cattle, Brenna," Robbie said patiently. "They're called cattle."

Jonah shot Robbie a look, but he only shrugged. He'd already ordered Brenna around about her clothes, he wasn't about to do the same over her name. If she was fine with the hands calling her Brenna, he'd act like he was fine with it too. No matter how much it scraped along his nerves.

Brenna rose from the bench seat and went into the kitchen, returning with two mugs of coffee. She handed one to Jonah, who thanked her quietly, and the other to Pete who'd eagerly taken a seat next to Robbie. She smiled at their appreciative sounds as they took their first sip.

"The bread won't be ready for another half hour, but I have fresh eggs that I'd be happy to cook up for you."

Robbie set his empty coffee mug down with a loud thump. "They need to get their work done."

"We've already put in a couple of hours, boss," Pete said. "I'm hungry as a bear."

"Which is more than you can say, Robbie." Unnoticed by the group at the table, Toby had come in through the back door that led into the kitchen, and was standing across the room, his arms folded over his chest. "We need to get that corral mended before Hopper can turn out the rest of the stock."

"I guess we can do that." Jonah started to rise but stopped when Robbie waved him back to his seat.

He might not like the idea much, but it wouldn't be fair to order the men back to work when he hadn't put in a lick of it himself yet. Besides, he'd seen Shue cross the yard, headed toward the barn. It was her habit to fetch Hopper every morning for breakfast, so she'd be in to help make the meal for the rest of the hands. He nodded at Jonah.

"Stay and get something to eat and come out to the corral when you're done." He jerked his head toward Brenna. "And make sure she gets a proper introduction to the rest of the hands when they come in to eat."

Jonah grinned at Brenna. "I'll sure do that."

Robbie picked up his hat and followed Toby out the front door,

being careful not to slam it behind him. There was no point in
giving the men something else to speculate on. Brenna had said she
was just another one of the hands, and that's how he intended to
treat her.

CHAPTER THIRTEEN

"ANYTHIN' ELSE YOU WANT ON THIS HERE LIST?" SHUE LOOKED over at the young woman standing by the stove.

Brenna pushed away a damp lock of hair as she continued to stir the steaming pot. "No. I think that's all."

"You put different sorts of things on this one," Shue observed. "Not sure Robbie is going to want some of this."

"Robbie needs everything on there if he wants to make it through the winter on that new ranch of his."

Shue shrugged and folded the paper neatly in half. "The boys will be makin' the trip into town in a week or so. If you think of anythin' else, you can always add it yourself."

"Hmm." Brenna made the noncommittal sound and bent further over the pot.

She'd been at the ranch almost a month and a half, and so far, had managed to avoid the need to confess that she had no idea how to add something to the supply list. That day would most likely come soon enough, especially since Shue had been dropping more frequent hints about going back to her own cabin on Shannon and Luke's place.

But she was happy to put off that moment of truth for as long as possible. And it could be for a very long time since she'd discovered that young Steph took weekly lessons with one of the hands, and could read and write just fine. Brenna had taken to asking him to add things to the list whenever Shue wasn't around, so she was sure the older woman had no idea that Brenna hadn't written it all out herself.

"Have I ever told you the story of how I got my name?"

Happy for the change in topic, Brenna turned her head and smiled at Shue. "No. You haven't, and I'd love to hear it."

Shue chuckled. "All right then. I got it from my pa. He used to call me that." She paused for a moment. "Well, the old coot didn't call me that exactly. He just always said that to me."

Brenna gave the pot one last stir. She set the spoon down on a small dish next to the stove before glancing over at Shue. "What did your pa always say to you?"

"He'd look over at me and say, 'shoo, girl. You go on now.' It's about the only thing I remember him sayin' to me until he sold me off." The old miner nodded at Brenna's startled look. "I guess he got tired of me bein' underfoot, cause one day he showed up with another man and said I was supposed to go live with him now. Since he never called me by a name, only said 'shoo', it just stuck, I guess."

The story took Brenna completely by surprise, and she blurted out the first question that popped into her head. "What about that man your pa told you to go live with?"

The old miner's eyebrows cocked upward. "What about him? I went with him and we were together about ten years, I reckon."

"How old were you?"

Shue's forehead wrinkled as if she was thinking it over. "I'm not sure since pa never mentioned my age, but I figure I was about eleven or so. Near as I could tell."

Eleven? Brenna had to fight to keep her chin from dropping to her chest. Shue's pa had sent her off with a complete stranger when she was barely more than a child? "What happened after ten years?"

"Oh, he went into town for supplies and come back with another woman. Told me that I had to leave. He'd given me plenty of time to give him sons to help around the place, and since I never had, he found another woman." Shue shrugged. "Didn't bother me none since I didn't care for livin' with him anyways."

When Brenna's eyes went soft with sympathy, Shue let out a lout snort. "I didn't tell you them things so you'd get all teary on me. I got a point I'm tryin' to make here."

Brenna sniffed then managed a smile. "What's that, Shue?"

"For a long time I thought most people were no good. Especially men, since I didn't know any women. Then one day I met Miss Shannon. I was sittin' in the square, tired and hungry, and she came over and started talkin' to me. Seems old Trapper, who I'd met up at the mines, had been at the mercantile when he overheard Miss Shannon speakin' to the owner about needin' a cook and housekeeper for her aunt's place. Trapper told her he didn't know nothin' about my housekeepin', but that I could cook fine and shoot pretty good, so she came lookin' for me."

Shue looked off in the distance, a smile playing around the edges of her mouth. "I've met lots of good people since then. Shannon's husband Luke is one." She glanced over at Brenna. "And Toby and Robbie are too. You can trust them both to be fair, and they don't have any meanness in them. They do right by people and take care of their women."

"I'm glad Miss Shannon found you, Shue," Brenna said with a soft smile. "And that you found a home with her and her family."

"Family don't come any better than this one," Shue declared. "We help each other out. Jules needs help trackin' a man, then Ethan comes. There ain't no better tracker than Ethan. Robbie needs a cook, then I come." Shue's head bobbed up and down. "That's the way families work."

"Yes, it is," Brenna agreed wholeheartedly. "When I needed a home, Meemaw and Gramps gave me one, and we became a family."

"And when they needed help to run their farm, you did the

work," Shue pointed out. She fixed her stare on Brenna. "And when Shannon figured out I couldn't read or write, she made sure I got the teachin' I needed so I could learn."

Brenna froze. She watched Shue's expression carefully, trying to discern if Shue knew her little secret, or had simply been making conversation. As the silence drew out, Shue looked down at the folded piece of paper in front of her.

"I've seen Steph's handwritin' before, Brenna. I recognized it. It got me to thinkin' that I ain't never seen you write."

"I haven't had a need to with Steph always underfoot." Brenna knew she sounded both guilty and defensive but couldn't help it.

"He is that," Shue chuckled before giving Brenna a knowing look. "No one in this family thinks less of someone who didn't have a chance to do somethin'. You just tuck that away in case you need to remember it someday."

"All right." Brenna said since it's what Shue expected to hear.

"How're you feelin' with yer new family?"

It took Brenna a moment to catch up with the sudden jump in Shue's thoughts. "New family?"

"Yer part of this family now, girl. The only one who needs to get used to that notion is you." Shue grinned at her. "Family can also be a pain in the backside. You about ready to send young Steph out to the high country without any map on how to get back?"

Brenna laughed. "He can be a handful. But I like having him around."

"That's a good thing, because it seems to me that boy likes to be around you," Shue said. "Maybe like Miss Shannon, you've found a brother of yer own."

Her attention caught, Brenna walked over to the table and sat down across from Shue. "Shannon found Ethan?"

Shue grinned. "It's a long story. You should ask Dorrie about it some time. Miss Shannon told me she gave Dorrie the journal to read."

"Journal?"

"Our Shannon writes down all the family stories," Shue said. "Puts them into this journal she keeps. Ethan's story is in there." She sat up a little straighter and her chest puffed out a bit. "So is mine."

"I'd love to hear them," Brenna smiled. She was already imagining all kinds of adventures with a doctor and two US Marshals in the family. Not to mention Ammie and the hints she'd had about her Uncle Charles and Aunt Lillian.

"All you have to do is learn to read," Shue declared and then gave Brenna a wink. "And of course, marry someone in the family. Any new spouse in the family gets to read the journal."

Since that wasn't going to happen, Brenna's enthusiasm instantly deflated. Shue might consider her part of this remarkable family, but the truth was, she was just the hired help. She wasn't as kind as Dorrie or refined as Ammie. Not wife material at all.

"This ain't too much work for you, is it?"

Over the past month, Brenna had gotten used to Shue's sudden conversational shifts, but it still took her a moment or two to adjust to it.

"No, it isn't too much work at all. I've had plenty of help putting the garden in, and haven't chopped even a stick of wood."

Shue looked toward the bedrooms off of the big front room in the ranch house, as if she could see right through the wall and onto the wide back porch. "You have a touch for growin' things. I saw some of them bean plants comin' up already. And you had them clear off double the space that was there before."

"I like to grow things," Brenna admitted. "And the garden was too small to feed this many people."

Shue laughed. "Them hands sure can eat."

Brenna diplomatically kept her mouth shut, but silently agreed with that assessment. She'd been astounded at how much food the men could put away at a single sitting. It seemed she was constantly adjusting upward the amount of food she needed to cook.

"And the hands, are you gettin' along with them all right?"

"They're fine," Brenna said, growing a little alarmed at Shue's persistent questions. Had she done something wrong? "All the men are very nice, and very sweet."

"Sweet?" Shue slapped a hand on her knee. "I wonder what they'd have to say if they ever heard you call them that?" She shook her head with a grin. "I have noticed that they do behave better when you're around, and even havin' a bath more often." She shrugged. "Well, at least most of them. I think Pete's downright afraid of water." She pursed her lips together. "So you like them all, do you?"

Brenna cautiously nodded.

"How about Toby? He can be a contrary old coot."

"He's not so bad." Brenna smiled at the older woman. She'd seen for herself what great friends Toby and Shue were. They were so comfortable around each other that she'd have thought they were an old married couple if she hadn't known better.

"Jonah? Do you like Jonah? He's certainly a handsome fella."

"I suppose he his." Brenna hoped Shue wasn't trying to play matchmaker between her and Jonah. She liked the charming and good-looking hand well enough, but didn't feel any kind of attraction for him. He stood out in a crowd a little too much for her taste. She liked her men a little more easy-going, so she didn't feel she had to be perfect all the time because he was so perfect.

At least that's the conclusion she'd settled on. Brenna really wasn't at all sure what she did and didn't like in a man since she hadn't had much experience with them. All she knew was that it wasn't Jonah, so if Shue did have hopes for the two of them, the old miner was going to be very disappointed.

"What about Robbie?"

"Robbie?" Brenna didn't even try to hide the surprise in her voice. "I don't know. I haven't seen him much since I've been here." The day she'd arrived, and the morning afterwards, had been the most she'd talked to her boss in the last month.

He was never around the ranch house during the day, and rarely came in for his meals. She certainly appreciated that he had a big job to do, but she'd been a little disappointed at his absence too.

"He's not helpin' much," Shue muttered.

"What?" Brenna wasn't sure she'd heard Shue correctly. Helping? Helping with what?

"We need to be sure this list of yers is fine," Shue suddenly announced. "We don't want to have to change the whole thing at the last minute."

She grabbed the list before getting up from the table and quickly skirting around it. Shue latched onto one of Brenna's hands and pulled her up and away from the long bench she was sitting on.

"I know where the boss is today. Let's see what he has to say."

———

ROBBIE RAN the brush in one last long stroke across Hayseed's back. He walked over to a low bench and set the brush down before reaching for a pick. Returning to Hayseed's side, he lifted one hoof and examined its underside. He smiled at the steady sound of a shovel against dirt as Toby worked at mucking out the stall next to Hayseed's.

"You've sure been gettin' lots of work done lately, boss," Toby tossed over the short wall of boards between them.

"We're running a ranch, Toby. We're supposed to work."

"Just wonderin' if you have somethin' on yer mind that's drivin' you out so early and comin' back so late."

Robbie set Hayseed's hoof down and rolled his eyes at the wall separating the two stalls. "Nope. Nothing is driving me out anywhere. I just want to be sure everything is in perfect shape for Aunt Lillian. I don't want to leave any problems for her."

The shoveling sounds stopped and Toby's head popped up over the wall. "She decided what she's goin' to do with the herd yet?"

His boss shook his head. "She hasn't said. I'm guessing she'll sell it. But whatever she decides, I intend to ask her if I can buy about one hundred head of her cattle."

Toby nodded. "I imagine she'll sell you whatever you want. Give 'em to you if you want."

"I'll buy them," Robbie said firmly. "She's given me more than enough over the years."

"We was just talkin' about that. It's what families do."

Robbie turned around and smiled at Shue, although his gaze immediately bounced to the brunette behind her. She was wearing the plain brown blouse he'd seen on her almost every day, and the skirt she'd been mending her first morning on the ranch. He could still see her sitting at the table while the smell of coffee and fresh bread drifted all around her.

"Hello, Shue." He looked past the old miner and nodded his head. "Brenna."

She didn't say anything, but she did give him a smile, which was good enough. He was enjoying it until Shue stuck a piece of paper in his face.

"Brenna has made up a list of supplies for the run that Pete and Hopper will be makin' into town, and we want yer approval of it."

Robbie stepped back and lifted a hand, taking the list from Shue. "I'm sure it's fine."

"We come out here fer you to take a look at it. So you just do that now," Shue insisted.

Robbie dutifully opened the sheet of paper and glanced down the column of items. He looked up and raised an eyebrow at his older cook. "Two pigs and two goats?"

Brenna stepped up beside Shue and nodded vigorously. "You'll need those for your new place and it would be best to start a couple of breeders now." When he gave her a skeptical look, she put her hands on her hips. "I ran a farm for years, Robbie. I know what I'm talking about."

She looked so serious, Robbie couldn't help but grin at her. "I told you, Brenna. I'm starting a ranch, not a farm."

She pursed her lips and kept her gaze on his. "And I keep

telling you, Robbie, that you'll be too far from town to get supplies as often as you can here. You'll have to make do on your own, and its farm animals and a garden that will help you do that in the middle of the winter. Not cattle."

He held the list out. "So you made this list?"

Shue nodded. "She's doin' all the cookin' now, so she made the list."

"Is that a fact?" Robbie said, borrowing one of Jules' favorite phrases.

"Toby," Shue snapped out at the foreman mucking out the next stall.

His head immediately appeared over the top of the wall. "Why're you yellin' at me? I ain't done nothin' to git yelled at fer."

"I need your help."

Toby scratched the top of his head. "What fer?"

Shue glared at him. "What do you care, you old goat? I said I need your help, that should be enough."

Toby's head disappeared and a minute later his whole body reappeared behind Brenna. He peered around her to look at Shue. "All right. Here I am. What kind of help do you need?"

Shue walked around Brenna and grabbed onto Toby's arm as she headed for the open barn door. "Come on and I'll show you."

CHAPTER FOURTEEN

ROBBIE WATCHED TOBY BEING DRAGGED OFF KNOWING FULL well that Shue had done it on purpose. What he didn't know was why. But whatever the reason, he really wished he wasn't alone in a semi-dark barn with Brenna. It put his nerves on edge.

Taking a deep breath, he stuck his thumbs in his belt and fixed a polite smile on his face before he slowly turned to face her.

"So this is your list?

The corners of Brenna's lips curled upward as her eyes twinkled back at him. "I believe you've already asked me that."

He looked down at the list he was still holding and smiled. She had him there. "Well, let me see what the rest of it says." He looked up at her. "There aren't any more farm animals on this list, are there?"

She shook her head. "We can get the chickens on the next supply trip."

He grunted, not at all sure about that, but took a quick glance down the rest of the list. "I still don't know if I want to be bothered with pigs or goats. And chickens are just plain noisy."

She rolled her eyes up toward the barn's rafters. "Then you'll be dealing with a bunch of ornery men who have biscuits without grease or lard to make them soft, and no bacon for breakfast." She lowered her gaze and looked at him. "I imagine even Hopper can make bacon and eggs."

Robbie didn't even look up from the list when he snorted. "Your imagination needs some work. Hopper burned the last pan of bacon he fried up for us. I think he needs to take a few lessons on how to cook."

Brenna laughed. "I think Hopper doesn't like to cook, which is why he burns all the food."

"Burning the supper is a good way to get hung up by your thumbs from the nearest tree," Robbie replied. He frowned and pointed at an item halfway down the list. "What's this cloth for?"

"Shue needs a new shirt. I can't patch the one that she wears the most anymore."

Robbie cast a sideways glance at Brenna. She was wearing the skirt she'd been mending her first morning at the ranch. And he could see there were several new patches on it since then.

"Is this enough cloth for just one shirt, or is there a little extra to make a few more things?"

The surprise was plain on Brenna's face. "It's only for one shirt. Do you need one too? Or one of the hands? I can make more."

He had no intention of her turning into the ranch's seamstress on top of being their cook and tending to the garden. Although it wouldn't surprise him if she was already doing the mending for some of the hands. The woman seemed determined to work herself to death.

But then he had a stubborn streak too, and he was just as determined that she not put herself into an early grave. But he let the subject drop for now and moved on to the next item that had caught his eye.

"Yarn?" He glanced over at her. "Are you planning on knitting us all something too?"

Brenna crossed her arms and stared back at him. "No. Just a scarf for Steph. It's his birthday next month. He'll be thirteen, in case you weren't aware of that."

"I know how old the boy is," Robbie said, his gaze returning to the paper in his hand. But he had forgotten that Steph's birthday would be here soon. He felt a little guilty that he couldn't recall if they'd done anything to celebrate it last year.

"I'll pay you back for the yarn from my wages," Brenna said quietly. "I should have put that on there, so you'd know."

"I'll pay for the yarn." He wasn't about to take any money from her, that was a sure thing.

"But if you pay for the yarn, then the gift is from you, not me," Brenna pointed out.

Robbie did a quick count to ten to hold on to his patience. "You'll be doing all the work, so that makes it from you. You aren't paying for the yarn, Brenna, so don't waste any more of the day arguing about it."

"All right. I'll give him the scarf. And what are you going to give him? I also think we should have a party for him with the hands." When Robbie's eyes shot wide open, she nodded at him. "He's still a child. And one who probably hasn't had much of a fuss made about his birthday. He's a good boy, works hard at his chores, and at the lessons he takes with Hopper. He deserves to be rewarded a bit on his birthday."

"Lillian and Ammie always come out and bring him something," Robbie said, although they weren't usually here on the exact day.

"I know, he told me," Brenna smiled. "And he's always happy to see them. But it's you he looks up to. He'd be thrilled to have a bit of extra attention from you."

"Me?" Robbie was astonished to hear that. He hadn't realized that, but thinking on it, maybe he should have. He'd gotten so used to seeing Steph right behind him whenever he turned around, that he'd stopped noticing it. Until lately. He hadn't seen the boy as much the last month or so, and the only thing that had changed on the ranch was Brenna's arrival there.

He smiled. "It seems to me he's taken to being *your* shadow. Maybe it's you he's looking up to these days."

She shook her head. "Now you're just being silly. Why don't you take him hunting with you, teach him how to shoot?"

"I could do that," Robbie said slowly. He remembered when Charles had taken him out shooting the first time. He'd been a little younger than Steph, but not much, and it had been one of the best days of his life.

"There's something I've been meaning to ask you." Brenna's hands were clasped in front of her. Robbie thought she looked pretty nervous and didn't have a clue why.

"All right." He waited, his head cocked to one side.

She chewed on her lower lip before taking a deep breath. "Are you planning on taking Steph with you to your new ranch up north?"

Not expecting that question at all, Robbie hesitated. "I haven't thought about it one way or another. Why? Has he said he'd rather not go?"

Brenna quickly shook her head. "He hasn't said a word. But I was wondering. If you don't think it's a good idea, I'll take him back to town with me."

Robbie shied away from the idea that Brenna was only in his life temporarily. He didn't like it, and didn't appreciate being reminded that the day she'd be gone was coming soon enough.

"I'll have to talk it over with Lillian," he finally said. Another thought crossed his mind. "Do you have a birthday?"

"What?" Brenna stared at him as if she hadn't understood a word he'd said.

He grinned at her. "A birthday. I was asking when your birthday is?"

"Of course I have a birthday. Everyone does. It's the tenth of May."

Robbie was back to frowning. "The tenth? That was last week."

"Was it?" Brenna shrugged. "I lose track of the days. And I've had enough birthdays. I don't pay attention to them anymore."

"Enough?" Robbie chuckled. "Aside from Steph, I'd wager you're the youngest person on this ranch." He gave her the boyish grin he was so famous for within the family. "I think some of the cattle are older than you."

Brenna gasped. "Robbie Smith, are you comparing me to a cow?"

He shook his head, his grin still in place. "I'm just making a point about your age, darlin'."

"Well if my birthday was last week, then I'm twenty-five," she sniffed. "I doubt if there's a cow on the place that old, although I don't appreciate the comparison."

"Twenty-five is barely getting your feet wet with living," Robbie teased.

She gave him a good look over. "Oh? And how old are you?"

"Twenty-nine on my next birthday, ma'am." He raised a finger to the brim of an imaginary hat since his was hanging on a hook on the far side of the stall.

"And when will that be?"

Robbie wished he knew, but the fact was, his ma had never told him. "I'm not sure, but we celebrate it in September." Not wanting to deal with any more questions about it, he remembered something Toby had told him the day before.

"I understand you want to have an outdoor dinner and some kind of get together for the hands?"

"Yes. Everyone has been working very hard, and it would be nice for them to be able to relax one night. Joe has a fiddle that he's offered to play." Brenna smiled. "And Shue wants to make her special mud pie. She claims she has some real chocolate stashed away."

He couldn't take his eyes off her. Standing there in her patched-over skirt, topped by an ugly blouse, her rich fall of hair tied back at the nape of her neck with a piece of twine, and her face lit up with amusement, she was the most beautiful woman he'd ever seen. Never in his life would he have believed he'd be captivated by any female, but this one might just do that. The thought had him taking a quick step back.

"Is something wrong?" Brenna asked.

"No." Robbie quickly dropped his gaze back to the list in his hand. "Is the licorice for this little party of yours?"

"No."

He winced inside at the sudden caution in her voice, realizing it was a reaction to the sharpness in his, but he simply sent her a questioning look.

"Pete's mentioned it a few times, and I know Shue has a fondness for it."

"All right." He continued on down the list. "And writing paper?" He looked up and smiled. "Are you planning on keeping a journal like Shannon does?"

"That's for Miguel. He's courting a girl in town, and they write to each other."

Robbie sighed. He doubted if there was a single thing on this list for herself. "This looks fine. Is there anything else you need?"

Her back stiffened slightly, but she nodded. "There's a stack of boards behind the barn."

Robbie looked in that direction before returning his attention back to her. "They're for a storage shed I doubt will ever get built."

"Can I use them? I'll need to build a pen for the goats and pigs."

He knew those animals were going to cause him trouble. Robbie rubbed a hand across his chin. "You can use the wood for that, but it'll have to wait until I can spare a man to build it."

"Steph and I can do it," Brenna added a nod when Robbie frowned.

He found himself once again doing a quick count to ten as his patience wore thin. He was tired of her always thinking up ways to work even harder. Cooking for all of them, keeping the ranch house clean, and tending the garden, was enough for any person to take on.

"You don't need to be doing that. The men can build it."

"So can I," Brenna insisted. "And the men have other work to do." She lifted her chin a notch. "I won't be a burden, Robbie. I can earn my way."

"You are. By doing what Lillian hired you to do. Cook. You don't need to work yourself into an early grave." Robbie set his feet apart. This was one argument he was going to win.

"Into an early...?" Brenna gasped then put her hands on her hips, squaring off with just a few feet between them. "I had no idea I was looking so poorly."

"You look fine," Robbie snapped. "You always look fine." He folded the list back up and stuck it into his shirt pocket.

She held her hand out. "I'll need that, in case something else has to be added to it."

Robbie shook his head. "You can let me know if you do, and I'll add it."

She lowered her arm and narrowed her eyes at him. "Fine."

He nodded back at her. "Fine." She could stand there and glare at him all day for all he cared. He was keeping the list. He had a few things he wanted to add to it himself.

"Then I guess I'll see you at supper."

Robbie didn't think so. Even when she was mad, he could still feel the mysterious pull she had on him. And he didn't like it much. He had his dream ranch close enough when he closed his eyes he could see it, not to mention the spread right here that he had to worry about. He didn't have time to figure out why one woman he hadn't even set eyes on a couple of months ago was intruding on his thoughts during the day and haunting his dreams at night.

So no, he wasn't coming in to supper. It was a much better idea to stay as far away from her as he could.

CHAPTER FIFTEEN

"Do you know why I'm riding with your agin' today?"

Robbie didn't even glance over at his foreman as he shrugged. "Because you enjoy my company?"

Toby snorted then urged his mount forward until he was in his boss's line of vision. "Not even a rattlesnake would enjoy yer company lately. And that's why I'm ridin' with you."

The rancher raised one eyebrow. "Because you couldn't find a rattlesnake this morning?"

"No. It's on account of no one else wants to be around you. Pete even said he'd fetch me another cup of coffee from the ranch house if I took his place with you today." Toby rested his hands on the saddle horn and leaned forward. "What do you think of that, boss man?"

"I think the hands are getting a mite pampered when they think they can pick out what work they want to do every day."

The foreman stared at him long enough that Robbie had to concentrate not to squirm in his saddle.

"It's because you've been in a contrary mood for a week now. You almost bit Pete's head off when he didn't catch that mare the first time he threw his rope, and Miguel damn near burned his hand tryin' to brand that calf with you standin' over him with a scowl on your face." He settled back into his saddle and frowned. "And Jonah's been out on the far pastures for days, and we brought the cattle in closer weeks ago, so we ain't got no cows out there." Toby paused and shook his head. "You got them all runnin' fer the bunkhouse and hidin' under their beds whenever you ride in at night."

"It isn't that bad," Robbie grumbled, although he suspected it was. Even caught up in his own thoughts, he'd noticed that there hadn't been anyone around whenever he'd been working in the barn or out in the corrals. "And I've had a lot of work to see to."

"No more'n usual," Toby countered. "What burr has gotten under yer saddle, Robbie? I don't recall ever seein' you so unhappy fer so long."

No burr, just a woman, Robbie thought, but wasn't about to voice that out loud.

"You've been this way ever since I left you in the barn with Brenna. What'd you do? Ask her to marry you and she turned you down?"

"Marr...?" Robbie's jaw dropped as he almost choked on the word. Where the hell had that come from?

Toby gave him a smug smile. "Strange way to look when a simple head shake and 'no' would've done."

"Fine. No, I didn't ask her to marry me." Robbie's mouth snapped shut and he took several deep breaths. "It was a fool question, and it took me by surprise, is all."

"Then did she ask you to marry her and *you* turned *her* down?"

Robbie made a growling noise deep in his throat. He was close to reaching over and busting a fist into Toby's jaw. "That's enough talk about marriage. No one is getting hitched to anyone around here. And that's the end of it. If you keep talking about it, you'll be riding out to look for another job."

His foreman didn't appear at all worried over that threat. Not if the grin on his face was any indication. "You know what? That Shue is a real smart woman."

Out of patience, Robbie's eyes narrowed into an unblinking stare. "Toby, I don't know what you're talking about, but find something without a woman's name attached to it, or keep your mouth closed."

The older man shrugged. "Okay. How about that new pen behind the barn? It looks fine."

When Robbie remained silent, Toby went on as if his boss wasn't visibly fuming.

"Bren... I mean the cook and young Steph sure did a fine job buildin' it. It's sturdy too. Took a good look at it jest to be sure."

"She should have waited until I could spare a man to build it for her," Robbie ground out. That pen was a real sore point with him. He'd told her he'd have one of the hands put it up, but he'd seen her working on it, since he'd taken to checking on the ranch house a few times each day from one of the hills surrounding it. Didn't the woman trust him to keep his word?

"She had help. I jest told you that. Steph helped her."

"A grown man. I told her I'd have one of the hands build it."

Toby's grin was back. "I guess she likes to do for herself."

Robbie glared at his foreman as his frustration with Brenna went from a simmer to a full boil. "She's contrary and stubborn, that's what she is."

Toby's eyebrows shot up. "Why'd you say that? Now if we was discussin' Shue, I could understand what you're sayin'. That woman was born contrary and stubborn. But Brenna ain't been nothin' but nice to everyone, especially young Steph. She's givin' him some of that motherin' he missed out on in his early years."

Robbie certainly couldn't argue with that, but it didn't change his mind any either. The woman thought she should work just like a man, and didn't seem to have any idea how much weaker she was. Every day he half expected to ride into the yard and get told she'd taken to her bed. He'd even considered sending for Doctor Abby so she'd be here when Brenna collapsed from overwork and exhaustion.

"She should do what she's told and not take it into her head she can do what she pleases."

"Now that's jest confusin'," Toby said. "She don't roam about doing only what strikes her fancy. She does what she's supposed to. She cooks fine meals, tends to that big garden of hers, keeps the house clean, and she don't complain none about any of it. At least not that I've heard."

"And that's more than she was hired to do," Robbie snapped out. "Not put up pens or make new clothes for everyone but herself." Having built up a head of steam, Robbie kept on going. "And if that isn't enough, she's planning parties, like this campfire supper of hers, and one for Steph's birthday next month. And that garden she put in is twice as big as the one we had before. Pete told me she'd turned over a good piece of the dirt herself before he got out there to help her. The woman needs to sit down and take a rest every day instead of digging up a mountain of weeds and building pens for farm animals."

Robbie finished on a huff of breath. Toby hadn't said a word. When the foreman's mouth started to twitch, he turned his head away and looked off toward the horizon.

"I can see why you have a problem with her," Toby finally said. He turned back to look at Robbie, and while his voice had been neutral enough, the big man's eyes danced with amusement. "But she's only temporary. We'll be gone come fall, and so will she."

"That's right." Robbie's jaw hardened. It was not only right, but exactly as it should be. He had a dream to chase, and Brenna needed to get settled back into town and start a new life. Without all the work on a ranch.

And without him.

Robbie pushed his hat down lower over his forehead and nodded. "That's right."

"I heard you the first time," Toby said. "But until then, she's your responsibility."

"I know that."

"So you should keep a closer eye on her if you think she's

workin' too hard, or the men are gettin' too attached to her."
When Robbie's gaze jerked around to him, Toby nodded. "I don't
want to be ridin' north with a bunch of mopin' cowhands, and
that's a fact."

"Is someone taking liberties with Brenna?" Robbie's blood
started to heat. Toby was right about Brenna only being temporary,
and about her being Robbie's responsibility until he could deliver
her safely back to town. He wasn't going to tolerate one second of
anyone bothering her until then.

"What are you talkin' about now?" Toby demanded. "I ain't
seen anythin' like that. I'm jest sayin' the men are goin' to
miss her."

"Never mind. I'll take care of it." Robbie lifted his reins and
looked over toward the next hill where a few head of cattle were
peacefully grazing. "We've got work to do. Let's ride."

———

ROBBIE STOOD on the spacious porch of the ranch house and
leaned against the front post at the top of the steps. Night had
barely taken over the sky, lending a soft gray backdrop to the green
hills surrounding the ranch. His gaze was drawn to the glow
coming from the large campfire burning on the far side of the large
corral. Laughter and fiddle music floated on the air, along with the
smell of roasting meat. Robbie took an appreciative sniff before
descending the steps and strolling across the yard. He stopped at
the corral fence, just beyond the glow of the fire, and watched as
all of the ranch's residents sat on bales of hay or mingled together
in the flickering light, with an easy camaraderie flowing through
the group.

A close-knit group, Robbie thought with a smile. A family he'd
had a big hand in building, along with Toby and Lillian and
Charles. After all, it was the place Lillian had built for orphans that
he'd come to live on.

And when that need had passed and no more children came to

grow up here, he'd stayed to build it into a working cattle ranch. One that helped feed the orphans in the churches and homes built for them in town, as well as supply meat for the kitchen at The Crimson Rose, Charles' gaming hall. Robbie was proud of that, and of the family of misfits who helped run the ranch right alongside him.

His smile grew wider when he saw Toby take a seat beside Shue on a wide log that had been dragged within the circle of light thrown off by the fire. But his gaze kept moving over the shifting crowd of people until he spotted a long fall of dark curls, tied at the nape of a slender neck. Brenna was bent at the waist, her hand on Steph's shoulder, carefully listening to something he was telling her with a good deal of excited hand gestures and head nods. He watched the soft smile play along her lips and wondered what it would be like to feel them beneath his own. Straightening up at the thought, he quickly shoved it aside and stuck his thumbs in his belt as he strolled forward, deliberately taking a path straight toward Toby and Shue. His foreman must have heard him coming because he turned his head and squinted into the darkness.

"That you, boss man? It'd better be, 'cause everyone else is already here."

"It's me," Robbie acknowledged, stopping just behind the log. He smiled at Shue when she looked at him and frowned.

"It took you long enough to git here. Everyone's mostly finished supper, and Hopper is already tunin' his fiddle."

"I heard." Robbie inclined his head toward the gray-headed fiddle player, who had a beard to match. "I wonder if he's learned any new songs."

"Don't need no new ones. The old ones sound jest fine," Toby declared. He chuckled when Hopper broke into a lively tune and Steph stepped forward and did a bow so low his nose almost touched his knees. "Looks like the youngest man here is goin' to do the honors."

Robbie couldn't help grinning as well when Brenna sank into a perfect curtsy and placed her hands on top of Steph's shoulders.

The young boy instantly bounced to the right and then back to the left as Brenna followed along, laughing when Steph whirled them both around in a wide circle.

Robbie was content to stand out of the light, watching the two of them enjoying themselves. He only started frowning when Pete stepped up and tapped Steph on the shoulder. The short, brash cowboy managed two full turns around the fire before Miguel cut in for a turn.

Robbie relaxed as he watched Brenna graciously dance with each man who stood patiently waiting for their chance to take a turn around the fire with her. There was plenty of space between her and her dancing partner, which was a good thing. She needed it to keep from getting her feet stepped all over. Robbie had to stifle a laugh. The hands were a lot better at chasing cows than they were at dancing with a woman. Robbie's frown didn't return until Jonah stepped up and made a far more practiced bow than Steph had.

When the handsome cowboy's hand settled confidently on Brenna's waist, Robbie's arms crossed over his chest. And when Jonah expertly guided Brenna around the fire, his steps matching perfectly to hers, Robbie planted his feet further apart and his eyes narrowed as he carefully followed their every movement. But when it seemed to him that Jonah had managed to cut in half the space that ought to be between them, Robbie's boots began to move.

He walked toward the fire, his eyes on the dancing couple. He didn't notice the other hands taking a long step backward as he approached Jonah and gave him a hard tap on the shoulder. The cowboy's eyebrows shot up when he saw who was standing behind him, but he inclined his head at Brenna before moving aside.

Robbie and Brenna stood in the firelight, looking at each other for a moment before he reached out and circled his fingers around her waist. He could see the uncertainty in her eyes as she hesitated before placing her hands lightly on his shoulders.

"Are you ready to dance, Miss Roberts?" Robbie smiled at her.

She nodded, her gaze on his. "I am, Mr. Smith."

He took one step and then another as she effortlessly followed him. They moved in a perfect rhythm, their bodies swaying together as the music slowed into a haunting melody. Robbie didn't notice as he automatically slowed his step, his eyes locked on hers. Every nerve in his body was tuned to her, as if he'd found the other half of himself.

Completely absorbed in the warmth flooding through him and the overwhelming rightness of the moment, Robbie tightened his arms and pulled her closer until he could feel the heat of her body reaching out to meet his. He didn't notice or care about anything beyond the woman he was dancing with. As she stared up at him, he started to lower his head, wanting the feel of her mouth beneath his before he drew in another breath.

Brenna stiffened in his arms, making him blink. That's when he heard the loud cough behind him. He quickly straightened up and extended his arms to put a proper distance between them.

"Song's done," Shue declared in a voice that was loud enough the coyotes in the hills probably heard it.

Feeling the heat rush up his neck, Robbie dropped his arms and stepped away from Brenna as if she'd suddenly caught fire. Resisting the urge to shake his head so he could clear it, he watched the blush flood over Brenna's cheeks as she stepped back. Feeling the wrench when the physical connection between them was broken, Robbie fists curled up at his sides and his jaw hardened as he stared at her.

"You shouldn't wear your hair down like that." His jaw clenched even harder at the hurt look that leaped into her eyes, but he simply gave an abrupt nod then forced himself to turn around and walk off. When he was standing next to Toby, who was staring at him as if he'd sprouted two heads, Robbie turned and crossed his arms over his chest. He maintained a bland expression for the rest of the hands who were all staring at him.

"Maybe it's time we got that cake we baked out here," Shue said into the silence.

A cheer erupted from the hands and Brenna closed her eyes for a moment before turning a smile on all of them. "I'll get it." Her skirt fluttered out around her as she quickly turned and headed into the dark toward the ranch house before anyone could offer to come with her. Robbie suddenly found himself at the center of a circle of condemning glares.

"You really can be worse than a mule's backside, boy," Shue snorted before getting to her feet and stalking after Brenna.

Toby slowly rose as well, his lips pursed together as he faced his boss. "And maybe I need to take you behind the barn and give you a talkin' to about manners. What's gotten into you, anyways?"

"I think we'd all like to know that," Jonah said quietly.

Robbie looked around at all the men he'd just told himself were a family he'd helped build, and sighed. He rubbed a tired hand across his chin before straightening his shoulders and facing them.

"She has. She's gotten into me. And I don't like it." Having confessed to all he was going to, Robbie turned on his heels and stalked off.

CHAPTER SIXTEEN

BRENNA STEPPED OUT ONTO THE PORCH. A SOFT BREEZE touched her face as she kept to the shadows, her gaze roving over the wide yard. It was filled with activity this morning, and she smiled as she spotted Steph practicing his roping by tossing it over an unsuspecting Pete. The cowboy wrestled his way out and turned to shake a finger at the boy who'd prudently stepped back several feet.

Knowing Pete wouldn't be too harsh over one of Steph's pranks, Brenna's gaze moved on until she'd looked over the entire yard. Satisfied that one Robbie Smith was nowhere in sight, she stepped further out onto the porch. So far she'd managed to avoid him for going on three days now.

Every night she'd left him a supper plate on the table, along with bread wrapped up in a cloth and set next to a pot of jam for his breakfast the next day. And every morning, as she stared at the empty plate and neatly folded cloth, she told herself the arrangement suited her just fine. But as a precaution, in case the man popped up unexpectedly, she made sure her hair was wound into a tight bun and pinned securely at the back of her head. Since she wasn't about to mimic Shue and lop it off, her ornery boss was going to have to be satisfied with that.

A shout from Hopper had Brenna looking back over her shoulder toward the house. The men looked like they had the wagons about ready to leave for town, and she didn't want to miss giving them the note that Shue had agreed to write out for her. She was about to go inside to hurry the older woman along, when the door banged open and Shue walked out, a folded piece of paper in her hand and a scowl on her face.

"He isn't here so you might as well stop stretchin' yer neck out lookin' fer him."

Brenna wrinkled her nose. "I'm not looking for anyone. I'm standing here waiting for you."

Shue rolled her eyes. "Now that's a lie and you know it, girl."

Brenna fought a smile. Shue rarely called her "girl" anymore. Only when the old miner was annoyed with her, and that wasn't very often. Although this morning seemed to be an exception to that.

"I'm not lying," Brenna said. "I am standing here waiting for you, and I've already stopped looking for Mr. Smith."

Shue snorted. "Mr. Smith, is it? I guess that means yer still mad at him." She added a shrug. "And you cain't avoid the man forever."

"Probably not," Brenna conceded. "But I can today, and maybe tomorrow, and I intend to for as long as possible."

"All that jest because he said somethin' about yer hair?"

Not just her hair, but that was a good start. Brenna was still smarting from the way Robbie had delivered his obvious snub by leaving her standing all by herself as all the hands had averted their eyes. She'd never pretended to be a beauty like Ammie, and wouldn't blame him for making that comparison and finding her lacking in many ways. But he hadn't hired Brenna for her looks. He'd hired her to work at the ranch, so he didn't need to point out all her flaws. Especially not in front of all the hands.

Brenna wasn't vain, but he'd hurt her feelings and she wasn't inclined to forgive him. Another one of her flaws, she supposed, but that was too bad. He'd have to live with all of them. At least until the fall. Then he'd go to his new place, and she'd go back to town to work for Dorrie.

That thought didn't cheer her up much either.

"He didn't mean he didn't like yer hair."

Shue's voice broke into Brenna's thoughts and set her own into fuming again. "Well, that's what he said."

"No he didn't. He said you shouldn't wear it down."

"Same thing," Brenna insisted. She'd never given how she wore her hair much thought until Robbie Smith had come along. Now she spent a good amount of time each morning considering what to do with it. It was plain annoying, that's what it was.

"And it hasn't been just my hair," Brenna went on. "He's mumbled things about my clothes, too."

"Yer clothes?" Shue looked Brenna up and down. "What about them?"

"He's taken a dislike to my skirt. And he's the one who insisted I wear it rather than my britches, which would be a lot more practical." Brenna's mouth set into a stubborn line. "And I've noticed he doesn't mind *you* wearing britches. It's just me he doesn't like looking at."

"Oh, I wouldn't say that." Shue grinned. "I think he likes lookin' at you jest fine."

"He certainly doesn't like looking at me working. He thinks I can't do the work." Brenna put her hands on her hips and pressed her lips together even more. "He's made it very clear that he doesn't like me much, and I haven't given him one reason to think that way. I put the meals on the table every day, the house is clean, the garden tended to, the washing and mending done. I even help out in the barn when I can." Brenna glared at Shue. "What more does the man want?"

"Fer you to sit down every so often?"

"He didn't hire me to sit down, Shue. He hired me to work."

Shue slapped the note against her thigh. "He hired you to cook. But that ain't the point."

Exasperated, Brenna threw her arms out wide. "What is the point?"

"He's a man." Shue nodded when Brenna crossed her arms and shook her head. "That means there's certain times when what comes out of his mouth ain't what he means."

"Certain times?" Brenna scoffed. "What times are those? Whenever he's awake?"

"Nope," Shue chuckled before her expression turned serious again. "When he don't know how to deal with his feelin's."

Brenna frowned. It seemed to her that Robbie wasn't having any problem at all saying what he felt. And none of it was good for her. Thinking Shue had too much of a soft spot for the usually charming ranch manager to see that the man could actually dislike someone, Brenna held out her hand. "Did you finish the note?"

Shue looked down, blinking as if she was surprised to see a piece of paper in her hand. "I almost fergot about it." She raised her gaze to Brenna's. "I finished it. Put in everythin' you asked. It's real nice that yer willin' to have Steph come live with you after all the men leave. He'll like that jest fine, I'm thinkin'. But what's this about a letter? I meant to ask you, but was concentratin' on rememberin' the words to write."

Brenna smiled. "Ammie wrote a letter for me to a man in St. Louis. He's my uncle, I think."

"You think?"

"I have letters that he wrote to my papa. Ammie read them to me, and they were signed 'Mathias Roberts'. That's the name papa called his brother."

The older woman slowly lifted her arm and held the note out. "You got family in St. Looey? Are you thinkin' of goin' there to be with them?"

"Oh, no." Brenna shook her head. "Ammie wrote to the place on the letter, but that came almost twenty years ago. I doubt if my uncle is still there. And I'm not expecting them to take me in now. I'm full grown, so there's no need." Brenna sighed and looked down at her feet. "I thought he'd like to know why papa suddenly stopped writing to him. I'm sure my uncle must have wondered about it."

"Well then. Let's git this note off so you can find all that out." Shue's gruff voice took on its normal no-nonsense tone as she pressed the note into Brenna's hand. "And you'd best hurry. Looks like them boys are about to leave."

Brenna spun around and saw Joe climb onto the high seat of the front wagon.

"And you tell them not to dawdle in town none," Shue said to Brenna's back.

Picking up her skirts, Brenna flew down the steps and across the yard toward Pete who was still talking to Steph. She skidded to a halt next to them, and all three waved their hands at the dust she'd managed to kick up.

Pete smiled, his long mustache moving upward with the curve of his lips. "What's got you in such a hurry, Brenna?"

Holding out the note, Brenna returned his smile before raising an eyebrow at Steph. "I wanted to give you this, and to tell Steph he should be more careful where he throws his rope."

"I already explained that to him," Pete said. "And now he's going to get started on his chores." The older cowboy stared at the boy who nodded vigorously before taking off toward the barn at an easy lope.

"That boy can sure be a handful." Pete removed his hat and held it down at his side. "Now then, what's this?"

"A letter I'd appreciate you delivering to Dorrie McKenzie. I know Mr. Smith has asked you to stop by the marshal's house."

"He has," Pete confirmed. He looked down as he shuffled his feet for a moment. "You know Robbie didn't mean nothing the other night." Pete looked up, his gaze soft. "He liked dancing with you, I could tell."

"Thank you for saying so, Pete." Brenna kept her tone polite as she continued to hold out the note Shue had written for her. "Can you be sure this gets to Dorrie?"

Pete looked down at her hand and backed up half a step. "Now there ain't nothing in that about you leaving is there? 'Cause I ain't taking no letter that says something like that." Pete backed up another step before hastily adding, "and neither will Joe."

Touched by Pete's words, Brenna could have hugged him. It really was wonderful to hear that someone, at least, wanted her around. Knowing a hug would completely embarrass the hand who looked as if he was prepared to run at any moment, Brenna quickly shook her head in denial. "There's nothing like that in this note, Pete. I love it here at the ranch." Which was the truth. Well, at least most of the time.

The cowboy immediately brightened up, a huge smile exposing every one of his slightly browned teeth as he took the note from Brenna's outstretched hand. "That's good, because we sure like having you here." He paused. "Even the boss does. You shouldn't pay him no mind. He's just tired, what with running this place and planning for the new one. And this hot weather ain't helping none either. Makes it hard to find enough water for the cattle. Looks like we'll have to be taking them further out in the hills again."

When he paused for the second time, Brenna was surprised to see the splash of red creeping along his cheeks. Pete drew in a deep breath as he held his hat in front of him, his fingers playing along its brim. "And your hair looks just fine any way you want to wear it. If the boss says otherwise, then I'll just have to set him straight about it."

Brenna laughed. "Thank you, Pete. As much as I might like that, it won't be necessary."

The short, thin man smiled as he plopped his hat back on his head. "Well, I will if I need to. So will any of the other hands. I thought you ought to know that."

"I'll keep it in my mind, Pete. Oh. And Shue said not to dawdle in town."

Pete cast a glare toward the porch where Shue was standing, staring back at him. "I know. I could hear her all the way across the yard." He raised his voice. "And I don't dawdle nowhere. You know that, Shue."

———

ROBBIE HAD TAKEN up his position on the tall hill behind the ranch house, staying in the shadow of an old oak tree that graced its top. Hayseed was contentedly chewing the grass ten yards down the backside of the hill and well out of sight of the people scurrying around the yard below them. The sun was climbing in the sky as Robbie frowned at the wagons still standing in the yard. Pete and Joe needed to get going. It was a two-day trek into town by the road the wagons had to take, and if they didn't start out soon, it would become a three-day trip.

His annoyance with his hands faded into the background the minute Brenna came into view. She hurried across the yard in a direct path toward Pete. Robbie had no idea what they were talking about, or what she held out to Pete, but he didn't really care either. Just seeing her was enough to put a shine on his day.

By the cold silence he'd been getting from Toby and the rest of the men for the last few days, Robbie was pretty sure they hadn't understood what he'd told them that night by the campfire. But there was nothing he was inclined to do about that. He had his own problem of trying to figure out how he felt about Brenna.

For three days she'd stayed in his mind, no matter how hard he worked chasing cattle, breaking in a horse, or digging new fence posts. And even as exhausted as he was every night, falling into his bed after he'd eaten the cold supper she'd left out for him, the woman invaded his dreams. And they weren't the innocent kind either. Which only put him further on edge. It was a cycle he couldn't seem to break out of.

But there were two things he knew for sure. He had to keep his mind on the ranch since the heat and drought were causing big problems, and he had to figure out a way to apologize to Brenna. So far he hadn't come up with an answer for either one.

When Brenna turned to go back into the ranch house, and Pete climbed up on his wagon, Robbie blew out a long breath as he watched until Brenna disappeared from sight. It only took him a minute to reach Hayseed and swing up into the saddle, and another twenty minutes to reach the point around the curve of the hill where he could intercept the wagon. He patted his shirt pocket, satisfied when he heard the crackle of paper beneath his glove. He had a list of his own that he wanted delivered to Ammie, who he was sure would get it all together in the short amount of time the men would be in town picking up the supplies for the ranch.

Robbie didn't have long to wait before the wagons rounded the curve. Since Joe was in the lead wagon, he spotted his boss first and hauled back on the reins as he let out a low whistle to the horses. Robbie gave the driver a friendly nod as he rode up.

"'Morning, Joe." Robbie glanced up at the sun. "You got a late start today."

The ranch hand jerked his thumb behind him. "Not me. Pete's the sociable one. Had to wait for him to stop talking to everyone he saw."

Nodding his understanding, Robbie set Hayseed into a walk back toward the second wagon where Pete was waiting. As he pulled his horse to a stop, Robbie removed his glove and reached into his shirt pocket for his list. He handed it to Pete.

"I need you to give that to Miss Ammie. You've been to her place before."

Pete scowled down at him from the lofty height of the wagon's bench seat. "I ain't no letter delivery service. I got the supply list to give over to Cook at The Crimson Rose, who ain't going to be too happy about some of the things on it. I don't think they got no goats or pigs at that gambling hall. And then I got to go to Miss Lillian's to give her a letter from Shue, and that old bird told me I cain't give it to no one at The Crimson Rose except the boss lady. I had to deliver it personal."

Not much in a sympathizing mood, Robbie only shrugged. "You've delivered notes for Shue before."

"It's not just hers. Now I got yours to deliver to Miss Ammie, and Miss Brenna's to go to the marshal's wife. Why cain't all of you write to one person and let them pass these letters around between them?"

Robbie immediately latched onto Pete saying he had a note from Brenna. He wrestled with his conscience for a long moment about whether or not to demand to see that note, but in the end his conscience won out and he decided against it. He already had enough to apologize to Brenna about, he sure didn't need to be adding snooping into her private mail to that list.

Lifting two fingers to the brim of his hat, Robbie gave a quick nod. "You be sure to deliver all three of them, Pete." He followed that declaration with a stern look before turning Hayseed back toward the hills and riding off.

CHAPTER SEVENTEEN

"It's been ten days since those wagons left for town. Where do you think they're at?"

Brenna barely shook her head in response. Shue had posed that same question at least a dozen times every day for the last three days. Brenna had no idea where Pete and Joe were.

"I'm surprised Robbie isn't mad as a stirred-up hornet at them two for bein' late." Shue was sitting on the bench pulled up to the large table in the kitchen. She leaned over and cast a long look out one of the windows overlooking the back porch, as if she were willing the wagons to magically appear. "But then I'm mad enough for the both of us. I told that no-good cowboy not to dawdle." She tapped her stubby fingers against the tabletop. "You heard me tell him that, didn't you?"

"I most certainly did," Brenna quickly agreed. She was only half-listening to the older woman's complaints. Standing next to the table, she leaned over it and turned the battered pitcher stuffed with daisies, looking for the best position to show off the cheerful little flowers. Brenna stepped back and looked the pitcher over with a critical eye.

"They looked fine the way they were, girl. Stop fussin'
with 'em."

Not at all put off by Shue's peevish tone, Brenna sent her a
sunny smile. "They're worth a little fussing." She glanced over at
Steph who was sitting across the table from Shue. "What do you
think, Steph? How do they look?"

In the grand gesture of males everywhere, the twelve-year-old
simply shrugged. "I don't know. They look fine to me."

Brenna laughed. If he'd been sitting closer to her, she'd have
reached over and given him a hug. Not that Steph wouldn't have
squirmed in embarrassment. But she knew by the grin on his face
he liked it whenever she hugged him.

"Ain't no flowers growin' near the house," Shue said. "You
must'a got up pretty early to go traipsin' up the hill to pick 'em."

"She didn't pick them," Steph immediately piped up. "Robbie
did. He was carrying them when I see'd him in the barn last night."

"You *saw* him in the barn, Steph. Not 'see'd'," Brenna automatically corrected then frowned at him. "And why were you out in the
barn so late last night?"

"I was waiting for Robbie." Steph's voice clearly conveyed the
underlying message that he thought Brenna had asked a foolish
question. "I had to see if he needed any help with Hayseed. That's
what a good hand would do."

"And good hands git up early in the mornin', Steph, so they
need their sleep. If Robbie wants to stay out until the night's half
gone, then he can jest take care of his horse on his own. He don't
need yer help with that." Shue pointed a finger at the back door to
the kitchen. "What does need yer help are them chores yer
supposed to be doin'. You go on and git to those now."

"Steph," Brenna said quietly, halting the boy in his rush toward
the door. "You don't need to worry about Robbie going back on his
word to take you on that hunting trip for your birthday. Or
showing him that you want to work on his ranch when you're
older. He won't forget."

"'Cause you'll remind him?" Steph grinned.

Brenna grinned right back at him. "Of course I will, and nag him too, if that's what it takes."

He let out a loud whoop as he raced to the back porch, carelessly shoving the door closed so it slammed shut behind him.

Shue gave Brenna a doubtful look. "You sure you want that boy livin' with you in the city? He's a loud one."

"I'm sure," Brenna laughed. "Just as I'm sure he'll grow out of it."

The old miner looked skeptical, but she returned her attention to the flowers. "So Robbie left them here for you to find this morning?"

"I'm sure he left them for both of us," Brenna said.

"He don't have much of a hand at how to put them in that pitcher. Never seen such a sorry-lookin' mess when I first saw 'em."

The flowery mass did overflow the sides of their dented container, with a number of them drooping down until they were almost doubled over no matter how much she'd fussed with them . But Brenna didn't care.

She'd loved the flowers lining up beside the houses in the city. It wasn't a luxury she'd had on the farm since all her energy went into growing food for the household, or a small patch of flowers to sell at the market along with her produce. And she'd been even more astounded by the showy arrangements gracing the tables all over Ammie and Charlotte's house. But this was the first time she'd ever had any flowers on a table of her own. Well, at least it was partly hers for as long as she was at the ranch. And Brenna thought they looked perfect.

"A man who leaves flowers is probably tryin' to say somethin', don't you think?"

Brenna's brow furrowed as she glanced over at Shue. "Like what?"

Shue rolled her eyes upward. "I don't know. Maybe the same thing he was tryin' to say when that mare showed up for you."

"Miguel brought the mare," Brenna pointed out. She'd been

surprised when Hopper had insisted she come out to the corral where he'd pointed out a pretty little pinto with a peaceful look in her eyes. He'd told Brenna that the mare was hers, and that he'd been ordered to give her lessons, so she'd get used to riding a genuine cow pony. She hadn't had a chance to start the lessons yet, nor had Hopper had any free time since the ranch was currently two men short. But she was looking forward to them.

"You don't think it was that cowboy's idea to ride over to the Simmons place and bring you back a horse, do you?" Shue chuckled. "I'm guessin' you must'a mentioned it to Robbie that you didn't know how to ride a horse on your own."

"I might have." Brenna pursed her lips. "But I wasn't hinting around that I thought he should get me one."

"I doubt if he thought you were," Shue said. "And did you also tell him that Steph would sure enjoy goin' huntin' with him?"

"Maybe I did in passing," Brenna said slowly.

"Well maybe in passin' you could leave the man some kind of sign that yer in a forgivin' mood, before he talks Lillian into deedin' the ranch over to you?" Shue cackled at her own joke and slapped a hand against her upper thigh before lifting it to point at the flowers. "That boy may act like a mule's hind end at times, but he sure does know how to apologize to a woman."

"Yes, he does." Brenna couldn't deny that Robbie seemed to be bending over backwards to keep her happy. And he was doing a good job of it too. But she didn't want him to feel guilty forever. She figured a week or two was enough, and it was time for him to stop. She tilted her head to one side and considered the possibilities.

She was still thinking about it four hours later as she was tending the garden. It was not quite noon, if the sun's position in the sky was any indication, and she was filling her second basket of weeds since Shue had insisted she would make the lunch while Brenna got off her feet for a change. That hadn't lasted long, but Brenna had appreciated Shue's thoughtfulness.

She stood up and put her hands to the small of her back,

stretching upward to work out some of the stiffness. A loud shout from the front of the house had her turning her head in that direction. Brenna immediately spotted the cloud of dust rising from the wagon wheels churning it up as two teams of horses made their way around the last curve of the road and headed for the yard.

With a wide smile on her face, Brenna picked up her skirts and did a very unladylike sprint across the garden and around the side of the house. Pete and Joe were back, so there would be plenty of supplies to put away, hopefully a few goats and pigs to put into the new pens, and maybe even a return note from Dorrie that she could nag Shue into reading out loud to her after the noon meal.

She came around the side of the house and into the yard just as the first wagon rumbled to a stop. Brenna blinked in surprise. It looked like a whole parade was coming into the yard. Aside from the wagons, and there looked to be three rather than two of them, there were four riders. And there were more people than Joe and Pete in the wagons. Brenna recognized Jules, who had dismounted and strode over to the lead wagon to help one of the women down. From the easy and familiar way the marshal's hands went around the lady's waist, Brenna instantly knew that it had to be Dorrie. Lifting her hand in a crazy wave, Brenna raced forward only to stop halfway as not one, but two bodies came running across the yard in her direction.

Before she knew it, she was engulfed in a group hug from Dorrie and Ammie. Brenna closed her arms around both of them, her eyes brimming with tears.

"I can't believe you're here." She pulled back slightly so she could look into their faces. "How did you get here?"

Ammie laughed. "On the back of my horse. How else? Poor Dorrie had to ride in the wagon though."

Now Dorrie laughed. "At least I didn't have to put up with Ethan's silence for miles and miles."

"Oh, that's all right," Ammie said airily. "I kept up enough chatter for both of us. He loved it."

Even Brenna, who'd already heard all about Ethan's stubborn

silence whenever Ammie was around, laughed. She imagined the man, who was supposed to be the best tracker west of the Rockies, hadn't enjoyed that at all.

"You do like to annoy him," Dorrie said.

"Why did you come in the wagon? I know how much you like to ride." Brenna leaned back and studied Dorrie's face. Her friend was positively glowing from within, making Brenna break out into a wide smile. "You're in the family way?"

As Dorrie happily nodded, Ammie wrapped an arm around Brenna's waist. "Our friend here is going to make us all aunts, of a sort. Or at least honorary ones." She winked at Brenna. "And her overanxious husband came along to be sure she did nothing more than lift a spoon." Ammie grinned at Dorrie. "Unless he's also taken to feeding you?"

"He might," Dorrie sighed. "He has reverted to his cotton-ball behavior."

Brenna looked from Dorrie to Ammie and then back again. "What's his cotton-ball behavior?"

"That's when he treats me like I should be wrapped in a whole barrel full of them."

"Oh. I told Robbie he shouldn't treat me like I was made of glass." Brenna grinned as she and Dorrie looked over at Ammie.

"Well don't look at me," the striking brunette said. "I haven't told Ethan anything. He doesn't speak to me, remember?" She looked over Dorrie's shoulder and put a finger to her lips. "Shh. Here come Lillian and Abby."

"Lillian?" Brenna's face went pale. She'd only met the owner of the ranch once, and that was over dinner at Ammie's house. She'd been too overwhelmed by Ammie's aunt to say much. Lillian wasn't tall or short, but somewhere in the middle, with a thick fall of platinum-blond hair. It had looked like moonbeams in the candlelight of the dining room that night as it had flickered over the curls that had been tied at one side of Lillian's neck and then flowed over her shoulder. After meeting her, Brenna had known instantly why that old miner she'd met in the middle of the square had talked about the famous Lillian Jamison.

She took a quick peek in the direction of the wagons and spotted Abby walking toward them, talking to the platinum-haired woman who Dorrie had once mentioned was the doctor's cousin. Lillian moved with an effortless grace and looked so perfect that Brenna's jaw dropped open exactly the same way it had at that first dinner.

She'd never even imagined anyone like Lillian Jamison. But then Ammie was a dark-haired version of her blond aunt, and just as beautiful. It was a wonder that Charles Jamison had time to do anything but fend off male advances to his wife and niece.

The mental image that brought up had Brenna smiling just as Lillian and Abby came up next to Dorrie.

"I take it Dorrie has told you the good news?" the doctor asked, a smile on her lips.

"Yes. And it's very good news," Brenna said. She blinked when Lillian held out a hand.

"It's good to see you again, Brenna."

Brenna tentatively took Lillian's hand, blinking again when Lillian gave it a good shake.

"That's the formalities from the owner of the ranch," Lillian said before she took a half-step forward and leaned in to give Brenna a warm hug. "And that's from me, greeting you as a member of the family."

"A member of...?" Brenna turned a confused look toward Dorrie. "I don't understand."

"Everyone should have a family," Dorrie said, a new firmness in her voice. "We've known each other for more than a decade, have told each other all our secrets. What's more family than that?"

"We've done the same," Ammie declared, aiming a brilliant smile at Brenna. "Well, without the decade. But we have shared clothing, so that puts the final seal on it. You're family."

"We didn't share clothing." Brenna couldn't stop a laugh as she pictured Ammie parading about in a much patched-over skirt. "You gave me some of yours."

"Which you left at my house," Ammie sniffed.

"They weren't suited for life on a ranch. I didn't want to ruin them."

Abby clapped her hands. "I think that proves the two of you are definitely family. I hear the same bickering from my children."

Lillian linked an arm with her cousin, the doctor. "And between all of us, on occasion." She smiled at Brenna. "We can get into the matter of clothes later. What we want to hear is how you've fared out here with Shue and all the hands."

"And Robbie," Ammie chimed in, batting her eyes when Brenna narrowed hers.

"And Robbie too," Lillian said smoothly. "Have you had any problems?"

Brenna glanced around at the four faces looking eagerly back at her. A warmth had grown within her when Lillian had declared her part of the family. Now her eyes started to mist over. She was happy beyond words to have them standing there with her in the dusty yard, and could hardly believe they'd come all this way to check on her.

"Is that why you're here? To be sure I haven't had any problems?"

All four of them broke into laughter. As usual, the very calm Abby recovered first.

"That's reason enough since we've all had our dealings with the men in the family." She added her nod to the other three around her. "But there was also the other thing."

Brenna's eyebrows drew together. "What other thing?"

Lillian, Ammie, and Dorrie reached into the waistbands of their skirts and each of them drew out a folded piece of paper.

"We got notes."

CHAPTER EIGHTEEN

ROBBIE APPROACHED THE LAST HILL SEPARATING HIM FROM THE ranch with a determined glint in his eye. He'd hoped Brenna would give him a sign that she knew he was trying to apologize to her, but had finally decided it must be the way Toby said. Women had to have the words.

Unfortunately, he didn't have a lot of experience with that kind of talk. Most of his life a smile and a wink had gotten him out of hot water with any woman. Since it had always worked for him, he'd never had to bother with much else. Never even given it much thought. Until now. Somehow, he didn't think his smile was going to work on Brenna the way it had on all the other women he'd met. But if she wanted to hear him say he was sorry for upsetting her at the campfire, then he could get the words out.

Probably.

Shaking his head at himself, Robbie set Hayseed into a quick trot as they came around the last bend in the road leading into the ranch. He pulled the horse up when he got a clear view of the yard. There was so much activity going on that it looked like Portsmouth Square in the middle of the day.

The two supply wagons were sitting in the center of the open space as several of the hands swarmed in and out of the beds, unloading the pile of goods that Pete and Joe had brought back with them. And it seemed as if there were double the number of people milling about than there should be. He squinted at one man in particular, trying to make out who he was, until Steph crossed his line of vision, leading a horse into the barn. Robbie might not have recognized the strange man who'd caught his eye, but he sure knew that horse prancing around as young Steph led him toward the barn. There was only one all-black Frisian, with that long, flowing mane and tail, in all San Francisco. Zeus was the grandson of the first Frisian Lillian Jamison had ever owned. He had been a gift from her husband.

And Lillian was the only one who ever rode that horse.

Wondering why the ranch's owner was paying them a visit, and who all those people were who'd ridden along with her, Robbie nudged Hayseed into an easy lope. It didn't take him long before he spotted Brenna, surrounded by a whole gaggle of other women, and when his gaze fell on Jules and Ethan standing together near the front of one of the wagons, he knew exactly who all his visitors were. Except for the one man he hadn't recognized and now seemed to have disappeared. But he'd ask about him later.

Robbie stopped Hayseed and stepped down from the saddle, giving his horse a firm slap on his rump to get him started toward the barn on his own. As the big horse ambled off, Robbie tugged off his gloves and stuck them into his belt as he made quick work of crossing the distance to where his friends stood, grinning at him. He gave them both a hard slap on the back before stepping away and raising one eyebrow at them.

"Didn't expect to see either of you here."

Ethan shrugged. "Wasn't planning on coming, except Lillian sent me a message telling me I needed to be here."

That surprised Robbie enough to have him glancing over at the women. "Did she give you a reason why?"

"Nope. But Jules has a theory about it, which I suspect he got from his wife."

The marshal nodded. "I did. Wives can come in pretty handy for that kind of thing."

"What kind of thing?" Robbie rubbed his hand across his chin. He had no idea what Jules was talking about, and he didn't have the patience to stand around and play childish guessing games.

But Jules only shook his head. "You'll have to ask Dorrie. I came along because my wife insisted on coming and I couldn't let her go alone. I need to keep an eye on her."

Robbie grinned. "Why? Does she have men following her about again? If she does, you need to take care of that problem on your own this time."

"No men. She's in the family way."

Ethan nodded, his whole face lit up with a smile. Robbie suspected that he looked exactly the same way as he gave Jules another quick slap on the back.

"Congratulations! You're going to be a papa." Robbie looked over at Ethan and wiggled his eyebrows. "And we're finally going to get the chance to be uncles. Lots of things I'll be teaching that boy." Robbie rubbed his hands together as if he was ready to do just that.

"It might be a girl," Jules drawled. "What do you intend to do then, Uncle Robbie?"

"Send up a daily prayer that she takes after her mama in looks rather than you?" Robbie suggested.

"Speaking of prayers," Ethan interrupted. "Lillian brought the preacher along."

Which explained the man all dressed in black that Robbie had spotted earlier, but not why he was here. He sent another frown in Lillian's direction, only to see her walking toward them, arm-in-arm with Brenna. He watched as the women approached, smiling when Brenna bent her dark head closer to Lillian's light one as the older woman seemed to be doing all the talking.

"Brenna's a real looker."

Robbie frowned at the soft statement from Ethan. He gave his friend a sideways glance, but didn't have time for anything more than that since Lillian and Brenna were now standing right in front of him.

Lillian gave each of the men a calm look before turning to smile at Brenna. "I think you've met Jules, Dorrie's husband? And of course, you know Robbie." She waited for Brenna's nod before inclining her head toward Ethan. "This is Ethan. I'm sure Robbie has mentioned him to you."

Brenna smiled at the dark-haired man with the intense brown eyes and held out her hand. "No, Robbie hasn't, but Toby's mentioned that you're the best tracker he's ever seen. And Steph has too."

"But not a word from Robbie?" Ethan asked as he took Brenna's hand with both of his, sandwiching hers in between them. "I'm pleased to meet you, Brenna. I'm sorry I didn't get a chance to say hello before you left for the ranch." Ethan smiled and gently pulled Brenna a little closer. "Did you get the rest of your things that you'd left behind that shack?"

Robbie stepped forward and wrapped his fingers around Brenna's wrist, pulling her hand away from Ethan. "She got them."

Ethan dropped his arms to his side as he grinned at Jules. "I think your wife's theory is a good one."

"Excuse me? What does Dorrie have a theory about?"

Brenna's polite question had Robbie tucking her hand into the crook of his arm and glaring at both his friends. "Why don't the two of you see to the women, then make yourselves at home while I go through the supplies with Brenna."

"And Shue? Is she invited to this supply check too?" Ethan's grin grew wider as he took a quick step back.

"And Shue," Robbie snapped out. He sent one last glare toward Ethan before leading Brenna away. He didn't know what had gotten into the man, but not even one of his best friends was allowed to take any liberties with Brenna. *Or any other woman who was his responsibility,* he quickly added to himself.

"Is something wrong?"

Robbie tipped his chin down and smiled at Brenna. "No. My

friends are just being jack...." He caught himself and quickly cast around for another word. "Silly. They're being silly."

Brenna laughed. "That's a very odd way for grown men to act, especially a US Marshal."

"Well, sometimes common sense is slow in coming to them." Robbie gave her hand a pat and slowed his pace. He was enjoying having her next to him with her hand resting lightly on his arm. "There's something I wanted to talk to you about, but I hadn't counted on having so much company come riding in today."

"I need to talk to you too," Brenna said.

"I got a few thin's I need to say myself," Shue announced.

Robbie's face bloomed with heat. He hadn't realized they'd almost run Shue over. While he was still getting his jumbled thoughts together, Brenna gently withdrew her arm from his and went to stand beside Shue.

"What did you want to say, Shue?" She smiled at the older woman who was shaking her head at Robbie.

"You've been actin' mighty strange lately, boy. I hope you start makin' a better accountin' of yourself."

"I haven't been doing anything wrong." Robbie clamped his mouth shut. Shue had a way of making him feel like a kid who needed to be taken to the woodshed.

"Yellin' at a girl one day and walkin' about with her on your arm the next is actin' strange." Shue snorted and latched onto Brenna's arm, turning them both toward the ranch house. They'd only gone a few steps when Shue turned back around and put her hands on her hips.

"Maybe you'd best stay out of the sun fer a spell." With a last decisive nod of her head, the older woman marched off with Brenna in tow.

CHAPTER NINETEEN

BRENNA LAUGHED AT THE FACE AMMIE MADE AT DORRIE'S STORY about one of their childhood pranks. Listening to her new friends banter back and forth made Brenna happier than she'd ever been. In a million years she never would have believed she'd be part of such an extraordinary family. And even if it didn't last long, she'd always cherish these memories — her first of what it felt like to have sisters and aunts.

Brenna, Ammie, and Dorrie were perched on the large bed that jutted out from one wall of the casita. The homey space also had a sitting area with two comfortable chairs that were currently occupied by Lillian and Shue, as well as a bathing tub with a screen that could be set up to separate it from the rest of the room. The colors were all softly muted, and the oversized bed had a third of its length covered in pillows. Brenna leaned back against one of them and tapped Ammie's knee.

"I know what was in the note that Dorrie received because I sent it to her. But who sent *you* one?" Brenna sent a questioning glance to Shue who shook her head.

"It wasn't me. I sent one to Lillian."

"Ah, a mystery then that needs solving." Lillian smiled at the three young women lounging together on the bed. "And I'd be happy to go first." She reached into her waistband and withdrew the note, opening it up. "Shue asked me to send some reading primers and the preacher." Lillian glanced at Shue, her crystal blue eyes twinkling with the same laughter that was in her voice. "Which was a very interesting combination, and the request came without any explanation. So of course I had to come myself to find out what is going on."

"You should learn to trust your elders, girl," Shue said.

Brenna's hand flew up to cover her smile as Lillian burst into laughter. It was good to hear Shue call someone else "girl", but somehow reprimanding Lillian that way sounded ridiculous.

"Yes, Miss Shue," Lillian said between her laughter. "Please tell us why you needed a preacher and the primers?"

"The preacher's for Steph. He needs to start learnin' some Christian ways, so I intend to tell the reverend that he needs to start stoppin' by regular-like. Jest the way the preacher did when we had a whole passel of orphans out here." She paused and clasped her hands together as if she were offering a prayer of her own. "And Robbie could use some guidin' from above. He ain't been himself lately."

"Oh?" Ammie sat up, her expression alive with interest. "What's our charming ranch manager been up to?"

Dorrie grinned. "Be careful what you say, Shue. Ammie has a theory and you might not want to encourage it."

"Why not? It's probably the same way I've been thinkin'," Shue said. The old miner turned toward Lillian. "Lately the boy's been makin' a point of keepin' his boots in place every mornin' until he can say 'hello' to Brenna, but he still don't bother to come in for his supper. And last week we had a beef roast and party outside, and he was dancin' with Brenna one minute as if there weren't anyone else around, and the next he's tellin' her he doesn't like her hair before he walks away from her." She took in a deep breath and plowed on. "And then he spends the followin' days tryin' to figure out how to apologize to her, so he buys her a horse, tells Steph he'll take the boy on a huntin' trip because Brenna asked him to, and even brings her flowers he must'a spent a good hour pickin'.'"

Ammie looked over at Dorrie, a smug smile on her lips. "I told you."

Brenna frowned at the brunette. "You told her what?"

"You'll find out when we get to *my* note." Ammie waved at Shue. "Please go on."

"Not much else to tell, exceptin' the boy still hasn't managed an apology." Shue leaned back in her chair. "He's actin' peculiar, so I told him to stay out of the sun."

"Somehow I don't think that's going to help him much," Lillian said dryly. "And what were the primers for?"

"Brenna. She can't read or write, and the ones Steph is workin' with are too hard for someone jest startin' out," Shue stated flatly, making Brenna's cheeks go red.

Lillian looked around the group, her gaze resting for a long moment on each face. "I gather I'm the only one who didn't know that?"

Wishing she could deny it, Brenna slowly nodded. "What Shue said is true. I can't read or write." Brenna winced inwardly at the words.

"And you'd like to learn?" Lillian asked.

"If Shue has the time to help me." Brenna had barely gotten the words out before Shue started shaking her head.

"I ain't no teacher. That's Hopper's job."

Brenna frowned. "I know he gives lessons to Steph, but why Hopper?"

"He used to be a teacher afore he decided to come west and try his luck at silver minin'. His luck wasn't so good. That's how he ended up here."

"Steph takes his lessons with Hopper," Lillian supplied quietly.

Brenna hadn't realized that. All she knew was that three times a week Steph disappeared into the bunkhouse, carrying his books under one arm.

Lillian smiled. "Well that's settled then." She nodded at Dorrie. "And what did your note say?"

"Mine was from Brenna," Dorrie said, drawing the note out of her skirt band and fending off Brenna's grab for it. "I also received two requests, although not mysterious ones. She wanted me to find a place in town for her to stay in the fall that was big enough for her and Steph, and she also wanted me to ask Ammie if she'd received any mail."

Lillian smiled at Brenna. "Who are you expecting a letter from?"

"Not expecting so much as hoping." Brenna shrugged when both Dorrie and Ammie shook their heads. "I, or I mean Ammie, sent a letter to my papa's brother, letting him know that papa and mama died eighteen years ago. Almost nineteen now."

"You have a family?" Lillian's perfectly shaped eyebrows snapped together. "Where have they been all this time?"

Brenna shrugged. "St Louis, I guess. At least that's where they were eighteen years ago."

"And you were too young to contact them," Lillian mused out loud. "What about the couple you considered grandparents? Didn't they try to find your family?"

"Neither Meemaw nor Gramps could read or write. They had no way to send word to anyone, and couldn't read the letters Gramps found in a tin on a shelf in the barn."

"I see." Lillian tilted her head to one side and considered Brenna for a moment. "And you've had no response to this letter Ammie sent on your behalf?"

"No." Brenna shot a look at her friends who both gave her a confirming head shake.

"And Steph wants to stay with you rather than go to the new ranch?"

"He does," Shue cut in. "He sticks closer to Brenna than a burr in a fox's tail."

"And that brings us to my note," Ammie announced.

Brenna looked around the room and frowned. "Who's left to send you a note?"

"Robbie of course." Ammie laughed at the dumbfounded expression on Brenna's face. "And he also had several requests." She held up one hand and started counting items off on her slender fingers. "Three skirts in Brenna's size with one split for riding, three blouses in Brenna's size, a warm coat, hair ribbons, and a pair of cowhide gloves. All of which I assume are for Brenna, unless Shue's suddenly taken to wearing ribbons in her hair."

Shue chuckled. "Not enough hair and too much fuss."

"So my theory is correct."

Brenda gave her an exasperated look. "Which is...?"

"That Robbie is completely taken by you, and on the verge of falling in love." Ammie declared as Brenna couldn't help but roll her eyes. As far as she was concerned, the man was only concerned with apologizing, and all that request was just part of it.

"I have to agree with her, Brenna." Dorrie chuckled, completely ignoring the astonished look on Brenna's face. "I think our Robbie has at last taken the fall."

"And how do you feel about him?" Lillian's head was once again tilted to the side and her intense gaze was fixed on Brenna.

Both confused and uncomfortable, Brenna squirmed against the pillow at her back. "I don't know."

Shue slapped her knee. "Oh, she feels the same. She's been actin' as peculiar as he has."

Offended, Brenna lifted her chin a notch. "I have not. And neither has Robbie. He's just got a lot on his mind, and he's certainly not falling in love with me."

The two young women sitting next to her on the bed responded in unison as Shue rolled her eyes and Lillian laughed.

"Yes, he is."

————

"No, I'm not."

Robbie stared back at the two men who were sitting cross-legged in front of the small campfire they'd all built. The preacher had retired to his assigned bed for the duration of his visit, which was in Robbie's room. Jules and Dorrie took up the second bedroom and Lillian and Abby the third, while Shue had taken to the loft and sent Steph out to the bunkhouse. Since Ammie had settled into the casita with Brenna, that had left Ethan and Robbie to fend for themselves.

Both men had been more comfortable spreading their bedrolls outside rather than taking up space with the rest of the hands and young Steph in the bunkhouse. Jules had joined them while Dorrie was visiting with her friends, bringing a bottle of whiskey and three tin mugs with him.

"What do you mean no?" Ethan demanded. "You have to do something with Brenna."

Robbie quirked an eyebrow upward. "Why? What's there to do? She'll be here cooking for us until we leave for the new place in the fall. Then she'll go back to San Francisco." He ignored the sudden wrench in his gut that happened every time those words passed through his mind.

"You don't look like that notion sits well with you," Jules observed as he poured whiskey into the mugs and passed them around.

Robbie took a swift drink from his before cradling the mug between his hands. "You're imagining things."

"Ah. I'm imagining things? So that wasn't you who was ready to put a fist into Jonah's jaw just for dancing with Brenna?" The marshal grinned when Robbie's eyes narrowed. "Toby told us about the campfire."

"Interesting story," Ethan added. "Telling her you didn't like her hair and then walking off like that." He glanced over at Jules. "How much groveling do you think he's had to do since then?"

"I'm not groveling, and Toby talks too much." Robbie scowled at them before taking another long sip from his mug.

Ethan chuckled. "Not groveling? So that new horse in the barn that Hopper told me you got for Brenna is an imaginary one?"

"Or what about that hunting trip you'll be taking Steph on?" Jules chimed in. "I hear Brenna asked him to take the boy." He grinned at the thoroughly annoyed Robbie. "Was that part of Pete's imagination?"

"I like the flowers." Ethan's grin turned into a smirk. "Are you trying to pretty up the ranch house? Or were those imaginary flowers too?"

Robbie sighed and rubbed his chin with the back of his hand. He might have known none of the hands would keep their mouths shut. But he was definitely going to have a talk with Toby.

"I'm just trying to be sure she likes it here. The men enjoy her cooking, and happy men make for an easier workday." Robbie thought that sounded reasonable enough, but wasn't surprised when both his friends gave him a skeptical look.

"When you can't stand to see another man's hands on a woman, then you've taken the fall," Jules laughed. "You can sit there and shake your head all you want, but if we've figured it out, then you can bet the women have too."

"Yep," Ethan agreed. "You've taken the fall, Robbie. You might as well give in to it. Be sure to let us know when you'll be getting down on one knee."

Robbie pulled his hat lower on his forehead and glared at them from beneath its wide brim. "You've both turned into gossiping ninnies. I haven't fallen for Brenna, and I sure as hell won't be marrying anyone soon. I have a ranch to build."

Jules grinned back at him. "Is that a fact?"

CHAPTER TWENTY

EARLY IN THE MORNING TWO DAYS LATER, ROBBIE STOOD IN THE yard with Brenna, Shue, and Toby and watched the wagon carrying most of his unexpected guests disappear around the bend in the road leading into the hills. He smiled at the audible sniffle coming from Brenna who was standing beside him. She seemed to have thoroughly enjoyed her visit with the women the last two days, and he'd enjoyed watching her fit in so effortlessly with the family. Just as she had at the ranch.

Brenna's appreciation for even the smallest gesture of friendship and kindness was a constant reminder to him of how much he'd had in his life, and how very little she'd had in hers. As she waved a last goodbye to her friends, smiling despite the single tear running down her cheek, he stuck his thumbs in his belt to keep himself from wrapping a comforting arm around her shoulders.

Being around Brenna so much in the last few days had only fueled his need to touch her. He could still remember the feeling of her hand on his arm, and just that thought alone had kept him awake long into the night. And he would always carry the memory of her thanking him for the clothes he'd had made for her. She'd looked at him with blue eyes swimming in gratitude, and looked so beautiful in the skirt and blouse he'd bought for her, he'd almost kissed her right then and there.

Robbie couldn't remember looking forward to a long day's work as much as he was right now. Having something else to occupy his mind, and tire his body out, would be a welcome relief from the constant onslaught of what Brenna made him feel. He needed to get away from her so he could get his feet firmly back on the ground.

"Now that we're done with our socializin', I need to talk to the three of you in the kitchen."

Robbie turned his head and looked at Shue. "Can it wait until later? We have a lot of work to see to, and the hands have already ridden out."

She put her hands on her hips and frowned at him. "No, it cain't wait. If it could, I wouldn'a said anythin'."

He glanced over at Brenna who only shook her head to indicate she had no idea what Shue was up to. His foreman did the same thing, which left Robbie without much choice. Whatever Shue wanted, it was better to get it over with so he could go back to work.

Giving the old miner a shrug and then a nod, he and Toby followed the women into the ranch house. Once they were all seated around the long table at the far end of the front room, Robbie politely removed his hat and set it down in front of him as he stared at Shue.

"Well? What did you want to tell us?"

The woman with the short, choppy gray hair took a deep breath. "I talked to Lillian. She's goin' to send out one of the men who help Cook every night at The Crimson Rose."

Toby frowned. "What fer?"

"To do the cookin', you old goat. What else would he be comin' fer?"

While the foreman scratched his head, Robbie nodded his approval. "Brenna could use the help. She works too hard."

"I do not," Brenna instantly protested before she bit her lower lip as she looked at Shue. "You aren't happy with my cooking?"

"You cook fine, girl. This ain't about you. It's about me."

There was a long silence around the table before Toby finally broke out into a grin. "You've decided to spend your time sittin' in a rocker on the porch? The streams are too dry to be pannin' for gold."

Robbie considered that a fine idea, so he nodded his agreement. Shue deserved to have her days to herself, and he was happy to have another resident on the ranch if that would give the old miner more time to rest.

"I might be sittin' on a porch," Shue said. "But it's goin' to be my own." She hesitated as she looked at the three astonished faces around her. "I've decided to go home. There's only a few months before you all will be leavin' fer the new place. Shannon and Luke's kids are growin' up fast, and I need to be there to teach them a thin' or two. You can git by without me fer a while. I told Lillian I'd be back to help her pack the place up if she decides to sell it after yer gone. And Brenna will be back to help too."

Robbie's eyebrows snapped together as Brenna's mouth dropped open.

"Why would Brenna have to come back when she'll already be here?" Toby asked. "That don't make no sense."

"Because she won't be here," Shue said calmly. "On account she'll be comin' with me. Or I'll take her to Dorrie or Ammie if she'd rather go there." The older woman turned and smiled at Brenna. "You got lots of choices now, girl. No need to fret about that. I suspect Ammie and Dorrie will be fightin' over who gets to have you with 'em, and Lillian said you'd be welcome at her place too."

"But I don't understand. If my cooking is fine, why can't I stay here?"

The hurt and confusion in Brenna's voice had Robbie clenching his hands into fists. He refused to think about her being so far away.

"If Brenna doesn't want to go, she doesn't have to," he said quietly.

"Yes, she does have to go if I do," Shue stated. "She ain't married and it wouldn't be right." She reached over and patted Brenna's hand. "You got family now, and they ain't goin' to be too happy about you stayin' here on your own without them around to protect you."

Toby jumped to his feet and leaned across the table, bracing his hands on top of it. "None of us would lay a hand on Brenna, and I don't like you thinkin' that we would."

Robbie grabbed his foreman's arm and forced him to sit back down, all the while keeping his stare on Shue.

"I know that, you old goat. It ain't that it will happen, it's that folks will say it has, and be talkin' about the family behind those fancy fans they like to carry around." Shue's snort of disgust made her views on the society gossips very clear.

"Shouldn't make no never mind. Brenna will be out here, and they'll all be in town," Toby grumbled.

"Well, she'll be livin' in town after you're gone, and you won't be around then to set them all straight, will you?"

"I don't mind the talk, Shue," Brenna shrugged as a smile fluttered across her lips. "The women in the market used to talk plenty about the way I looked and dressed."

Robbie frowned at that, but he set his mouth into a firm line when he looked at Shue. "I'm part of the family and I'm here, so that should be enough to satisfy everyone else."

"You bein' here is the problem, Robbie Smith." Shue sniffed when he gaped at her. "So are all the rest of the unmarried men around the place. When I'm gone, Brenna would be alone in the casita. Those gossips can dream up all kinds of shenanigans about that."

"All right. Then she can move into the ranch house," Toby said.

Shue pointed at Robbie. "And live here with just a wall between him and her?"

"I'll move into the bunkhouse," Robbie quickly offered. Since that would be a lot further away than just a wall, he thought it should solve the problem quite nicely.

"And then she'd be alone in the ranch house?" Shue scoffed. "How's that any different from bein' alone in the casita?"

Frustrated, Robbie ran a hand under his chin and looked at Brenna who'd been silent through the whole argument. She suddenly glanced over at him, and he saw the moisture gathering in her eyes, making his gut clench even tighter.

"This family has been good to me," Brenna said softly. "I won't do anything to shame them."

Toby cast a helpless look at his boss, who gritted his teeth to keep from lashing out at Shue for bringing this whole thing up and upsetting Brenna.

"You haven't done anything to be ashamed of," he finally said. "And if you don't want to leave, you don't have to." He glared at Shue. "And that's the end of it."

"I won't do anything to make you think less of me, Shue." Brenna's head was bent but her words were clear enough. "Or bring shame to Ammie and Dorrie. They're my friends." She looked up with watery eyes. "They're the only friends I've ever had."

Brenna slowly rose to her feet and wrapped her arms around her waist. "If Lillian is sending someone right away, it won't be long before he's here, so I'd best start packing a few things and get to cleaning the casita." She managed a tiny smile. "He might want to stay there."

Robbie watched her walk away, a tic evident in the side of his jaw. He kept his silence until he was sure Brenna was out of earshot.

"You had no right to upset her that way." His voice was low with anger as he stared at Shue.

"I got every right," Shue countered. "I'm part of that girl's family too, and I'm not leavin' her here with a bunch of unmarried men."

Toby's head came up as he considered Shue, but Robbie wasn't in the mood to notice. "If Brenna doesn't want to leave, then she doesn't have to," he repeated.

"You heard her. The girl has gone to pack up because she don't see any other way." Shue stood and looked down her nose at Robbie. "Maybe you can think of somethin' to solve this little problem."

Robbie watched Shue stomp off, her back stiff and her head held high. He wished he'd ridden out this morning instead of following her into the ranch house. But then he might have come back that night only to find Brenna gone.

Robbie's shoulders were stiff and he rolled them back to give himself some relief from the tension running through them. *Shaming the family by staying on the ranch*, Robbie thought with disgust as he gazed out the window. He'd never cared what the gossiping busybodies in town thought, so why should anyone else?

But a piece of his anger was already fading into guilt. He knew if Ammie or Dorrie or any other woman in the family was left behind with a bunch of men, no matter who those men were, he'd be riding out to bring her home quick enough. So would Jules, or Ethan, or any of his uncles.

"Yer the boss. You need to fix this."

"Fine. You got any suggestions?" Robbie slanted a look at his foreman before returning his gaze to the front window where he could see the casita. It suddenly seemed a lot closer to the bunkhouse and the main house than he'd realized. Wouldn't take much for a man to cover that distance under the dark blanket of a starless night.

Toby's long face dropped into a frown. "You ain't thinkin' this through properly. The whole problem here is that our Brenna ain't married. How hard can that be to fix?"

"Sure." Robbie rolled his eyes. "All we'd need is a husband lying about."

"Well, we got plenty of men here," Toby ignored Robbie's sound of protest. "Let's jest look 'em over." The tall, thin foreman crinkled his forehead. "I'm a mite old for her, and so is Pete, even if he won't ever admit it. And Joe already has a wife."

Robbie frowned. He'd forgotten that Joe was married.

"They don't git along too good, which is why he's here and she's back in Texas. But he's got one, so he can't go marryin' someone else." Toby pursed his lips. "That leaves Hopper..."

Robbie let out a loud snort at that. There was no way Brenna would ever consent to marry Hopper, even if the man was willing.

"... or Jonah," Toby finished. He paused as if he was considering the idea. "I'm thinkin' Jonah might not mind having Brenna for a wife."

"*She* might mind it," Robbie ground out. The memory of Jonah's hands circling Brenna's waist popped into his head. His eyes narrowed at the mental image.

"Don't know why. He's nice enough, and all the ladies think he's good-lookin'. But the pickin's here are a mite slim. Maybe we ought to make a quick trip to town. Plenty to choose from there. She's bound to find one who'd suit her fancy."

The thought of Brenna looking for a husband in town had Robbie fuming. "And be willing to come out to the ranch to work?"

Toby shrugged. "Shouldn't be that hard."

Having enough of this entire discussion, Robbie stood and slapped his hands on the table. "It could be that Brenna doesn't like the idea of a husband at all. And there's only one way to find out."

When Toby's eyebrows rose with an unspoken question, Robbie picked up his hat and shoved it down on his head. "I'll go ask her."

CHAPTER TWENTY-ONE

ROBBIE STALKED ACROSS THE YARD, HIS MOOD AS BLACK AS THE sludge Hopper used to try to pass off as coffee. He couldn't tolerate the idea of Brenna searching about the city for a husband, and even less the notion that she might like the idea of Jonah filling that role.

He halted in front of the door into the casita and gave it a sharp knock, pushing it open when he heard Shue's shout to "quit that bangin' and come on in."

Robbie took several long steps inside, his gaze immediately going to Brenna who was sitting on the bed, the old burlap sack lying next to her. Seeing it only made his temper spike even higher. Brenna had looked up when he'd come into the room, and now her gaze was locked with his.

"I guess you come to say somethin'." Shue looked between the two. "Even though I don't hear no talkin' goin' on." As the silence drew out, she walked over to the door. "I'll be jest outside." Shaking her head, Shue went outside and closed the door behind her.

Brenna blinked at the loud snap of the door shutting. "What did you want to say, Robbie?"

"I'd appreciate it if you'd get up off that bed."

She blinked again as she looked down. "Why?"

Feeling his whole body tighten at the picture she made, Robbie gave her an exasperated look. "I'll explain it later."

Frowning, Brenna stood up and put her hands on her hips. "All right. Now will you explain?"

You. The unbidden thought had Robbie tensing up even more, but he nodded as he stuck his thumbs in his belt.

"Toby thinks you ought to get married so you can stay on the ranch," he baldly stated.

"He *what?*" Brenna's eyes flew open so wide it looked as if they might pop right out of her head.

"Married," Robbie repeated. "He thinks Jonah might do as a husband."

"Then maybe Toby should marry him," Brenna retorted.

A wave of relief swept through Robbie, but he kept his expression neutral. "Then you don't want to?"

"Marry Jonah? Certainly not," Brenna stated. "That's a lot to ask of a man simply to keep a cook about the place."

"Would you marry him if Shue was staying and Jonah was asking for himself?" Robbie persisted. He had to know if she felt anything more than friendship for the handsome cowhand.

But Brenna gave him a look as if he'd gone loco. "No. I wouldn't. Why should I? And why would he? We don't love each other."

That was fair enough. And good to hear. Robbie grinned. "But what about the idea? Are you opposed to having a husband?"

She stared at him for a moment before finally giving in to a long sigh. "I suppose not."

"Then it shouldn't bother you any to marry me."

Brenna froze. "Marry you?" The words came out on a squeak.

Robbie had no idea why that had come out of his mouth, but now that it was said, he wasn't going to take it back. He aimed his best smile at her. The one that had never failed to make a lady melt like butter in the hot sun. "I'm told I'm a pretty good catch."

But rather than become a puddle at his feet, Brenna shook her head. "You can't marry me."

That certainly was not what he'd expected to hear. "Why the hell not?"

"Because I'm not good enough to marry you," Brenna pointed out, her voice patient as if she were talking to someone who had a hard time understanding things. "And that's taking an apology too far, Robbie. I appreciate all you've given me, but I can't marry you."

"And I'm asking you again, why not?" Robbie's eyes narrowed. "What did you mean that you aren't good enough?"

Brenna sighed, and disregarding his earlier command, she sank back down onto the bed. "You should marry someone like Ammie."

"Ammie?" The whole idea revolted Robbie. Ammie was a sister to him. He couldn't marry her if she were the only woman he'd ever laid eyes on. And he couldn't believe it when Brenna gave her head a vigorous nod.

"She'd be perfect for you. Or at least someone like her would be." Brenna clasped her hands in front of her and looked down at her feet. "Smart, beautiful, rich."

Robbie's gaze shot upward as he counted to five. The woman made no sense at all! "You're smart and beautiful, and I don't care that you aren't rich."

Brenna looked up. "But your wife should have something to bring to the marriage, and I don't have anything. No money, no land, not even a father to give me away at a wedding."

He was astonished that she felt that way. "You have yourself to give, Brenna. That should be more than enough for any man. It is for me."

Her mouth drooped down at the corners. "I'm poor, Robbie. And ignorant. I can't read or write. You can't marry someone like that."

Robbie waited a full minute before he realized she was through talking. That was her objection to marrying him? That she couldn't read and write? He looked at her with a great deal of curiosity. "You don't talk like you're ignorant."

"Papa read to Mama and me every night, teaching us how to talk like what he called refined folks." Brenna's voice dropped a notch. "Oliver Twist by Mr. Dickens was my favorite."

"I liked that one too," Robbie agreed. "Lillian read it to me when I had trouble sleeping at night." His brow furrowed. "He read to you but never taught you to read or write?"

"He meant to. At least I remember him saying he would. But there was always a lot of work on the farm, and Papa never had the time." She shrugged. "I suspect Mama couldn't read or write either."

He turned and paced to the door and back as he turned a thought over in his mind. When he returned to standing in front of her, he squatted down so they would be eye level.

"Do you think not being able to read or write is worse than being the son of a whore?"

"What?" Brenna's eyes searched his before they went soft with sympathy. "Your mama...?"

"Was a whore," Robbie confirmed. "So that's what I am. The son of a whore who got sick and didn't know what to do with her child. The only decent act she probably ever did before she died was to take me to Lillian so I'd have a roof to sleep under and food in my belly. I don't know who my father is, or the date I was born, or even where I was born. But I do remember loving her even if I can't remember her face." He shrugged. "You'd be getting a far worse bargain thant I would if we get married. You can learn to read and write, darlin', but I can never change what I came from."

Brenna reached over and took one of his hands in hers. "What you came from is for your mama and papa to answer for, not you. None of that is any fault of yours."

Robbie nodded. He'd accepted that long ago, thanks to Lillian. He rose to his feet in one fluid motion, pulling her up with him. "Then we have a bargain?"

She looked skeptical. "It doesn't seem like my staying on the ranch is a good enough reason to get married, Robbie."

He grinned down at her. "Well, I have another reason."

Before she could ask him what it was, Robbie lowered his head and captured her lips with his. The kiss turned to fire in a heartbeat as Robbie's mouth and tongue insisted she open for him, and when she did, his arms tightened around her pulling her against his chest. He almost groaned at the feel of her breasts crushed against him as his tongue engaged in an age-old dance with hers. When Brenna's arms rose and circled his neck, his mind went blank. He hadn't even realized he had her down and lying across the bed until a hand shook his shoulder so roughly it broke them apart. He kept his arms around a stunned Brenna as he glared over his shoulder into the amused gaze of Shue.

"I guess the two of you have come to an agreement?"

At the sound of Shue's voice, Brenna gasped and did a quick scramble to get to her feet. Robbie didn't have a choice but to let her go. He got up just as quickly and faced Shue.

"I'm sorry," Brenna stammered out. "I didn't mean to be so shameful."

Robbie took issue with that and frowned.

"Ain't no shame in enjoyin' yer husband," Shue said, keeping a baleful eye on Robbie. "And that's what he will be the minute I round up the preacher."

"Right now? But that's not..."

"Sounds good to me," Robbie cut in. He didn't care much how it came about, but he wanted to get married before Brenna was given a chance to object. He clamped an arm around her shoulders. "Let's go find him."

Robbie and Shue marched across the yard with a shocked Brenna in tow. He got his soon-to-be bride into the kitchen where the preacher was enjoying a cup of coffee with Toby. Both men looked over when the trio burst in on them.

Shue pointed at the man all dressed in black with the white

collar. "Can you do a marriage, or do you need to fetch yer Bible first?"

The Reverend Matthews looked from Shue to Robbie who had Brenna between them and plastered to his side. "I take it the haste is necessary?"

Toby broke into a huge grin. "It is if we want a good meal tonight." He got to his feet and hurried over to stand on Robbie's other side. "We're ready if you are."

The preacher cleared his throat and took another sip of coffee as he got to his feet. "All right." He smiled at Shue and lifted the Bible that was on the table in front of him. "I never need to fetch it." He quickly thumbed through it, finally settling on a page before he looked up at the young couple standing on the other side of the kitchen table.

"Dearly beloved..."

Less than five minutes later, Robbie was giving his bride a chaste kiss on the cheek and accepting a hearty handshake from Toby.

"So, what do we do now?" the foreman asked. "I guess we don't got no cake or nothin'."

"I'll make us one fer supper tonight," Shue promised.

Robbie looked at Brenna and smiled. "What would you like to do, darlin'?"

Brenna, who had only said two words that were required to get married since they'd walked into the kitchen, simply shook her head.

Shue waved her arm at Robbie and Toby. "You two git to your work. Brenna and I will clean up the breakfast dishes and move her things into your room in the ranch house."

When Robbie felt the tremor run through Brenna, he looked over at Toby. "You go on and get the horses ready. I'll be out in a moment." As Toby disappeared out the back door, Robbie took Brenna's hand and pulled her into the front room, away from the prying eyes of Shue and the preacher. When they were afforded a bit of privacy, he turned and put his hands on her shoulders.

"Everything's going to be fine, Brenna. I'll take good care of you, I promise." He leaned down and whispered close to her ear. "And when I get back tonight, we'll finish that discussion we were having in the casita."

He grinned at her sudden gasp and the blush staining her cheeks before he leaned down and gave her a lingering kiss. Breaking it off before he wouldn't be able to, Robbie ran the back of his fingers down her cheek.

"I'll see you later. Don't work too hard, darlin'."

CHAPTER TWENTY-TWO

As the sun reached its daily midpoint in the sky, Robbie rode up to the makeshift camp the hands had set up underneath the far-reaching limbs of an old pine tree. The heat had risen to a level where cowboy and horse were drenched in sweat, and even the sheltering branches of the towering pine gave little relief from it. Since Robbie was the last one coming in from scouting for strays, most of the men were already either sitting or sprawled out on the ground, chewing on hard tack and biscuits and washing it down with small sips of water that had grown hot in their canteens.

"Hey, boss," Pete called out as Robbie grabbed the canteen attached to his saddle and left Hayseed to find his own meal. "We got something on our minds."

Robbie looked around at the small group who were all staring back at him. Toby shrugged and went on chewing the rough edges of a piece of cured meat.

"What is it, Pete?"

"We heard that Shue is fixing to leave, and Brenna's going with her."

"Where did you hear that?"

Pete jerked his thumb back toward the ranch. "Hopper said he heard it when he took our canteens to fill them in the kitchen."

"Is it true that Shue's going home?" Jonah asked.

Nodding, Robbie uncorked his canteen and took a short sip, making a face when the hot water almost scalded his throat.

"And that Brenna will be leaving with her?" Jonah prompted.

"She don't have to do that," Pete cut in. "Hopper said Shue's worried about what folks will think about her being a spinster-woman out here with all of us." He looked around at the rest of the men. "We've been talking it over, and it seemed to us that all she needs to stay is a husband."

"That's what I said." Toby nodded then shrugged again when Robbie shot him an annoyed look.

"I said that she could marry Jonah." Miguel poked the cowboy sitting next to him.

Jonah batted Miguel's finger away and gave Robbie an apologetic glance.

Ignoring them both, Miguel warmed up to the subject. "All the ladies think he's handsome. They make smiles and batt their eyes at him."

"It's that purty face of his," Toby agreed. "Gits him lots of attention from the ladies."

Jonah had to give Miguel a good shove when the hand made a second attempt to give his handsome friend a jab in the ribs. "Stop poking that finger at me, Miguel, and I'm not going to marry Brenna. A man would have to be crazy to marry a woman his boss is in love with."

A sudden quiet fell over the group as all eyes turned on Robbie. He stepped back and made a show of loosening Hayseed's girth strap to hide his discomfort at the turn in the conversation.

"You don't have to worry none about it," Toby broke into the silence. "Brenna ain't goin' with Shue. Robbie took care of the problem and married her."

A pin dropping onto the pile of pine needles beneath the tree would have made more noise than the five men sitting underneath its canopy. Robbie couldn't even hear them breathe. Deciding he had to face them sooner or later, he turned around and crossed his arms over his chest.

"We're married." He hoped that would be an end to the subject.

But those two words started a landslide of questions, and Robbie had a hard-enough time sorting them out that he finally raised his hand until they all fell silent again.

"I can only answer one of you at a time. Since you brought it up, Pete, you can start."

"Exactly when did you get married? You've been out here with us all day."

Robbie grinned. "After breakfast and before Toby and I rode out.

"You asked her to marry you, and she said 'yes'?" Jonah looked so shocked at the notion, that Robbie's back stiffened.

"We talked about it, and she said her 'I do's'." He gave the cowboy a hard look. "Do you have a problem with it?"

Jonah stared right back at him. "Not as long as Brenna was in agreement."

"She was," Toby announced in a loud voice. "I was right there and heard her say so. Didn't even bat an eyelash when she said she'd take him on as her husband."

The mood around the circle instantly lightened up as the men lined up to give Robbie a hard slap on the back.

"I can't believe she'd marry someone as ugly as you when she knew I was available," Pete declared. "I guess there's no accounting for taste."

"Well, she needed a husband this morning, and you weren't there," Miguel said.

Pete's mustache twitched as he laughed. "That would explain it."

Toby walked over and kicked the bottom of Jonah's outstretched boot. "We'd best get to it. This heat ain't goin' to get any better, and Shue said she'd have cake waitin' for us when we got in tonight."

Robbie added his own eager nod. He might not be looking forward to the cake, but he sure was to the rest of the evening.

———

THE SUN WAS BEGINNING to set when Robbie walked out of the barn behind the rest of the men. They were all tired from a long day of chasing down cows in the hot sun, and dirty from all the dust that was kicked up, but every one of them walked with a lightness to his step. It wasn't often they'd been promised the treat of cake along with their dinner. When they were almost to the foot of the porch that led into the main house where the meals were always served, they came face-to-face with Shue.

Toby was the first to spot her, waiting for them on the top step. He stopped dead and scowled at her. "Now don't you go tellin' us that supper ain't ready and there ain't no cake."

She glared at him. "I said I'd make one, didn't I?"

"Then let us by so we can git to it."

"Yer supper ain't in there, and neither is yer cake." Shue pointed a finger behind them. "Everythin's been set up in the bunkhouse. You all will be eatin' in there tonight. And fer yer breakfast tomorrow too."

"Why in blazes are we eatin' in there?" Toby complained. "Ain't no table in there fer us to sit at."

"You can sit on yer bunk, you old goat. The food'll taste the same."

Robbie paid little attention to the grumbling men shuffling by him as his gaze wandered across the porch looking for Brenna. When he didn't see her anywhere in sight, he started up the steps only to have Shue's hand shoot out to keep him from coming any further. "You git yourself to the casita and make good use of the bath water in there."

Robbie glanced at the small building set off from the main house. "I'll do that. Right after I see Brenna."

Shue gave her head a hard shake. "No you won't, boy. Bath first, bride second." She gave him a light push to get him going in the right direction. "And mind you don't take more'n thirty minutes, or yer dinner will git cold."

Robbie looked down at his hands that were covered in dirt. Maybe Shue had a point. He was in no condition to be greeting his brand-new wife. And considering how he was hoping their evening would go, a bath might help things along considerably. With his mind made up, Robbie changed directions and headed for the casita. Once inside he'd stripped down before he'd made it halfway to the large copper tub in the corner. He smiled at the towels folded neatly on the small stand by the tub, and clean clothes lying out across the bed. Idly wondering if all this was Brenna's or Shue's idea, Robbie stepped into the tub and made quick work of washing the dust and grime away until his bathwater was too cloudy to see to the bottom of the tub. He dried himself off and put on the clean britches, tucking his shirt into the waistband. He looked down at his boots for a moment before grabbing his damp drying cloth and wiping most of the dirt off of them. He doubted if Shue would be very happy about the poor condition of the cloth, but it was worth her wrath to show up all clean and presentable for his bride.

Night had taken over the landscape when he emerged from the casita, and with the disappearance of the sun, the air had cooled down to an almost pleasant temperature. Robbie walked toward the house when he heard his name called out. Recognizing Toby's voice, he reluctantly changed directions, hoping the foreman hadn't come across a problem in the last half hour.

"I guess I need to talk to you, Robbie," Toby blurted out once Robbie was standing in front of him.

Puzzled, Robbie leaned against the wooden side of the bunkhouse. "About what?"

"The way things are between a man and a woman."

Even in the dark, Robbie could see Toby's face was beet-red. "What are you talking about?"

"I know you've never had a pa to explain things to you, so I figure it's up to me." Toby cleared his throat. "I know you grew up on this ranch, so you just think about them animals. It works about the same for a man and a woman, but our females have..." Toby stopped and fumbled for a word. "Well they got certain expectations."

It suddenly hit Robbie exactly what his foreman was trying to explain, and a horrified look crossed his face as his jaw dropped to his chest. "We aren't going to talk about that kind of thing, Toby. Have you gone loco?"

"A boy needs to know these things," Toby insisted, a stubborn set to his chin.

Robbie gave a quick glance around as he lowered his voice. "I'm not a boy, and I already know everything you're going to say."

"Well if you don't know what I'm goin' to say, why do you think you already know it?"

Robbie ran a hand across his chin and inclined his head toward the bunkhouse. "Toby, you go back inside and enjoy more cake and let me go about my own business."

"Well, if yer sure you know..."

"I know, I know," Robbie hissed. "Don't worry about it." He gave his foreman a none-too-gentle push. "Go on now."

Praying for patience, Robbie turned on his heel and walked off toward the main house, keeping up a brisk pace in case any of the other older hands thought he needed a talking to.

He walked through the front door and shut it quietly behind him. Brenna was standing near the long table, her back to him as she lit a short stubby candle. When he took a step forward, she turned at the sound and smiled at him. And he'd have sworn his heart stopped right then.

She looked beautiful. The dress she'd put on was light blue, with long sleeves and lace on the cuffs and its high-necked collar. Her hair was tied back, and the candlelight played seductively over her skin, giving it a shimmer that made her seem innocent and seductive all at the same time. Robbie almost forgot to breathe as she walked toward him. She stopped less than a foot away. Gently placing her hands on his chest, Brenna tilted her head back to look up into his face.

Robbie's hand automatically went to her waist. He had to stifle a groan when the tips of her silky black hair brushed across the back of his knuckles. If there was a heaven on this earth, he was standing in the center of it now. Giving in to the rush of emotions, he lowered his head and settled his mouth on hers, pulling her close until his arms were wrapped around her back and hers around his neck. He leaned over slightly, bending her backwards as he took the kiss deeper, his mind going blank when her tongue eagerly met his and she pressed herself closer. Not caring about his supper, or anything else but the woman in his arms, Robbie bent his knees and lifted her up into his arms, not breaking their kiss as he carried her into the bedroom and slammed the door shut with the back of his heel.

He set her on her feet next to the bed and she turned and lifted her hair, peeking back at him from over her shoulder.

"You'll have to undo the buttons."

That's all it took for him to go from a slow burn to a raging fire. Robbie had her out of her dress and undergarments in record time, and took even less to shuck his own clothes off and toss them on the floor. She laughed when he pulled her down with him on the bed.

"Do you find this amusing, darlin'?" He grinned at her when she shook her head and gently pushed a lock of golden hair away from his eyes.

"I'm hoping it might go a bit faster, though. I've waited all day for you."

Robbie's breathing went choppy, but he gave her a wicked smile. "I'll do my best. Toby says a woman has expectations."

Her brow wrinkled at that. "He said what?"

Robbie lowered his head, and when his mouth was within an inch of hers he whispered, "Never mind, I'll show you."

When her lips parted in an open invitation to his, Robbie

placed a kiss on the tip of her chin, ignoring her sound of disappointment as his mouth slid lower, leaving a trail of kisses in its path down her neck and over the swell of her breast. He didn't stop until he'd taken the pebbled peak into his mouth, smiling at her gasp as she began to squirm beneath him. He continued to kiss and caress every inch of her skin until she was begging him to take her. When he was absolutely sure she was ready for him, he slid into her, gritting his teeth at the exquisite sensation, fighting for control as he started to move gently. When she wrapped her long legs around his waist, he couldn't hold back any more. Their pace became frantic as they both took from, and gave to, each other, their arms tangled and their lips locked together. As the huge wave of sensation crested, they both rode the pleasure until they had no strength left.

It took Robbie several minutes before he could open his eyes, and another full minute to realize he was probably crushing Brenna beneath his weight. With a great deal of effort he managed to shift to his side, keeping one hand splayed across her stomach. When his breathing finally evened out a bit, he propped his head on one elbow and looked down into her face. Her eyes were closed, her breathing soft and even, and there was a smile on her lips. When she made a soft sound and reached for him, Robbie laid back down and tucked her against his side.

His wife had worn him out and then gone to sleep with a smile on her face. A man couldn't ask for more than that.

Pulling Brenna closer, Robbie shut his eyes.

CHAPTER TWENTY-THREE

"How many head are there?" Brenna sat easily in the saddle, shading her eyes with one hand.

The last two months had been a slice of magic, and she'd never imagined how happy she could be. She smiled at her still-new husband as he kept a firm hand on the reins to keep Hayseed from dancing away. Brenna watched the big stallion with a smile as she reached down and gave Dolly a solid pat on her neck. The pretty chestnut bobbed her head as if to say "thanks", making Brenna turn an amused gaze on Robbie who was still wrestling with Hayseed.

"Lillian never intended this to be a big outfit, so she's only got about seven hundred head of cattle roaming out here. I think she started out with two hundred or so. The herd's grown over the years." Robbie frowned as he had to have another push-and-pull match with Hayseed. He gave Brenna a mock glare when she laughed at his horse's antics.

"Don't encourage him. He's just showing off for Dolly."

Brenna loved the new mare Robbie had gifted her with on their one-month anniversary, and even more the compliment when he'd said she was a natural with animals and needed a better mount.

Not that she hadn't enjoyed riding Fancy, the horse he'd given her as part of his apology for treating her badly during their first camp-fire dinner. But Dolly had more spirit and wonderful manners at the same time. She was lively but not nearly the handful that Hayseed was.

"Showing off for the ladies seems to be something every male likes to do, even the four- legged ones," Brenna observed with a knowing look at her husband.

"Well, darlin', that's because you never know where all that showing off is likely to land you." Robbie gave a suggestive up and down wiggle of his eyebrows.

Brenna tried sending him a shaming look, but failed miserably and finally gave in to her laughter. "It's certainly worked for you, I guess."

He leaned over in the saddle and slid a big hand along the back of her neck. Gently urging her forward, he gave her a kiss that belonged more in the bedroom than out on the open range where any of the hands wandering about could see them.

"Robbie." Brenna's protest sounded weak even to her own ears, and the hand she'd placed against his chest wasn't pushing him away at all.

"Brenna," he responded, smiling as he drew back and let his hand drop away from her. "I guess that'll have to wait until sundown."

Her lips still warm from his, Brenna nodded and looked back at the herd. "Why didn't you buy this ranch from Lillian? I'm sure she would have sold it to you."

Her husband snorted. "Steal it from her, more likely, and I prefer to start out in a different spot." He leaned his hands against the saddle and looked into the shallow valley below them. "The water's better north of here and closer to the mountains. That Texas fever that's been killing off the cows doesn't like the cooler weather. At least that's what I've seen." He looked toward a distant set of hills. "Some of the other ranchers would disagree with me."

"Then it sounds as if going further north is the best idea,"

Brenna said. She certainly had no objections to it since there was nothing holding her here. As long as she was with Robbie, she didn't care where they lived.

"We leave in six weeks." Robbie turned in his saddle to look at her. His mouth thinned out and his gaze grew serious as he studied her for a long moment. "It won't be easy, Brenna. There's no house, and I don't know that we can put much of one up before winter comes. We'll need to cut the lumber to build the barn first. And the corrals. Then the house." He gave her an apologetic look which made her love him all that much more.

"That's fine, Robbie. I don't need much."

And she didn't. After a hard day's work on the farm, she used to lie on her straw mattress and dream of pretty dresses and leisurely walks in a lush green garden. When she'd made that confession to him one night, the very next day he'd taken her to a wooded copse about an hour's ride from the house, and they'd walked under the green canopy along the banks of a small stream. It wasn't the flower-strewn path she'd imagined, but she'd been deeply touched that he'd done his best to make her dream come true. She was pretty sure that was the day when her attraction to the tall, good-looking rancher had begun to have love blossom at its core. And every day that feeling had grown, until now she couldn't even remember when she hadn't been in love with Robbie Smith.

"I know you don't. But I promise you it won't always be that way. You'll have whatever is in my power to give you. And I'll work hard to make sure of it."

"And I'll work hard to make a good home for you, Robbie, and help you build your ranch."

"And take care of all the kids we're going to have, since I refuse to keep my hands off you. That just wouldn't be natural." Robbie grinned.

Brenna pursed her lips as if she were considering the matter. She finally gave in to a smile. "That sounds fine to me."

He sighed and settled more deeply into his saddle. "Before you tempt me to get started on them right now, why don't you tell me what Ammie had to say?"

She'd received a short letter from her friend yesterday, and hadn't had a chance yet to share it with Robbie. There hadn't been anything really important in the letter, but Brenna had taken a great deal of pleasure in being able to read some of it, and the rest she'd made out with a little help from Steph.

"Ammie says we'll be staying with her when we come into town tomorrow night. And that Jules is acting like a nervous ninny around Dorrie."

Robbie chuckled. "It seems there are one or two things our US Marshal is terrified of, and being a papa is one of them."

Brenna shook her head. "I don't think it's being a papa that has Jules scared. It's knowing Dorrie will be going through the birthing that has him worried."

Like most men, Robbie visibly cringed at the mere mention of giving birth. Taking pity on him, Brenna continued on about the letter. "She said Helen is now claiming daily that the dark storm is coming nearer."

"Dark storm?" Robbie rolled his eyes. "She usually says it's a shadow. So now it's a storm?"

"That's what Ammie wrote. And she hasn't received so much as a single word from St. Louis."

"She's talking about that uncle you told me about?"

"Yes." Brenna sighed. "It's been a while since Ammie sent off that first letter to him, so I guess he doesn't live at that address any more."

"Are you disappointed he hasn't answered?"

The quiet question had Brenna frowning. Was she? As far as she recalled, she'd never laid eyes on the man, so she had no real feelings for him. But it made her sad to think of him wondering why his brother out in California had suddenly stopped writing. Or maybe so much time had passed, he no longer thought about the brother who'd vanished, or the small niece he'd never met. In any case, it didn't seem likely that she'd ever find out.

"It's hard to be disappointed when I don't know him at all," Brenna finally said.

Robbie gave a non-committal grunt before he reached for his canteen. Uncorking it, he handed it to Brenna first, smiling when she made a face at her first sip of the water already warm from the hot morning sun.

"We'll need to leave for town at first light, as soon as I see the wagons safely on their way."

Brenna nodded, "I'll be ready."

———

IT WAS LATE in the afternoon when they turned up the quiet street where Ammie and Charlotte lived. The stately home, with its old-fashioned wrap-around porch, looked positively wonderful to Brenna after the long eight-hour ride in from the ranch. They'd come across the hills, brown in the summer heat and without a drop of rain for several weeks. Brenna had enjoyed the freedom of riding far off the public roads. She and Robbie hadn't encountered one other rider. Just after the noon hour, they'd stopped alongside a trickling creek to share a quick meal while Robbie regaled her with the story of how Jules had encountered a gang of bank robbers who'd made their camp right where they were sitting. Brenna had already heard the story from Ammie, but she didn't let on as she listened wide-eyed, to a few more embellishments than Ammie had related. Once they'd finished eating, Robbie had pulled her close, and they'd made love by the stream as the horses grazed peacefully nearby.

As wonderful as the day had been though, Brenna was glad to finally reach their destination. A good meal, a hot bath, and a soft bed sounded just perfect, and she was looking forward to each one. They'd barely turned their horses into the short drive leading to the stable when Ammie came flying out of the house, with Dorrie following at a more sedate pace, a shawl wrapped around her shoulders and covering her extended belly.

"You're finally here!" Ammie exclaimed.

She almost pulled Brenna off Dolly to engulf her in a tight hug as Robbie shook his head and led the horses into the stable. Ammie had barely let go when Brenna found herself exchanging another hug with Dorrie, who had tears in her eyes when she finally stepped back.

"I don't know what's gotten into me," her friend sniffed, swiping a hand across her cheek. "I cry at every little thing these days."

"It's the baby," Ammie announced making Brenna smile. The lively brunette sounded as if she knew all about having babies, which Brenna doubted very much.

"Well, she's certainly making her presence known," Dorrie said.

Brenna grinned. "She?"

Ammie nodded. "Of course Dorrie's having a daughter."

The expectant mother's eyes went soft as she gently rubbed a hand across her stomach. "I can't wait to meet her, or him. I don't really care, and neither does Jules."

"It's a girl," Ammie repeated. "It's only fair. We were always outnumbered by the boys."

"Then she'll need a companion to share secrets with," Dorrie teased.

Ammie linked one arm through Dorrie's and the other through Brenna's. "You'd better talk to our Brenna about that. She's the married one."

"Which we need to talk about in every detail," Dorrie announced. "I cannot believe that the minute we rode off you married Robbie!"

"I told you she would." Ammie gave Brenna an assessing look. "And she even seems happy about it."

When Robbie let out a loud snort from behind the trio, Brenna looked over her shoulder and gave him a wink. "Oh, he has his good points."

"Probably the same ones Jules has," Ammie laughed. She gently pushed an elbow against Dorrie's side. "Which means Brenna will be in the same condition as you are pretty soon."

"Ammie, behave!" Dorrie gave her friend a return shove in the side as the three women made their way toward the house.

Brenna let the chatter flow over her, basking in the warmth of being part of a large family. When they walked into the parlor, Charlotte, Jules, and Ethan were waiting for them. While the men greeted Robbie, Brenna exchanged a brief hug and kiss with Charlotte before the women all hurried her to a seat on the divan, leaving the men to sip their whiskeys on the other side of the room in peace.

"We'll get into all the details later," Ammie said, wrinkling her nose when Robbie turned his head and narrowed his eyes at her. "But tell us how you happened to get married so fast?"

"Not that we're objecting," Charlotte said, raising her voice so the men could hear her as well. "It's an excellent match, of course."

"Of course it is," Ammie agreed with a note of impatience in her voice. "But what happened?"

Brenna blinked. "Nothing happened. Shue decided she wanted to go home and that it wouldn't be right for me to stay there with all those men."

"So then what?" Dorrie laughed. "They all lined up and you picked one?"

Ammie gave a dramatic gasp then raised her voice to carry across the room. "And you picked Robbie instead of Jonah?"

"Of course I would have." Brenna raised her voice to the same level as Ammie's, making her friend grin back at her. "But Robbie and I decided to get married. And the preacher was there, so it didn't take any time at all."

"Just one moment," Dorrie frowned. "No time at all? Where did you get married?"

"In the kitchen," Brenna admitted, hunching over a little when all three women stared at her and then over at Robbie.

"So after a nice supper, you decided to get married in the kitchen?" Charlotte asked.

"It was after breakfast, and the hands had already left," Brenna explained. "Except for Toby."

She waited as she got another stare from the rest of the group who then collectively turned their heads again to stare at Robbie.

The marshal's wife glanced over at Ammie with a raised eyebrow. "What do you think of this wedding?"

"I think it was very convenient that Shue happened to have a preacher handy." Ammie shrugged. "I can't say the ceremony surprises me much, but we can certainly rectify that with a big party right here." When a sound of protest drifted over from the other side of the room, Ammie continued right on as if Robbie hadn't made a peep. "Which is the least the groom can do to make up to his bride for saying his vows over the breakfast biscuits."

"I couldn't agree more, and the rest of the aunts will too, so you can just stop that moaning back there, Robbie Smith." Charlotte folded her hands in her lap and nodded when she heard the "yes, ma'am", from behind her. "Well, I'm sure since you had a talk before the wedding that Robbie managed a wonderful proposal. He can be very charming when he puts his mind to it."

When Brenna remained silent, the other three women stood up and turned to face the men, their hands on their hips. Brenna got to her feet and started to say something about it not being important, but the guilty look on her husband's face was too priceless to ignore.

Switching tactics, she gave Robbie an innocent smile. "It wasn't a proposal exactly."

"Exactly what did he say, dear?" Charlotte asked, her stare still not budging from Robbie.

"Hmm." Brenna drew out the sound, enjoying the fun of the moment. "As I recall, he told me that it shouldn't bother me to marry him."

"And that was it?" Dorrie crossed her arms over her enlarged stomach. "Is that what you consider a proposal, Robbie Smith?"

"Of course not." Robbie shook his head. "I just haven't gotten around to one yet."

"Wonderful," Ammie declared. "I've always been partial to getting down on one knee in the middle of Portsmouth Square."

Now it was Ethan who snorted. "You've been saying that since you were a child, Ammie, and it's just plain foolish."

"I'm sure whatever is is will be just fine," Brenna hastily spoke up to head off an argument, since Ammie and Ethan were already glaring at each other. "But it will have to wait until we get back from rounding up the herd."

Robbie grinned at her. "Brenna's going along as the cook. She and young Steph will be handling the wagon together."

"Really?" Ammie sounded fascinated. "I've never done anything like that. Would you like some company?"

"No, she would not," Ethan said, setting his whiskey glass down on the sideboard with a sharp snap of glass against wood.

"I don't believe you have any say in the matter, Ethan Mayes."

Brenna sent a look to her husband, clearly conveying the silent message to distract his friend, before turning a bright smile on Ammie. "I guess we should give up waiting to hear from my uncle."

Ammie sent a last sniff in Ethan's direction as Robbie handed the tracker another drink and Jules rolled his eyes at both of them.

"I was thinking I might go to St. Louis and search for him on your behalf." Ammie nodded when Brenna's mouth opened in surprise. "With the new train service, I could be there in no time at all."

As much as the idea appealed to her, Brenna hesitated. It was a lot to ask of her friend. Especially since she couldn't afford to go with her or had the time to go. Before she could say anything, Helen appeared in the doorway to the parlor.

"I guess you were all carrying on so loudly that you didn't hear the knocking on the front door?" She shook her head and stepped to the side. "This gentleman says his name is Mathias Roberts, and he's looking for Brenna."

CHAPTER TWENTY-FOUR

ROBBIE STOOD BEHIND THE DIVAN WHERE HIS WIFE AND HER new uncle were seated, chatting away. Just as they had been for the last two hours. His arms were crossed over his chest, and he ignored the sideways looks he kept getting from Ethan and Jules. If his friends thought that Robbie might put a fist into the man's nose, then they had good reason to worry. As far as he was concerned, every word out of Mathias Robert's mouth was meant to lure Brenna to St. Louis.

Almost vibrating from his growing anger, Robbie narrowed his eyes and aimed a deadly stare at the merchant. As much as he'd like to, he couldn't deny that Mathias was related to Brenna. They had the same dark hair, the same shade of blue in their eyes, and Mathias' smile was an exact mirror of his wife's. It only added to Robbie's growing black mood, since it would have been an easy fix to the problem if he could have tossed Mathias back out the door as an imposter.

"We've done well and have a house large enough that you and your husband could stay as long as you like." Mathias nodded to the group surrounding him. "And of course, all of you are invited for a visit as well." He returned his attention to Brenna with a smile. "I have to say it again, niece. I'm beyond happy to have found you at last."

"I'm sorry I didn't know about all the letters you wrote to the city sheriff," Brenna said, for what Robbie was sure was the third or fourth time.

Why did she think she had to apologize for that? It wasn't her fault. She was a child for most of that time. And why had the man given up so easily? He should have made the trip to California to look for his family.

I would have, Robbie thought.

"You'd love St. Louis, Brenna," Mathias went on. "We have a garden bursting with flowers, and the city's streets are lined with all kinds of shops." The merchant smiled at Dorrie. "It might be worth a trip for you to take a look at several of the sweet shops that are thriving there."

"Maybe sometime after the baby," Jules said diplomatically.

Since Robbie translated that to mean "never", he nodded his agreement.

The merchant leaned forward, reaching across the table between the divans to gently pat Brenna's knee. "Well, I'm grateful you've found such wonderful companions to help you through this difficult period until I could find you."

Robbie dropped his arms to his sides. That was the last straw! They weren't companions, they were Brenna's family. And *he* was her husband, not someone she was barely acquainted with. This uncle from St. Louis sounded as if he meant to take Brenna away on the next train.

"She has family right here," he growled. When Brenna turned her head to look up at him, her astonished gaze met his angry one.

"So she does," Mathias said smoothly. "But she also has a large family she's never met waiting for her in St. Louis."

That was it. Robbie stepped around the divan and held his hand out to his wife. "We're going to bed."

"Robbie!" Brenna frowned at him, but stood up and put her hand in his as she gave her uncle an apologetic smile. "I hope you'll stay in San Francisco for a few days, so we can talk some more."

Mathias also stood and inclined his head toward her. "I intend to. It's an interesting town, with what looks like excellent prospects for a good mercantile."

"We already have a lot of stores here." Robbie's voice was flat as he drew a wide-eyed Brenna away from the divan and toward the parlor doors.

The man could stay in town as long as he wanted because he was taking Brenna back to the ranch. Tomorrow.

———

ROBBIE GAZED off into the distance, barely acknowledging Toby as he pulled his horse up next to Hayseed. The lanky foreman pointed to a pair of mostly brown hills on their right.

"Pete and Jonah found ten head in a gulch about half a mile that way."

"That's good." Robbie didn't even turn his head to see where his foreman was pointing to.

Toby frowned and shifted in his saddle. "That only makes us about fifty head short."

"All right."

"But Miguel found 'em, and he's takin' 'em on up to Oregon to start his own place."

"That's fine."

The foreman rolled his eyes. "Well, I'll be sure to let Miguel know that you said so."

Robbie rubbed a hand under his chin before he shot his foreman a sideways glance. "Let Miguel know what?"

"That you jest gave him the rest of the herd." Toby pulled off a glove and slapped it against his thigh. "You ain't listening to me. Agin."

"I heard you," Robbie growled. "Fifty head in a gulch, ten still missing, and some nonsense about Miguel."

"It's ten head in the gulch and fifty still missing, and like I said — you ain't listening." Toby shot back. "And you ain't heard a word durin' this whole roundup since yer too busy fightin' with yer wife."

"We aren't fightin'," Robbie snapped out.

"And meaner than a snake the whole time." Toby glared at him. "What happened in town to put both yer backs up?"

That was easy enough to answer.

"Family." Robbie gave a curt nod to go along with the single word.

Toby shook his head. "You cain't mean you let Ethan git under your skin that bad. You know he don't mean nothin' of what he says. He's jest joshin' with you."

Robbie wished it were Ethan who was the problem. *That* he could deal with.

"Not my family. Brenna's family. Her long-lost uncle to be exact."

"Uncle?" Toby reached up a long finger and scratched his head. "When did he turn up?"

"While we were in town." Robbie sent his gaze back to the far-off hills. "He lives in St. Louis with a whole passel of kin, and they're rich. They own a lot of land and a couple of businesses too."

The whole evening had left a sour taste in Robbie's mouth, and led to the first fight between himself and his wife. He vividly remembered how enthralled Brenna had looked during her new uncle's description of his life in St. Louis. The man had been so brazen in his attempt to lure Brenna to go with him that Robbie had felt more than justified at literally dragging Brenna up to their bedchamber. Which is where their fight had started. A week had passed and it was still going on.

Brenna thought he should apologize to her uncle, but he'd be damned if he would. The man was trying to turn their lives upside down, and Robbie wasn't going to apologize to anyone for doing that.

"Well, the men are about to set up a separate camp from the two of you, and I might jest join them if you don't straighten things out with yer wife. This is a roundup, and we need to keep our minds on the cattle, and that includes you." Toby picked up his reins. "And you'd better get to it."

Robbie watched Toby ride off, his head high and his back stiff. As tempted as he was to follow his foreman back to the herd, Robbie knew that Toby was right. He and Brenna had to come to an understanding about her uncle. She wasn't going to St. Louis, they were going to the new ranch, and there was nothing more to say. In a few weeks he and Lillian would have an agreement about him purchasing a hundred head or so, and then he'd help her sell off the rest of the herd. And The Orphan Ranch too. They needed to start driving the herd up to his piece of land and get started on building a place for themselves. There wasn't any time, or space, in their lives for a bunch of Easterners from St. Louis.

Thirty minutes later he rode into the campsite the hands had set up two days ago. He didn't see anyone about until Steph popped out from behind the wagon holding all their supplies and which was also doubling as a bed at night for Brenna and him.

"Hey, Robbie!" Steph peeked around him as Robbie dismounted from Hayseed. "Everyone coming in early today?"

"They'll be in later." Robbie took another look around. "Where's Brenna?"

Steph pointed over Robbie's shoulder. "By that tree over there, practicing her reading."

"Get Hayseed some water, would you, Steph?" Robbie handed over the lead rein and turned to walk in the direction of the tree.

Brenna saw him coming and closed the book she was holding, laying it down in her lap. She looked like an image out of a painting, sitting there with the dappled sunlight coming through the branches and playing in her hair. The polite smile she gave him set his teeth on edge. He wanted the smile he'd grown used to. The one she gave only to him. But he hadn't seen it since Mathias Roberts had walked into Ammie's house.

He dropped his hat onto the ground and sat down beside it, facing his wife. She cocked one eyebrow at him, but didn't say anything as he crossed his legs and set his elbows on top of his knees.

"We need to have a talk."

"All right." She tilted her head to the side. "You start."

"I'm not apologizing to your uncle."

Brenna huffed out a breath. "You were very rude to him, Robbie, and he didn't do or say anything that you should have taken offense with."

"He wanted to take you to St. Louis."

"Only for a visit so I can meet the rest of the family."

"You already have a family right here."

"And more family in St. Louis." Brenna shook her head. "I don't understand why you took such a dislike to him."

Robbie didn't either, he just knew that he had, and he wasn't inclined to let go of it. "He's a little late deciding to be your family. Where was he when your folks died?"

"He explained all that."

The exasperation in Brenna's voice did nothing to improve Robbie's mood.

"Well he didn't explain it enough. And why is he all of a sudden showing up now?"

"I sent him a letter, Robbie. Remember?"

"You told him what happened to your parents, and that's all you had to say. You didn't ask him to come visit you."

Brenna's chin came up. "I would have if I'd thought of it. I've dreamed of having a big family ever since I was a little girl, and I won't say I'm unhappy that they've found me."

"Would you rather be spending your life with them?" Robbie wished he could take the words back the minute he'd said them. He held his breath and braced himself to hear something that would break his heart in two.

"I never said that," Brenna answered quietly.

Robbie got to his feet and stared down at her. "But you aren't saying otherwise, either. I'll be taking watch on the herd tonight." He heard her call out after him as he stalked off, but he didn't turn around. Steph stared at him as he stomped over and vaulted up onto Hayseed's back. Giving the boy a curt nod, Robbie gave a quick jerk on the reins and took off at a gallop.

CHAPTER TWENTY-FIVE

"YOU THINK STAYIN' WITH THE HERD ALL NIGHT IS GOIN' TO solve yer problems?"

Robbie wanted to ignore Toby, but it wasn't easy to do since the foreman was standing right in front of him. He knew Toby was telling him the truth. He'd spent a miserable night watching the herd rather than face Brenna again. He shouldn't have lost his temper with her, but then she shouldn't have defended the man who seemed determined to rip them apart. In his heart he knew that wasn't all of it. It wasn't even the biggest part of it.

But right now all he wanted to do was drink the coffee that Jonah had brought out to him, even if it was stone cold.

"You've had enough time to mope about," Toby persisted. He untied his bandanna and wiped the sweat off his face. Even at this hour of the morning it was hot enough to fry an egg on a rock. "You'd better patch things up, and right quick.

"I don't know if I can." Robbie grimaced at the words being said out loud. "I can't give her what she's always dreamed of."

"Cain't or won't?" Toby asked. "Seems to me Brenna don't ask for much."

"She hasn't asked for anything, but she dreams about walking in gardens with flowers all around her, and waking up late with nothing to do but whatever she wants." Robbie glanced over at Toby, anger churning in his belly. He couldn't give that to her, but Mathias Roberts could. And the man had made that perfectly clear.

"Everybody dreams about somethin'," Toby said. "I still make up a ma and pa from time to time, and you've had that ranch in your head for a long time."

"But I'm going to build that ranch," Robbie said quietly. "It's going to be a lot of work for everyone, including Brenna, and there won't be any garden with flowers everywhere."

"You're a horse's patoot if you think Brenna is goin' to give up a life with you for some fancy garden in St. Looie. That girl's in love with you. I might not know much about wives and marriage, but I got eyes in my head and I do know that much."

Robbie was tired of the whole battle raging inside of him. He didn't know how he and Brenna would work out their differences, but right now he had a herd to take care of, and fifty more head to find. He threw out the rest of his coffee and looked over at Hayseed grazing peacefully on a small patch of grass behind him. He frowned. There was smoke coming up from behind a hill that looked to be about a mile away.

Toby stepped up beside him, his gaze fixed on the same point as Robbie's. "What's that?"

Robbie walked over to Hayseed and reached into his large saddlebag, drawing out a small telescope he always carried with him. Stepping away from his horse, he peered through the eyepiece, quickly quartering the hillside that had an orange haze all along its top. With his blood suddenly turning cold, Robbie watched as the flames came into focus and started to rapidly eat their way down the front side of the hill. Within a minute, the whole hill was engulfed in flames as the fire continued on, fed by the wind at its back. Robbie mentally calculated the direction it was traveling before he snapped his telescope shut. Within seconds he was swinging up onto Hayseed's back.

"Fire," he shouted at his foreman. "And it's moving fast."

As Toby leaped for his own horse, Robbie set Hayseed into a gallop, heading for the herd in the small, shallow valley below him. Several of the hands looked over as he pulled up to a quick stop next to Pete, Hayseed's hooves sending dirt flying as Robbie put two fingers to his lips and let out a shrill whistle.

It only took a minute for the hands to make their way over to where Robbie was waiting, a panting Toby beside him.

Pete frowned as he stuck his nose into the air. "Smoke."

"There's a wildfire, and it's headed this way. Get the herd together and start moving them southeast."

The cowboys immediately split up, heading for the back and sides of the herd as they, and their horses, started moving the restless cows away from the danger. Robbie paused to take a long look at the smoke billowing up behind him, and then turned his head to look to the south. They'd already moved the cattle enough earlier, that the campsite was now a good forty-minute ride from the herd, and luckily far enough south it was out of the path of the fire. But not wanting to take any chances, he headed over to where Joe was riding.

Twenty minutes later, already caked in the dust and dirt flung up by the constant movement of hundreds of head of cattle, Robbie took out his spyglass and turned it to the west. The flames leaped into view, taller and more fierce than ever. And the smoke was getting thicker by the minute. Even at the quick pace they were moving, the fire was gaining on them. Not only gaining, but he was sure there was a subtle shift in the direction of the wind that had been blowing steadily north. Even as he studied the flames through his glass, Robbie felt the wind shift across his face. Alarmed, he looked up at the red ball that was the sun shining through the smoke, watching the air twist and swirl. South. He held his breath, but the proof was there in front of him. The wind had shifted. It was no longer blowing northeast, it was now taken a more southern track. Which meant it would drive the fire southeast. And they would be right in its path. So would Brenna. And the ranch.

He turned Hayseed and waved at Toby who left his position at the side of the herd and set his mount into a quick lope. When he'd pulled up beside Hayseed, Robbie ran a hand across his forehead to wipe away the sweat and dirt as he kept his eyes on the hills to the northwest that had already begun to take on an orange haze.

"The wind has shifted."

Toby turned in his saddle to look in the direction Robbie was pointing. Even through the grime covering his foreman's face, Robbie could see the foreman go a pale.

"We won't outrun it at this pace," Robbie said. His mouth was set in a grim line as his gaze shifted from the fire to Toby, whose eyes widened as he caught the underlying meaning to Robbie's words.

"You want to stampede the herd?"

Robbie looked over just as one of the cows broke out of the group and had to be chased down while the remaining hands struggled to keep the surrounding cattle from doing the same thing.

"They're close to it now, and we need to get more distance between them and that fire. Have the hands get to the sides near the front of the herd and keep them going straight east, just in case the wind shifts again." Which Robbie fervently hoped that it would. "And Toby," he paused until his long-time foreman looked over at him. "Have the men make noise so we know where they are. If one of them goes down, we won't leave him."

Toby nodded and rode off. As Robbie took up a position near the front of the herd, he sent up a prayer that Joe had reached the campsite.

———

"Brenna, what's that?"

Looking up from the task of chopping vegetables for the stew she was making for supper, Brenna looked over at Steph. He was pointing to something on the other side of the wagon. Curious, she walked around to the front of her temporary home for the last few days. Smoke was drifting up from a hillside in the distance.

"Think the men have set up their noon meal already? Or maybe those are rustlers following the herd!"

"Hush, Steph," Brenna admonished. "Your imagination is getting away with you. There aren't any rustlers after the herd, and even if there were, Robbie would take care of them."

"I suppose."

Brenna smiled at the disappointment in Steph's voice, but it soon disappeared as she watched the smoke move closer. It was only another minute before she saw an orange flame spike into the air. Steph had already lost interest and had turned away when Brenna laid a hand on his shoulder.

"Let's get the horses, Steph. We need to hitch them up to the wagon."

Steph looked over at the two horses and then back at Brenna. "I've never done that by myself before."

"I've hitched up a wagon plenty of times," Brenna assured him. "You get the hobble off Sam and bring him over to that log we sat on last night. We'll work together and be done in no time." At least she hoped so. Already the smell of smoke was drifting into the campsite.

It was well over an hour before they had the team and wagon ready to go. Brenna threw the last blanket under the high bench seat and climbed up to sit beside Steph. His eyes were huge and his mouth pursed into a tight line as he strained to hold the horses in check. Brenna took the reins from him and expertly turned Sam and Henry until the team was headed south, back toward the ranch house.

"What about the hands? And the herd? Shouldn't we go warn them?" Steph twisted to look behind them, and for a moment Brenna thought she might have to grab onto the back of his shirt to keep him from jumping off the wagon.

"They'll be fine. Robbie knows what to do." At least Brenna hoped the fire wasn't anywhere near her husband and the rest of the men. But feeling the heat grow in the air, and the jerky movements of the horses she was already fighting to control, Brenna was sure Robbie was in the same kind of trouble she and Steph were. Sending up a prayer for him, she kept the team moving.

It was almost an hour later when she saw one of the hills in between them and the ranch explode with fire. Brenna immediately turned the team, heading them directly away the sun. They needed to head east and get ahead of the flames.

"Brenna?" The waver in Steph's voice broke her heart. She couldn't do anything about his fear, and was afraid it would get much worse before they got through this.

"Don't worry, Steph. We'll manage." It wasn't much, but it was all she could offer at the moment.

She leaned over to the side and took a quick peek beyond the rear of the wagon. They'd gained some on the fire, which seemed to be headed more south than east. But not enough. And the horses were tiring at the pace they had to keep.

If they were going to survive this, she needed to act fast. Making her decision, Brenna pulled Sam and Henry to a stop, tying off the reins as she handed two blankets to Steph.

"Go put these over the horses' heads and then begin unhitching Sam." She reached out and caught Steph's arm as he started to scramble off the high seat. "Don't worry about getting the harness off. Just unhitch them from the wagon."

She waited for his short nod before releasing his arm and leaping to the ground, thanking her lucky stars that she'd chosen to wear her britches today, even if it had been just to annoy her husband. Stepping up to Sam, she moved as fast as she could to get the horse free from the wagon. She gave Steph an encouraging smile as he came up beside her.

"That fire is getting awfully close, Brenna."

"I know. Now you help me with Sam. Get that buckle on the side."

It took another frantic ten minutes before Steph led a nervous Sam away from the wagon, the harness still on his back. Brenna took the lead rein and pointed at Steph.

"You get up on Sam.'"

"What?" Steph stared at Brenna then stuck his lip out. "I'm not riding out on Sam and leaving you here."

Brenna straightened her back and narrowed her eyes on the boy who she held in her heart as a younger brother. "There isn't time to have an argument, Steph. You do as I say and get up on that horse or you're going to get us both killed."

Brenna had thrown that last threat in without any thought, but it seemed to work because Steph grabbed onto the harness and hauled himself up onto Sam's back.

"Now you go straight east. And don't stop until you can't see any more smoke. Do you hear me?"

"I'm going to stay right here until you have Henry unhitched," Steph said.

"I'll be right behind you," Brenna promised as she turned Sam to face east and then tossed Steph the lead rein. "Remember what I told you. Straight east, away from the sun." Without another word, Brenna reached over and pulled the blanket away from Sam's head. She gave the horse a hard slap on the neck, and another one on the rump as he moved past her, setting him into a fast trot as Steph yelled out a protest. She nodded in satisfaction when Sam broke into a gallop with Steph still clinging to his back. Having no choice but to trust that the riding skills the boy had learned under Robbie's watchful eye would keep him there, Brenna turned toward Henry. She started to work on the harness as fast as she could, praying the horse wouldn't bolt on her, while the heat slapped at her back and the surrounding air took on an orange glow.

CHAPTER TWENTY-SIX

"WE STILL GOT OVER HALF OF 'EM." TOBY PUSHED HIS HAT further back on his head and swiped his bandanna across his face.

Robbie nodded as he looked at the milling herd. Men, horses, and cattle all looked as if they were ready to drop to the ground right where they were. It had been a long hard run, but even losing half had been worth it. At least they still had a herd. And the fire was moving on well to the south of them.

That was the good news. But it didn't come close to outweighing the bad as far as Robbie was concerned. His eyes were glued to the south where smoke still plumed over the hills... and where he'd left Brenna.

"She's all right," Toby said quietly. "I'm sure Joe got her and young Steph stashed someplace safe."

"I should have gone after her." Robbie's eyes swept the hills, hoping against hope to see a wagon and rider coming their way. The worry had spread from his gut up through his chest and felt like it was choking him, and the chant in his head wouldn't stop. He should have gone.

He should have gone.

"Joe's horse was faster than Hayseed," Toby reminded him.

"I should have taken his horse and gone myself."

Toby sighed and leaned back in his saddle. "There wasn't time fer that kind of thinkin', and Joe knows that horse better'n you."

"Maybe," Robbie said, but he didn't believe it. Brenna was his to protect, not Joe's. He should have gone, but that didn't mean he couldn't go now. He straightened his back and glanced at Toby. "I need to ride out. You stay with the herd."

Quick as a snake's attack, Toby reached over and grabbed onto Hayseed's reins, almost pulling them out of Robbie's hands.

"Let go, Toby, before you get hurt." Robbie meant every word of it. He was going to find Brenna if he had to knock Toby to the ground to do it.

The foreman shook his head and held on. "You think you're goin' to ride out when it's almost sunset and you don't even know where yer goin'?

"To the ranch," Robbie ground out between gritted teeth. "I told Joe to take Brenna and Steph to the ranch. Now let go."

"We're a good eight-hour ride from there, and you won't be helpin' your wife none if you have to cover most of that on foot. And that's what you'll be doin' if you try to make that horse take one more step."

Robbie could feel the droop in Hayseed's shoulders. He had no doubt his horse would take another step for him, despite what Toby thought. But it might also be his last step. Hayseed was spent. A quick look around told him every other horse was in the same shape.

"We'll camp here, eat what we can shoot or find, and make a fresh start in the mornin'," Toby said. When Robbie jerked in reaction, the older man kept a firm grip on the reins. "It'll be dark soon. We cain't travel in the dark and risk a horse breakin' its leg on a rock or a hole we cain't see." His voice softened. "Whatever happened is already done, Robbie. A few more hours ain't goin' to make any difference."

Robbie's spine was rigid and his jawline rock hard as he stared off into the distance. He'd walk if he thought it would do any good.

But that was as foolish a notion as Hayseed being able to make it back to the ranch. Burning inside at what couldn't be helped or changed, Robbie swung his leg over his saddle and stepped to the ground. Without a word he turned away from Toby and walked off.

———

THE FIRST RAYS of the morning sun had Robbie getting to his feet. He'd been watching the horizon for over an hour, waiting for enough light to head out. Even though deep shadows still splayed across the hills, he figured he could see well enough to ride. He picked up his saddle and walked softly along the edges of the camp so as not to disturb any of the sleeping men. It only took him a couple of minutes to round up Hayseed. Robbie was still putting the saddle on his horse's back when Jonah passed by him, carrying his own saddle.

"'Morning, boss."

Jonah dropped his saddle just a few feet away and strode off, calling out for his horse. Robbie was still looking after him when Pete strolled up, his saddle slung over one shoulder.

"I'll be ready to ride before you can wink your eye." Pete grinned as he also dropped his saddle and followed Jonah out to the open field.

"You aren't coming with me," Robbie called out, but only got a shrug and Pete's back for an answer.

"We're comin'."

Robbie spun around and faced his foreman. "No, you aren't. You're going to stay with the herd and see about rounding up the strays, and then drive them east until you come to the main road. Keep it in sight once you get there and follow it south. I'll meet you at the crossroads in a few days."

"All right. I'll tell Miguel and Hopper."

Surprised at how fast Toby gave in, Robbie turned back to finish saddling his horse.

"We drew twigs last night, and those two got the short ones.

They'll be stayin' with the herd, and the rest of us are goin' with you."

His temper already running on a short fuse, Robbie didn't bother to hide the irritation in his voice. "They can't handle the herd alone, but I can make the ride by myself. You're all staying."

Another voice chimed in. "No we aren't."

Robbie looked over his shoulder at Jonah. "I'm the boss, now follow orders."

Jonah grinned, the white of his teeth a stark contrast to the grime on his face. "Then we'll all quit and go along with you anyway. And there will be no one to watch the herd."

Robbie turned and faced the hands who were all standing in a line next to Toby, staring back at him. "I don't have time to argue."

"Neither do we, boss. Hopper and I need to get out to the herd." Miguel gave the former ranch cook a hard slap on the back. "Those cattle are so tired, they won't be giving us any trouble."

Hopper didn't say anything, but nodded his agreement.

"And you might need help lookin' fer the extra stock, if Joe had to turn 'em loose," Toby said.

When Robbie looked around the group, every man was staring at his boots. None of them wanted to say that they might have to search for Brenna, Steph, and Joe too, but it was hanging in the air. It only took Robbie a moment more to make up his mind. If Miguel and Hopper lost control of the herd and they lost it all, it didn't matter. Finding Brenna was the only thing he cared about. And he'd take any help he could get.

"Saddle up and make it quick."

———

SEVEN HOURS LATER, Robbie crested the hill directly behind the ranch house. The group had ridden steadily, only stopping for short breaks to rest the horses. They'd first headed for the last spot they'd left Brenna, Steph, and the supply wagon. Robbie had walked Hayseed slowly into the clearing, his stomach clenched into a tight knot as he'd braced himself. The ground had been completely black, with only small patches of dried grass showing up at sparse intervals. Robbie had seen the charred remains of the log they'd sat on for their meals, and the ring of now-scorched rocks the men had built to contain the campfire. But he hadn't seen anything remaining of a wagon. The wood and canvas might have burned to nothing, but the metal parts would have survived.

The relief he felt was so sudden and severe, Robbie had been forced to dismount or risk falling off his horse. He'd stood, hanging onto the saddle with his head resting against its leather side, while all the hands tactfully kept their distance. When he'd felt his balance return, Robbie had straightened up and pushed away from Hayseed.

"We've been all around the camp and cain't find no tracks. The ground's too burned up," Toby had called out. "And there ain't no sign of the wagon, so Joe must'a got here and helped hitch up the horses."

Robbie had nodded and taken a deep breath before he'd swung up onto Hayseed's back. "Let's ride."

Now the hope that had wiggled its way into his thoughts died a little as Robbie looked down at the house and yard. The only thing left standing was the shell of the casita. All the other buildings — the house, the bunkhouse, barn, and corrals — were gone. The four men rode down the hill in silence, quietly following Robbie when he stopped and dismounted where the barn used to be. Without a word they spread out, kicking through the ash as they searched for any clue that might tell them where Brenna, Steph, and Joe had gone.

Robbie walked over to the remains of the ranch house, stepping carefully, his eyes glued to the ground. But he didn't see a footprint anywhere. Nothing to show that someone had been there before him. He had no idea if Brenna had made it back to the ranch or not. He hoped with all his being that she, Joe, and Steph had headed somewhere else. He finally returned to the horses where the rest of the hands were already gathered.

"I didn't find anything," Jonah reported. Pete quickly said the same.

"Found one of the hogs out back under some wood. He's dead but mostly in one piece." Toby removed his hat and ran a hand across the top of his head. "Didn't find no other animals, so I'm thinkin' the rest got loose."

"Or maybe they were let loose before Joe, Brenna, and Steph lit out again," Pete suggested.

Robbie scanned the surrounding hills. He still didn't see any wagon or rider, but that didn't mean they weren't out there. He sure hadn't found anything to tell him they weren't.

"We'll camp here tonight, so start clearing off a space." He looked at Toby. "Let's have hog meat for supper, and see if there's any water in the well for the horses. If not, they'll have to have what's left in our canteens." He shifted his gaze to the east. "I'm going to scout out that way for a while, see if I can pick up anything. You take the road to the south. We'll meet back here in an hour."

———

SEVERAL HOURS LATER, the sun started to sink below the horizon. Robbie was sitting on an upside-down bucket, holding his hat out for Hayseed to drink from. Fortunately, they'd found plenty of water still in the well. Pete had done a good job of butchering the pig with a large knife Jonah had found among the ashes of the former kitchen. Nearby was a small mound of things the men had uncovered from where the various buildings used to stand. Robbie looked around, wondering why he didn't feel more saddened by the complete destruction of his childhood home. But then, it had never been the buildings that had made it a home.

"Hello in the camp!"

Robbie's head snapped up at the sound of the voice rolling through the yard. Two horses appeared on the other side of the corral, their hooves making no noise in the soft mix of ash and dirt covering the ground.

"It's Joe!" Pete called out. "Joe! Where ya been?"

The cowboy waved and kept on coming as Robbie strained to see who was on the big horse next to him. He recognized Sam's ambling gait, but he only saw the silhouette of one rider on top of him. He strained to make out who it was, finally recognizing Steph. The boy had his head down and his shoulders were hunched over. Robbie's gaze moved past the duo, looking for any sign of another rider, but no one else appeared.

Joe pulled up and dismounted to the hearty handshakes and backslaps of the other hands. Robbie slowly walked up to the small group, his eyes on Steph.

"Joe, Steph." Robbie drew in a breath and waited for his stomach to settle.

"Hey, boss."

The other three men went silent as Joe turned to Steph. "You might as well get down, boy. Robbie needs to hear what you have to say."

A cold deeper than anything he'd ever felt crept through Robbie's limbs. All he could move was his head as he turned to stare at Steph. The boy slid off of Sam's broad back and raised his eyes, swimming in tears, to Robbie.

"She made me go. I didn't want to, but she made me."

"Go?" Robbie slowly turned his head back to look at Joe. "Go where?"

Joe moved over to put a bracing hand on Steph's shoulder. "Pistol ran like the wind boss, but that fire had already turned south and we couldn't get to the camp. We tried, but we ended up running for our lives, and that's a fact." The hand paused and looked around at his audience. "I went straight east. It looked like the only way out. Barely got breathing space in between me and that fire when I ran across Steph, heading in the same direction. As soon as we got to some safe ground, we had to stop." He gave a quick shake of his head. "The horses were done in."

Robbie didn't say a word. He couldn't. All he could do was stand and wait, hoping he didn't hear the one thing that would put an end to his world.

"Steph, you tell Robbie what happened."

The boy visibly braced himself. "As soon as we saw the smoke coming over a hill that was off a ways, Brenna had us hitch up the horses."

"You and Brenna hitched up them two horses to the wagon all by yerselves?" Toby's expression was as astonished as his voice.

Nodding, Steph doggedly plowed on. "Brenna mostly. She knew how to do it. It took us a while though. Then we started for the ranch, but Brenna, she saw the smoke coming from that direction too, so we headed east. But we couldn't stay far enough ahead of it. So she stopped and we unhitched Sam. She told me to get up on him and ride out, then slapped him into a dead gallop before I had a chance to do anything." Steph sent a pleading look toward Robbie. "I didn't want to go. She said she would unhitch Henry and be right behind me, and I kept looking. But there was lots of smoke, so I thought maybe I just couldn't see her."

There was a full minute of silence as Steph broke down into sobs and Robbie tried to understand what the boy had said.

"It's all right, Steph," Robbie finally managed to get out. None of this was the boy's fault. That was all on him. "You did the right thing." Robbie closed his eyes to deal with the pain.

Joe nodded along with the rest of the hands. "As soon as the horses were rested up, we came here, boss. I was sure this was where you'd head to first thing."

Robbie didn't say anything to that, but kept his attention on the boy. "Steph, can you remember where you were when you and Brenna unhitched Sam?"

Steph looked up, the tears still running down his cheeks, but he squared his shoulders and nodded. "I can take you there. I know I can."

Robbie reached over and gave the thin arm a firm pat. "That's good. Then we'll ride at first light."

———

THE MORNING SUN ROSE, spreading light over the charred hills and floating through the fine dust of ash and dirt raised by the six horses as they made their way across a wide field.

Steph sat up in his saddle and pointed to the far side of the open space. "Over there, Robbie. I'm certain of it. There was a tree there, and we unhitched Sam right beside it. I remember looking over after I got up on Sam, and seeing the fire burning at this edge, just about here." The color had drained from his face and his eyes were haunted as he looked up at Robbie. "It was too close for me to leave. I shouldn't have left."

"I don't want to hear that out of you again, Steph. You did the right thing, and that's all there is to it." Robbie looked across the field to where Steph was pointing and thought the boy was right about the fire, though. It had been close.

The five men and one boy made quick work of crossing the field, finally pulling up next to the gnarled remains of the burned-out tree. All six dismounted and began to silently quarter the ground. Robbie's jaw was clamped tight and his mind blank as he slowly moved through the ashes, not even sure what he was looking for.

"What's this?" Jonah squatted, reaching down into the dirt. When he stood back up, he was holding a blackened chain with something dangling on it.

Robbie leaped across the space and snatched it out of Jonah's hand. He stared down at the object, rubbing off the grime from the small oval surface until the relief of two women appeared. He stared at it, not saying a word, everything inside of him screaming out in denial. His thumb kept rubbing over the oval's surface, searching for the warmth of the woman who had sworn she'd never taken it off since the day her mama had placed it around her neck.

"It's Brenna's. Her mama gave it to her." Robbie looked up, blindly staring at the horizon. "She never would have taken it off."

There was no sound except the slight breeze stirring the air. Robbie couldn't even hear himself breathe.

"It must'a fallen off when she was unhitchin' Henry," Toby finally said. "Best hang onto it. She'll be wantin' it back."

Robbie felt numb but managed a nod. "We'll rest a bit and ride on to the Reeves' place for some fresh supplies. It's a couple of hours due east from here, and we can keep searching on our way."

"You just let us know when you're wanting to start out again, boss," Pete said.

Robbie automatically inclined his head in response as he walked away, not stopping until he was beyond the spot where they'd left their horses. A dark cloud of hopelessness had descended on him, so he saw everything around him in a gray shadow. The only thing he could see clearly was the charred necklace he held tight in his hand.

A few yards beyond the horses, Robbie's knees buckled and he sank to the ground. His head lowered until his chin touched his chest, and clutching the necklace to his heart, he let the tears roll down his cheeks.

CHAPTER TWENTY-SEVEN

FOUR HOURS LATER THEY RODE INTO THE REEVES' YARD. ROBBIE dismounted as Jim Reeves strode out from his barn, his young son trailing along behind him.

"That you, Robbie Smith?" The big bear of a man strode over to Robbie and shook his hand. "I didn't expect to see you here. I thought I'd have to make the trip out to your place."

"It's burned to the ground, Jim," Robbie said quietly. "There's nothing left."

Jim shook his head. "I'm sorry to hear that. What about the herd?"

When Robbie remained silent, Toby stepped up next to him. "We saved about half." The foreman took in the house at the other end of the yard. "Looks like the fire didn't git to yer place."

"Nope, but you weren't the only one who got burned out. We've had lots of folks stopping by, dropping off animals that need tending to, looking for family or hands who have gone missing." The big rancher frowned when Robbie's fists suddenly clenched.

"We were hopin' you could spare a few supplies," Toby said. "We're doin' some lookin' ourselves and need to be movin' on."

Nodding his understanding, Jim looked at his son. "Jake, go tell your ma to put a food sack together for Robbie Smith and his men." As the boy scampered off, Jim pointed at the barn. "I got one of your animals in the barn so that will be one less piece of stock you'll need to search for."

Robbie looked up. Besides the cattle and escaped goats, the only other stock on the ranch had been horses. A fresh mount would be welcome since Pete's horse had taken a hard stumble over a rock and had developed a limp a few miles back, slowing them all down.

He handed Hayseed's reins to Toby. "I'll take a look to see if it's in good enough shape to carry Pete." Robbie followed Jim across the yard and into the dark interior of the barn. The only light was from the wide-open door in the front, so he stopped for a moment to let his eyes adjust to the dimmer light as Jim walked over to a stall about halfway down a row of them on the right-hand side. Robbie waited as the rancher led out a horse with thick shoulders and a brown coat.

Robbie's jaw dropped open, and he leaped forward, yelling for Toby as he raced toward an astonished Jim who let go of the lead rope on Henry's halter and backed up two steps. Robbie threw his arms around the horse's neck then began to run his hands up and down his shoulders and back.

Toby raced into the barn and stopped short when he saw Henry. "Well I'll be damned."

Robbie stepped in front of Jim Reeves and looked him directly in the eye. "Where'd you find him?"

"I didn't," Jim said as his gaze shifted continually between Robbie and Toby as the other hands and Steph poured into the barn. "The Putnams got burned out too and were bringing some stock this way when they found her wandering across a field, looking for a road. She said she was lost.

Robbie pounced on the one word as if it were a lifeline in a raging sea, grabbing onto the front of Jim's shirt with both hands. "She?"

The big man frowned as he easily batted Robbie's hands away.

"Your wife. She said she was her wife. Went by the name of Brenna."

"Where is she?" Robbie looked wildly around the barn. "Where is she?"

Toby strode forward and placed a heavy hand on his boss' shoulder. "Calm down, Robbie. She ain't dead. Jim knows where she is, so give him a chance to tell you."

"Dead?" Jim shook his head, understanding dawning in his eyes. "Your wife isn't dead. She'd gone for a day or two without food, and she looked kind of puny. One of my hands was headed into town with the wagon for more supplies so he took her on in with him. I told him to take her to Doctor Abby's house, since she's your kin and all..." The rancher blinked when Robbie disappeared out the barn door.

A few seconds later there was the sound of hooves pounding the ground before they quickly faded away into silence.

Toby finally chuckled, setting off a roar of laughter from the rest of the men.

"Well. I guess that's the last we'll see of him fer a while." He grinned at a perplexed Jim Reeves. "If you'll give us some fresh supplies, we'd be much obliged. We have a herd to catch up with."

————

IT TOOK Robbie until nightfall to reach town, and another twenty minutes to make his way to Cade and Abby's house. He guided Hayseed straight to the barn and left him standing at a feed stall, munching on a mixture of hay and oats. He didn't bother to knock on the kitchen door, but barged straight in, startling Dina who was sitting at the table, next to her husband, Cook. Dina let out a startled gasp, while the lanky Cook, who had spider-like arms and legs, merely raised an eyebrow at the man caked in dust with a wild look in his eyes.

"Robbie? Whatever is wrong?" Dina asked.

Cook shook his head and pointed a finger to the back hallway. "She's in the second bedroom on the right."

Robbie didn't stop his forward momentum, but kept going right through the kitchen door, down the back hallway, and then took the front stairs two at a time, not even glancing at the small group of people gathered in the parlor. He burst into the bedchamber his gaze skipping right over Ammie, who managed to move barely fast enough to keep from being plowed over. Robbie sat down next to a smiling Brenna and wrapped his arms around her, pulling her close enough he could feel her heart beating against his.

"I'm sorry, I'm sorry," he kept repeating, not hearing Ammie's quiet exit from the room.

Brenna's hands ran up and down his back, her voice soft and reassuring. "I'm sorry too. I didn't mean to worry you."

Robbie raised his head and pressed his lips to hers, groaning at the feel of her kissing him back. He didn't want to stop, and only did when Brenna gave a soft gasp as he pressed her tighter against him. He instantly lifted his head and eased off, looking into the most beautiful eyes he'd ever seen.

"Are you hurt?"

"Just a bruise," Brenna whispered. "I fell off Henry." She gave him a rueful smile. "I guess I'll need a few more lessons." She leaned back a little further, her eyes suddenly filling with moisture. "I didn't know where you were. And I couldn't find Steph." She threw her arms around his neck and buried her head, her voice muffled against his shoulder. "Ethan and Jules went to look for you, and Steph, and the hands." She raised her head. "I sent Steph off on Sam, but I never caught up with him. We've got to find him, Robbie."

He pulled her back against him and began to rock slowly back and forth. "Shh, darlin'. I've got you, and we found Steph. He's with Toby and the other hands at the Reeves' place." When she began to sob, soaking his shirt with her tears, he held her even tighter, more than content to let the storm pass. He felt the wetness on his own cheeks and didn't care. When you held your whole world in your arms, a few tears made no difference at all.

His gaze went to the door when it opened and Ammie's head appeared around its edge.

"Is everything all right?" She whispered the question as if she were afraid of the answer.

The ranch and everything he owned was gone, along with the start-up stake he'd been keeping in a tin under his bed. And half the herd might well have been lost in the fire. So he'd be starting out with nothing but his strong back, determination, and the land up north.

Robbie smiled over the head of the woman he loved, and nodded.

"Everything is perfect."

EPILOGUE

Robbie held tight to Brenna's hand as they walked through the garden in the back of Ammie's house. Of course the predominant color of flower was pink, but there was also a liberal sprinkling of reds and yellows. He reached down and plucked a daisy growing by the side of the path, handing it to his wife with a smile. He knew she loved daisies.

Two weeks had passed since the fire. Two weeks of walking with, talking to, and making love with the woman he thought he'd lost. It had been two weeks of heaven as far as Robbie was concerned. And not something he'd ever take for granted again. Which is why he'd sweet-talked her into a walk in the garden when there was a whole roomful of people gathering in the house, and all of them were intent on finally having their chance to celebrate his marriage to Brenna. He'd made up his mind about the future, and he needed to tell her about it. And he wanted to do it before the party.

"Robbie, we really should go back inside." Brenna looked over her shoulder. Through the parlor window they could see the family greeting yet more new arrivals.

"We will. I need to talk to you first." He stopped by a bench and urged her to sit.

He still worried about her. She'd gone through a hard ordeal, and he didn't want her to overdo things. So far he'd been successful in keeping his wife from doing any work, and he intended for that to be a permanent situation. He could work enough for the both of them.

"All right, Robbie, I'm sitting." Brenna smiled. "Again. What did you want to talk about?"

"Us."

"Us?" Brenna repeated slowly. She folded her hands in her lap and took a deep breath. "What do you want to say?"

Robbie propped a booted foot on the bench and leaned his forearm on his knee. "Ammie told me that your Uncle Mathias is still in town. I invited him to the party tonight."

Brenna blinked up at him. "You did?"

He nodded. "Partly because I knew it would make you happy, and partly because I wanted to talk to him."

"About what?"

"Well, first to apologize." Robbie gave her a rueful smile when she raised an eyebrow at him. Given their last argument on that particular subject, he couldn't blame her for being a bit skeptical. "I'm going to apologize, then I'm going to ask him if he can find a job for me in that mercantile business of his."

Brenna jumped to her feet, her eyes wide. "What? A job? Here in town?"

"No, in St. Louis." Robbie frowned. "Why would you think it would be here in town?"

"Because my uncle is going to open a mercantile here. He has a son and a nephew who want to come west, and he thinks this would be a good place for them to start a new business." Brenna's hands went to her hips. "Why do you want to work in a store in St. Louis, of all places?"

"Because it will make you happy to be with your family, and in a place with all those gardens and their flowers." He straightened up wrapped his hands around her upper arms. "And I swore I'd do anything within my power to make you happy. Living near your family in St. Louis would make you happy and I can do that. It's within my power."

He wiped away the single tear rolling down his wife's cheek. "Don't cry, darlin'. It will be fine." Robbie was determined to make that true. If he'd learned to run a ranch, he figured he could learn to run a store.

Brenna brushed a hand across her cheek then leaned over and kissed him. When she drew back, there was a smile on her face. "I'm not crying because I'm happy to move to St. Louis, Robbie. But because I can't believe you'd make that kind of sacrifice for me. It's your dream to own a ranch."

"I can have other dreams. Dreams we share, so it isn't just mine."

"Would you be willing to share your dream of a ranch with me?"

Brenna asked the question so softly, Robbie wasn't sure he'd heard her right.

"I doubt if my uncle is going to show up here today," Brenna continued, smiling at his startled look. "I went to see him yesterday. To say goodbye." Her smile grew a few inches. "That's how I knew about my cousins' plans to start a life here. I'm looking forward to meeting them."

"You what?" She went to see her uncle yesterday? Robbie shook his head to clear it. "You don't want to go to St. Louis?"

"I want to go north and start building our new home, our new life. And I know you've said it isn't the place for a young boy yet, but I'd like to take Steph with us."

"But you have family in St. Louis, and flower gardens, and you wouldn't have to do a lick of work," Robbie protested.

"I'll have you and Steph and all the hands around me, and that's more family than I've ever had," Brenna countered. "If I want to see flowers, I'll just look at the hills right outside our door." She shook her head at him. "And I'm tired of doing nothing all day long. It brings my spirits down. I like to work at building a life, and I'd like to teach Steph and our children the same thing — to love, to work hard, to dream, and well, to never give up at reaching for a good life." She lifted a hand up to his cheek. "Like their father."

When Robbie reached out for her, she backed away and turned around.

He smiled when she looked over her shoulder at him. "Now's not the time to be teasing your husband, darlin'."

Brenna walked back toward him, her hands behind her back. "Now I have something I need to say to you."

He grinned. "What is it?"

She gave him that smile he loved so much. The one that was just for him. He took a step forward, but was stopped when something bumped against his chest.

He looked down and saw the single crimson rose in her outstretched hand.

"I've never done the proper thing in my life. Instead of cleaning a house or shopping for fancy dresses, I learned to work the farm, hitch up wagons, and wore britches to the market. So I'm thinking there's no reason to change now." Her eyes softened as she held his gaze with hers. "Marry me, Robbie Smith. I want to spend my life dreaming with you."

Robbie covered her hand with his, and keeping it there, he sank to one knee. "Sometimes the proper thing to do is the only way. And I'm glad you've left it to me to say first." He leaned forward and placed a gentle kiss on the hand he held captive with his. "I love you, Brenna Roberts Smith. I will always love you. And I'd be the proudest and happiest man on earth if you let me spend my life dreaming with you. I say 'yes' to your proposal, and hope you'll say 'yes' to mine."

When the tears started to flow down her cheeks in earnest, Robbie grinned and got to his feet. He lifted her chin with one finger. "This is where you say 'yes', darlin'."

"I love you too, Robbie Smith. So I say yes." Brenna smiled

through her tears. She wrapped her arms around his neck and rose on her toes. "Yes, yes, yes!"

Robbie was laughing when she placed her lips on his, sealing their promise to each other as he held her close and kissed her back with all the love in his heart.

AUTHOR'S NOTE

To My Readers ~

I hope you enjoyed Robbie and Brenna's story. There's something about a romance novel that will never go out of style. No matter when or where it takes place, a romance novel is a great way to pass the time. I loved writing about Robbie and Brenna—two orphans who always made the very best of whatever life handed them, and refused to be prisoners of a past they had no hand in making. These two deserved love, and to have found each other.

I want to take this opportunity to thank you, the reader. Time is precious, and I so appreciate you spending some of yours to read my books. I enjoy writing, and am very lucky to be able to do just that. And even luckier to have someone read my stories.

Thank you, and happy reading!

Cathryn Chandler

You can pick-up the any of my other romance novels on Amazon, or read for free with your Kindle Unlimited membership!

Be the first to receive notification of the release of the next novel in the Crimson Rose series. **Sign up** today at:

http://eepurl.com/bLBOtX

If you'd like to know what my latest projects are, and how they're coming along, drop by my website at:

www.CathrynChandler.com

Follow Cathryn Chandler on your favorite media:

Facebook:

https://www.facebook.com/cathrynchandlerauthor/?fref=ts

Twitter: @catcauthor

Website/blog: www.cathrynchandler.com

All authors strive to deliver the highest quality work to their readers. If you found a spelling or typographical error in this book, please let me know so I can correct it immediately. Please use the contact form on my website at: www.cathrynchandler.com Thank you!

And finally: If you like mysteries, I also write those under the pen name: Cat Chandler, and they are also available on Amazon.

Made in the USA
Las Vegas, NV
16 December 2023

82950968R00125